A native Northwesterner with the pale skin to prove it, Stefanie Sloane credits her parents' eclectic reading habits – not to mention their decision to live in the middle of nowhere – for her love of books. A childhood spent lost in the pages of countless novels led Stefanie to college where she majored in English. No one was more surprised than Stefanie when she actually put her degree to use and landed a job in Amazon.com's editorial department. She spent over five years reading for a living before retiring to concentrate on her own stories. Stefanie currently resides with her family in Seattle. You can find out more about Stefanie and her books at www.stefaniesloane.com or by following her on Twitter: @stefaniesloane

Praise for Stefanie Sloane:

'Captivating . . . With her fresh, original voice, Stefanie Sloane will charm her way into readers' hearts' Susan Wiggs, *New York Times* bestselling author

'Fabulous . . . everything readers of Regency romance crave' Amanda Quick, *New York Times* bestselling author

'A powerfully emotional, sexually charged story that will keep you up all night' *Romantic Times*

'An engaging, refreshingly original storyteller' Stephanie Laurens, *New York Times* bestselling author

'Perfect blend of tender romance and heart stopping adventure!' *Fresh Fiction*

# The Scoundrel
## takes a Bride

# STEFANIE SLOANE

**ETERNAL
ROMANCE**

Published by arrangement with Ballantine Books,
an imprint of The Random House Publishing Group,
a division of Random House, Inc.

First published in Great Britain in 2013
by ETERNAL ROMANCE
an imprint of HEADLINE PUBLISHING GROUP

1

Cataloguing in Publication Data is available from the British Library

ISBN 978 0 7553 9667 2

Offset in Sabon by Avon DataSet Ltd, Bidford-on-Avon, Warwickshire

Printed and bound by CPI Group (UK) Ltd, Croydon, CR0 4YY

Headline's policy is to use papers that are natural, renewable and
recyclable products and made from wood grown in sustainable forests.
The logging and manufacturing processes are expected to conform to the
environmental regulations of the country of origin.

HEADLINE PUBLISHING GROUP
An Hachette UK Company
338 Euston Road
London NW1 3BH

www.eternalromancebooks.co.uk
www.headline.co.uk
www.hachette.co.uk

For Junessa Viloria, my brilliant editor.
You are one in a million, with kindness, grace,
talent, and intelligence to spare.
I don't know how you do it all.
But you do it so, so well.
~XO, S

## Acknowledgments

The following is a list of people so awesome, so powerful, so ridiculously talented and insightful that, should they ever all be in the same room at one time, the world would explode, sending confetti, unicorns, and rainbows flying everywhere: Jennifer Schober, Franzeca Drouin, Lois Faye Dyer, Randall, and the Girls.

## Prologue

*Winter, 1796*
AFTON MANOR
COUNTRY ESTATE OF THE EARL OF AFTON
PETWORTH
SUSSEX, ENGLAND

"Will this snow *never* stop?"

Nicholas Bourne, the second son of the Earl of Stone-cliffe, turned to look at Sophia Afton and rolled his eyes at her question. "Of course it will. This is Sussex, not Siberia, you ninny." His words held a depth of exaspera-tion only a nine-year-old boy could convey.

"You needn't be so mean, Nicholas," Sophia scolded as she tucked a wool throw over his chilled bare feet. "I am, after all, only eight years old."

Nicholas returned his gaze to the scene just beyond the frosty glass panes before him. The butler had reluc-tantly agreed to move a small sofa nearer to the French doors so that he might watch his brother, Langdon, and their friend Dash frolic in the downy cloak of snow that had covered Afton Manor for more than a fortnight.

A stuffiness in his head continued to plague Nicho-las despite his fervent prayers that the Almighty might intervene on his behalf. And this morning Sophia had announced she would selflessly forgo all outdoor merri-ment in favor of playing nursemaid to the boy.

Clearly, God was punishing him.

"Well, I am older than you," Nicholas replied in a superior tone, wiping at his nose with the sleeve of his cotton nightshirt. "And can take care of myself, thank you very much. Which begs the question, Sophia, why are you here? Shouldn't you be out-of-doors? I'm sure Dash and Langdon are missing you."

A snowball collided with the window, the audible *thwack* eliciting a threatening shake of Sophia's small but determined fist. "That would have been my face!" she exclaimed, sticking her tongue out as the two boys raced by outside, their mad grins accompanied by fits of laughter.

"Besides, you should be pleased I decided to stay in today," Sophia continued. "You'd never get the rest you need on your own. Mama said so."

Nicholas adored Sophia's mother, Lady Beatrice Afton. And he suspected she'd not meant for Sophia to take her words so closely to heart.

The girl *never* stopped talking. And she'd brought her costumes. There was, in all likelihood, a play in his future. God *was* punishing Nicholas. There was no other explanation for his torturous predicament.

He stared at the irksome girl, frustration creasing his forehead. There were so many reasons to *not* like Sophia. But he did like her. Very much so.

"Why are you looking at me like that, Nicholas?"

He focused his stare in earnest. Her neat braids shone in the mid-day aura of wintry light like his pony's mane after a good brushing. Her skin reminded him of the cream the kitchen maids skimmed off the top of the milk each morning.

"Are you going to be sick?"

Sophia's presence made Nicholas feel odd; uncomfortable and cross, but strangely excited and buoyant, too.

"Mama just had this dress made for me. She'd be quite upset if you lost your breakfast all over it."

His head ached mournfully from the stuffiness and the thinking.

And the talking.

"Shouldn't you be looking after Langdon? He's the one you're going to marry, after all," he finally replied.

"Ewwwwww," Sophia uttered contemptibly, her face twisting with dismay. She sat up to fuss once again with the thick throw. "Don't say such things."

Technically, Nicholas had a point. Shortly after Sophia's birth, she'd been promised to Langdon. Oh, not officially. According to Lady Afton, only royalty put such promises down on paper anymore. Either way, it didn't make any sense to Nicholas. And it angered him. Which didn't make any sense, either.

"But it's true," he continued to needle. "One day you and Langdon will be married. With ten babies—no, twelve babies. I'm sure I heard Langdon say he wanted twelve."

Sophia's green eyes grew round with revulsion. "You're lying, Nicholas Bourne. Tell me you're lying!"

"I will do no such thing," Nicholas countered with indignation, knowing full well Sophia would take the bait.

She shot up from the damask sofa and bolted toward the drawing room door, stopping mid-stride and returning to stand in front of Nicholas, arms akimbo and eyes lit with fury. "I hate you, Nicholas Bourne." Sophia curled her fingers into a fist and punched him, landing a stinging blow to Nicholas's left arm. "And I always will!"

"Promise?" Nicholas fired back, feeling even more quarrelsome and out of sorts.

Sophia stamped her foot in response, letting out a feral growl before turning on her heels and marching from the room.

"I hate you too, Sophia Afton," he said under his breath, rubbing his arm's tender muscle and wincing. "And I always will."

# 1

*May 24, 1813*
CARRINGTON HOUSE
LONDON, ENGLAND

"I loathe weddings."

Lady Sophia Afton smiled wryly in response to Langdon Bourne's drawling statement. "Do you think it wise to share such views with the woman you intend to marry? At a wedding, no less?"

"Tell me you feel otherwise," the Earl of Stonecliffe petitioned with easy confidence.

Sophia arched one feathered brow and acquiesced. "I would be lying if I did."

"And you, my dear Sophia, never lie," Langdon softly answered. "One of your most remarkable traits, that."

Sophia tipped her head in recognition of the compliment before turning to watch the newly wed Viscountess Carrington as she accepted a warm embrace from her husband, Dashiell Matthews, Viscount Carrington.

The newlyweds remained in each other's arms slightly longer than was acceptable, Elena's chaste yet lingering kiss upon Dash's cheek at their eventual parting prompting onlookers to sigh with approval. A decidedly besotted grin had settled on the viscount's face as he gazed at his bride.

"That may be. Still, I'll not ruin Dash's wedding day—

nor will you. He is, after all, one of our dearest friends. Now, look as if you're bowled over by sentiment. Or filled with happiness, at the very least."

Langdon reached out and captured Sophia's hand in his, giving her a conspiratorial wink. "In that case, all I need do is gaze upon your enchanting face."

Sophia squeezed his hand and smiled brightly, attempting to infuse her response with the depth of emotion she *should* feel for her betrothed.

But as Langdon had just mentioned, lying would never be considered a special talent of hers.

At that moment, Lady Whitcomb and her daughter Mariah walked by the couple, nodding graciously in greeting though they looked reluctant to interrupt the intimate moment.

Sophia and Langdon returned the salutation in unison, his strong, square chin dropping at precisely the moment hers dipped, as if both were controlled by the same strings.

They were perfectly suited for each other, Sophia thought. Everyone within the swirl of society that surrounded them agreed upon this fact. Their parents had begun planning on the very day Sophia was born; the impending marriage written into the detailed schedule of Sophia's life, sometime after perfecting the pianoforte and well before the birth of her first child.

But then her mother had been brutally murdered at the Afton country estate and neither the killer nor his motive was ever found. Many wondered why Sophia had not taken comfort in Langdon's arms the moment she was old enough to marry. Even more whispered today, many years since a trip down the aisle had been expected.

Sophia wondered, too. She leaned into Langdon's bulk, the feel of his arm against hers familiar and pleasing. Theirs was a perpetual state of suspension. Neither unwanted nor deeply desired, the interminable engagement was just *there*, much like Sophia's love for Langdon. There was no need to question their regard for each other. They would marry, someday.

Perhaps they would not embrace with passion at their own wedding celebration. Nor, Sophia suspected, would Langdon wear an unguarded grin that betrayed his feelings for the entire world to see. But they would be happy and settled, married and the best of friends. What more could there be?

Unbidden, the swift image of Nicholas Bourne, second son of the late earl and brother to Langdon, flashed before her. He stared hard at her, his eyes so deep a brown that they seemed to hold the darkness of night when he was angered—a constant state of being for him whenever Sophia was present.

She frowned, eyes narrowing. Why was she allowing Nicholas to occupy her thoughts? She shook her head slightly, determinedly banishing the mental image of the man that both irritated and ignited her mind.

"Ah, there's Carmichael," Langdon announced in his steady tone, releasing Sophia's hand. "I'll go say hello—unless you would like to accompany me?"

Henry Prescott, Viscount Carmichael, was a dear family friend to both Sophia and Langdon. A high-ranking official within the Young Corinthians, a covert governmental spy organization, he'd been instrumental in the search for Lady Afton's killer. Sophia shouldn't have known about the spy syndicate that Langdon and Dash belonged to, but the ever charitable Carmichael took pity on the young girl who'd lost her mother and let her in on their secret, promising to do everything he could to capture the killer.

Sophia would always be indebted to Carmichael for all of his efforts. Still, she found it difficult to be near the man, the gnawing sorrow of her mother's fate only magnified when she looked in his eyes.

"No, no," Sophia replied politely. "Go on. I believe I shall indulge in a glass of champagne."

Langdon nodded approvingly, then courteously waded into the fray of family and friends that stood between him and his superior.

Sophia daintily waved down a passing footman carrying a silver tray laden with champagne flutes. "Thank you," she told the man, taking up a slim glass and smiling appreciatively.

A sturdy finger tapped a tattoo on her shoulder, followed by Dash's familiar voice in her ear. "You look lovely, Sophia."

She turned to face him, schooling her features into abject surprise. "Really? I should go searching about the rag bin more often."

Her elegant pale green gown, made especially for the occasion, was banded at the hem and waist in a narrow strip of cream and darker green embroidery. The toes of her matching slippers peeped from beneath the hem. Emerald drop earrings echoed the larger, single-drop jewel of her necklace, and a dark green silk shawl was draped artfully over her arms.

"I am attempting to behave myself, Sophia," Dash countered with mock ruefulness. "The old me would have likened your green dress to a hearty cucumber. Or perhaps a head of spring lettuce."

"Vegetables? Ah, there is the Dash I know," Sophia murmured with pleasure, brushing a stray thread from her dear friend's dark blue coat.

Dash mirrored her efforts and reached out to pluck playfully at her shawl. "But I am a husband now. And will be a father one day. It is time for me to grow up. To embrace my future—that is what they say, isn't it?"

There was a certain obligation to agree upon such sentiment at weddings. Talk of plans and fairy-tale endings were meant to roll off the tongue as one would welcome a stray ray of sunlight after an English winter—without thought or effort.

Why then did Sophia feel as if she balanced on the dizzying and wholly unwelcome brink of crying? She loved Dash as if his blood ran in her veins, and believed most fervently that he completely and without reservation deserved absolute happiness.

"Are you ready, then?" she asked, the words sticking like treacle in her throat. "To grow up?"

"More than ready, Sophia," Dash replied, bending his knees until he was eye to eye with her. "Elena saved me. Let Langdon do the same for you—as he did at the frog pond."

Sophia had been nine. Nicholas had enticed her down to the frog pond with the promise of seeing the largest frog to have ever graced all of Sussex. She could not refuse, such a creature was surely far too abominable to ignore.

The monstrous beast, not surprisingly, turned out to be wholly fictitious. Nicholas had only craved the opportunity to shove Sophia into the pond. Which he'd done the moment she'd knelt on the muddy banks.

And Langdon had jumped in after her, nearly killing the both of them with his enthusiastic, albeit unskilled, efforts. Nevertheless, she'd proclaimed him her hero.

"I am not drowning, Dash," Sophia assured her friend, turning to take in Langdon as he conversed with Lord Carmichael across the room.

She did not lie. Drowning was surely a startling occurrence, full of fear and desperation. In contrast, Sophia's life continued on in predictable fashion as she held tight to the belief that one day she would find her mother's killer, then move on to secure her own happiness with Langdon.

"Treading water, then?" Dash suggested bleakly.

"Stop," Sophia warned, tears pressing at the back of her eyes, "or you will make me cry, which I know for a fact you cannot abide. Besides, it is normally Nicholas's responsibility to upset me."

Her mind wandered toward the man for the second time that day. Sophia searched the crowd for him. "And do you know, I don't believe I saw him at the church."

Dash brought his glass to his lips and drained the last of the champagne before turning to set the empty flute on a nearby mahogany table. "Didn't you?"

His evasive answer sent a warning prickling over Sophia's skin. "No, I am sure of it."

"That seems rather strange," Dash answered, staring at Sophia with what seemed to be abject honesty.

Only he was lying. The pupils of his eyes were dramatically dilated, something Sophia knew happened when an individual was not telling the truth.

"Has he disappeared somewhere to drink again?" she pressed, unease settling between her shoulders. "There is no need to protect me, Dash. We might not be particularly close, but I am well aware of Nicholas's lamentable habit."

"Interrogating me at my own wedding?" Dash chided affably, looking over her head to the guests milling about. "Perhaps the Runners have trained you *too* well."

He referred to the Bow Street Runners, of course, though "training" was a rather overblown description. Sophia's interest in criminal behavior had taken root following the death of her mother. Once of age, she had cajoled her way into a limited apprenticeship of sorts. There was not a file she did not know forward and back, the details of every captured criminal in London available for her perusal. Through her highly controversial access to the Bow Street Offices, Sophia had witnessed a number of interrogations as well. The Runners had widened her knowledge exponentially; her own personal research into criminal behavior shoring up any area that might have been found lacking in her unique education.

Much to her surprise, Sophia had discovered that unearthing lies, deceits, and unnatural inclinations was her talent and her passion. Still, it did not give her permission to upset a dear friend.

"I am sorry, Dash," Sophia apologized. "Please forgive me."

Dash patted her on the head as he'd done since they were four and three, respectively. "There is nothing to be sorry for, my dear Sophia."

Sophia attempted to ignore the slow, steady intake of breath that gave away Dash's relief.

And failed. "Though Nicholas's proclivity for troublesome behavior would make anyone wary." Sophia caught the telling flare of Dash's nostrils with dread. "Please, go and find your wife. Ply her with champagne and allow her to repay you in kind. Forget all about this regrettable conversation. Langdon and I will deal with Nicholas—"

"Bourne has taken himself off to the Primrose Inn. Again. Which is hardly cause for concern," Dash interrupted. Only mild annoyance colored his tone but emotion darkened his eyes—and gave him away. "There is no need to bother Stonecliffe with such uneventful news."

Sophia smoothed her gloved fingers over the silk skirt of her gown nervously. "You are lying, Dash. To *me*. Why?"

"Let it go, Sophia."

She turned toward the crowd with every intention of joining Langdon and Carmichael. "We are not children any longer, Dash—you admitted it yourself only moments ago. There's no need to protect me from the truth, whatever it may be."

Dash's hand closed over her forearm before she took one step. "It concerns your mother's killer," Dash warned in a low voice.

Sophia could not have been more shocked by Dash's words. Her vision narrowed, her mind rejecting all other thoughts until its only focus was Dash's sentence. The buzz from the chattering members of the ton gathered in the salon blurred into incomprehensible syllables. She leaned into Dash's grasp for support as the room swayed precariously.

And then everything went black.

※ ※

A sharply medicinal scent filled Sophia's nostrils and her eyes flew open in response. "Dash?" she cried out, bracing her palms against the soft cushions of a settee and pushing herself upright.

"Calm yourself, Lady Sophia. You fainted," Dash's wife explained from where she sat on the Aubusson carpet at Sophia's side. "My husband told me you had an aversion to weddings. Not that I would blame you. It is my *own* wedding and I find myself in need of a quiet room and a good book. But fainting? Stroke of genius, if you ask me," she said dryly.

"It does appear rather drastic, doesn't it?" Sophia answered hesitantly. She glanced about the room, recognizing the graceful lines of the Adams fireplace surround, the delicate curves of a feminine writing desk, and a beautifully rendered portrait of Dash's grandmother that hung over the mantel. "I see I've been spirited away to the viscountess's quarters, no less. My, I do know how to draw attention. I must apologize, Lady Carrington. I had no intention of ruining your wedding celebration."

"There is no need to apologize. First, you managed

to extract me from the festivities, which as I mentioned before was not a wholly unwelcome thing. And secondly—and rather more importantly—you received some startling news."

Elena's statement quickly brought Sophia back to her senses. "Then you know about my mother's killer?" she asked, her heart beginning to pick up speed with equal parts anticipation and fear.

The viscountess nodded again. "That is why I am here—and why Dash is currently keeping Langdon occupied. Not an easy task, as I am sure you are aware. He is a most congenial man in all matters, with the exception of you. I suspect he will soon be pounding at the door, demanding entry."

"Then we haven't a moment to waste, wouldn't you agree?" Sophia asked, carefully swinging her legs from the settee and settling her slippered feet firmly on the carpeted floor.

Elena rose from the lavender patterned carpet and joined Sophia on the sofa, her expression cautious, but resolute. "Very well. In the interest of time, I will be brief. A journal belonging to Dash's late father was recently discovered. In it, he recounts a visit from a prostitute who sought him out in an effort to clear her conscience. She'd suspected for years that one of the brothel's clients was in fact the man who'd murdered your mother. Though his true identity had been concealed from her, Dash and Nicholas were able to successfully piece the clues together and identify the killer."

"Why did Dash not come to me?" Sophia protested. "He should have—from the very moment the journal was discovered."

Elena reached out; her upturned palm a silent request for understanding. "Lady Sophia, you do know how dearly Dash cares for you, do you not?" she asked plainly.

"Yes," Sophia answered reluctantly, accepting Elena's hand in hers.

"He knew you could not be kept from searching for the man if you were told. And putting you in such a dangerous position was something Dash wished to avoid at all cost."

Sophia wanted to rail against the woman's reasoning, to put into words the fiery indignation building in her chest. But it was no use. In the same position, it was entirely possible she would have spared Dash for her own selfish means.

"And the murderer's name?" Sophia asked, squeezing Elena's hand tightly in hers.

"Francis Smeade," Elena said warily, clearly watching Sophia for signs of distress.

*Francis Smeade?* Sophia had known very little of the man, his unappealing personality having discouraged her from pursuing anything beyond mere acquaintance. Then Mr. Smeade had managed to get himself shot and killed . . .

Sophia closed her eyes against the oncoming wave of nausea. "Is that it, then? The reason Nicholas decamped for the Primrose Inn? Did he shoot Smeade?"

"Dear me, no," Elena instantly assured her. "Both Dash and Mr. Bourne were there that night on the bridge when Smeade was killed. In fact, Dash was the last to speak with Smeade; their conversation lasted long enough to confirm that he'd been hired to murder your mother."

"For money? Then Smeade had been hired by someone else. Who?"

"We do not know," Elena answered. "Mr. Bourne pursued the shooter, but the man jumped into the Thames before he could be captured."

"And Nicholas blames himself?" Sophia's heart ached with a swift stab of empathy.

The abject silence that met her question confirmed Sophia's fears. She gently released Elena and folded her hands in her lap, striving for calm even as tension tightened her fingers.

"So that is why he is at the Primrose." Her voice trembled. She found it surprisingly difficult to speak clearly. "I cannot imagine how deeply the man's escape has affected Nicholas."

"Deeply enough that he refuses to speak with Dash—or is unable to due to drink," Elena replied in a somber, almost regretful tone. "Which is why I must ask a favor of you."

"Anything," Sophia answered distractedly, her mind attempting to keep pace with the volume of information.

"Though I understand you and Mr. Bourne do not often see eye to eye, I need you to convince him to take up the case again," Elena implored Sophia. "I cannot ask Stonecliffe; he is too dedicated to keep such information from the Young Corinthians. And Lord Carmichael would never stand for his involvement, as you well know. There is no one else but Mr. Bourne now."

Years before, Lord Carmichael had expressly forbidden all four of the children from pursuing the case. He'd assured them that time and distance was what they required.

"And, should you wonder why I'm being so monumentally selfish, I am with child," Elena finished, sinking down to the carpet until her wedding gown pooled all about her. "I cannot ask Dash to abandon the case. Still, I am terrified he'll come to harm. And how can I ask Mr. Bourne to continue in Dash's stead when I know the danger he will surely face?"

A storm cloud had settled on the woman's brow, tears threatening to break through at any moment. Sophia may have fainted at her dearest friend's wedding, but she would not make his bride cry.

She fought down a rising tide of dread at the knowledge that it was up to her to convince Nicholas. Such an appeal would take time and patience, two things that were always in short supply whenever they conversed.

Sophia focused instead on the surge of elation she felt over the very idea of joining the search for her mother's killer. After too many years of being told to let the matter rest, she would at last be involved.

"Please, Lady Carrington," Sophia crooned, patting the woman's hand reassuringly. "Do not worry yourself. Nicholas and I have our differences, that much is true. This is one matter, though, on which I feel certain we will agree."

Because she would give him no choice.

# 2

The Honorable Nicholas Bourne could not decide which was worse: the rattle of metal rings over the curtain rod as the rough linen hangings were pulled back, the excruciatingly loud crash of the shutters slamming against the outer stucco and timber siding of the Primrose Inn, or the sudden flash of blinding sunlight.

"Mrs. Brimm, are you trying to kill me?" he asked the innkeeper's wife in a low, even tone as he willed the relentless pounding in his head to stop.

Something soft yet painfully unwelcome landed on his face in response to his query. Nicholas cautiously opened his eyes but could see nothing through the folds of his linen shirt. "I see no need for clothing at this juncture, my good woman, as I intend to stay abed for at least another two hours. Now, off with you. I'm sure there are other guests who would welcome your attention."

"I am neither Mrs. Brimm nor am I trying to kill you. Not yet, anyway."

Nicholas startled at the sound of the woman's voice.

He grabbed the bedcovers, yanking them higher over his bare chest as he levered himself upright. "Sophia?"

Lady Sophia Afton stood in front of the open window, illuminated by the late-morning sun. The warm golden rays silhouetted her graceful form against the gloom and dark of the rented room. All about, empty bottles of brandy and Cognac, sheets of foolscap and discarded quills, and Nicholas's clothing were carelessly tossed hither and yon—the evidence of a messy and misused life.

And in the middle of it all stood Sophia. The faint pink of her rosebud printed gown appeared to be the exact hue of her full lips. Her dark hair, gleaming like autumn's burnished oak leaves, was artfully pinned up, a few stray curls expertly arranged about her face. And below the feathered arch of brows, her eyes were the deep green of emeralds, framed with dark lashes and spaced just far enough apart to give her an exotic air. One could get lost in those immeasurable depths, a fact Nicholas knew all too well.

Sophia stole his breath away. She always had and without even knowing that she did so. He'd long ago learned it was useless to fight the fascination. His sanity would return again. Or not. It did not matter in the least.

"Surely you're not surprised," she said, slowly walking toward the bed until she stood within touching distance. "Someone had to fetch you."

Nicholas fought the urge to disappear beneath the coarse bed linens, aware that doing so would only make him appear even more the fool. "Well, *someone* usually means Carrington or my brother. How on earth did you draw the short straw—and where's your Mrs. Kirk? This is feeling more scandalous by the moment." He gestured abruptly. "Turn around, Sophia, while I make myself decent."

With an unfathomable glance from beneath her lashes, she did as he bade her, turning to face the opposite wall.

Nicholas tossed back the covers and swung his bare feet to the plank floor. He swore under his breath as the sudden movement sent his head spinning. Then swore again as he reached for his shirt from the pile of clothing flung carelessly on the edge of the bed and pulled it over his head, tugging it into place.

"Mrs. Kirk is waiting in the coach so that we may speak privately," Sophia replied, her back to him as Nicholas buttoned his breeches. "As for Dash, he's celebrating his wedding trip."

"Dammit," Nicholas cursed for the third time in as many moments. "I thought he was to be leg-shackled on the twenty-fourth."

Sophia turned back to face him, pity pooling in her eyes. "He was, Nicholas. Today is the twenty-sixth."

He froze, staring at her, shame snaking its way around his heart. He'd lost a week. In the past there had been a day here or there that had disappeared into the ether, consumed by drink and his need to forget. Never before had there been so many lost days in a row. Too many days.

Sophia crossed the room to a slat-backed chair. She turned it around and clasped the worn wood, tipping the chair onto two legs and dragging it toward the bed.

Nicholas winced as the scrape of wood against wood set hammers pounding inside his skull.

She placed the chair to face Nicholas, then took her seat.

He narrowed his eyes at her. "What are you up to, Sophia?"

"Do you promise to listen?" she asked sternly, extending her arm, her palm up in silent plea.

He scrubbed his hand across his unshaven jaw. "Are we children again, then?" he growled.

"Do you promise, Nicholas?" Sophia pressed. "Or have I come all this way for nothing?"

"Honestly, Sophia," Nicholas muttered, reaching out and taking her hand in his. "I don't recall inviting you, so yes, I would say you have."

Sophia laced her fingers with his and shook four times, just as she'd done during their childhood. "Say it."

"I promise to listen with open ears, wide eyes, and a closed mouth," Nicholas bit out, his displeasure with her presence clearly conveyed in every last syllable. "There, will that do? They're only words—strung together by children, if you'll remember. Hardly anything that would hold water."

It killed him to touch her, her soft, small hand in his akin to torture. Yet he wouldn't let go. He knew he would never be an honorable man. Never marry nor know the joys of family. He would take his love for Sophia to his deathbed. Even if it destroyed him, which, he ventured to guess, was precisely what would happen.

"Thank you, Nicholas," she sighed, relief easing the strain from her countenance. She squeezed his hand in hers, then let go.

Nicholas lowered his arm, the tips of his fingers still tingling where they'd gripped Sophia's mere seconds before. "Well, out with it, then. I don't have all day."

"I need your help."

Nicholas stared hard at the only woman he'd ever loved. He'd often imagined what it would feel like to hear Sophia say she needed him. And the emotion was nothing like the growing sense of unease that crept up his spine now.

"And my brother?" he asked bitterly, desperate to maintain some sense of dignity though he knew it to be a pointless struggle. "I would venture to guess Langdon would be more suitable. Or sober, at the very least."

"I do not need Langdon. I need you."

Sophia folded her hands in her lap and stared at Nicholas. When she'd thrown back the curtains earlier and turned to look at him, she'd been stunned, frozen into stillness and too distracted to move or speak. The sunlight had arrowed through the window behind her and directly onto the bed. In that brief moment before Nicholas recognized her, she'd been shocked at the powerful, dangerous man sprawled on the rumpled bed.

The blankets were pushed to his waist, his upper torso bare. Though she'd known him since they were children, he was suddenly unrecognizable. She'd been unable to look away from the flex and smooth ripple of well-defined muscles in his chest and arms as he pushed himself upright. It was only the sound of his sleep-roughened, deep voice as he spoke her name that convinced her she'd not wandered into the wrong room by mistake.

Now that she was nearer, she could see deep crease marks from the crude inn bedding that ran the length of the left side of his face. He'd clearly been abed for some time and yet the dark crescents beneath his eyes intimated exhaustion.

An air of dissipation and soul-deep weariness shrouded his handsome countenance. She wanted badly to know why he felt driven to drink when it only led to this—a dank room in a hedge-inn, surrounded by nothing that could hope to bring him any peace. Despite their shared history, she felt a reluctance to question him. He'd always held some part of himself back, denying Sophia access for his own personal reasons. And it appeared his years in India had only increased the territory she was not allowed to traverse.

He rubbed his knuckles over his jaw for the second

time in as many minutes, the muscles beneath the un-shaven skin rigid. "I find such a notion impossible to believe."

He was clearly exhausted. Still, there was more. There always was with Nicholas. Her presence at the Primrose wasn't merely an irritation to the man; was he angry? Or perhaps embarrassed?

Sophia felt her nerves tighten with the queer tension that always accompanied their interactions. She was never quite sure how he would respond to her. He was a wild animal and she the hapless human who'd had the nerve to disturb him. It could not be said that Sophia ever felt fearful in Nicholas's presence, though at the moment the sudden quickening of her pulse gave her reason to pause.

Theirs had never been an easy friendship. Her unqual-ified need to be near him was matched in intensity by his impatience at her very existence. Sophia had come to believe that he truly disliked her, although she'd never been able to discover what she'd done to earn his en-mity.

Despite the distance he kept between them, she found herself unable to ignore the inexplicable pull his pres-ence always exerted on her. "Langdon would refuse me. And as much as I chafe at the very idea, I cannot do this alone," Sophia replied honestly, willing her heartbeat to slow.

Nicholas captured her with a look of shock. "I'm sorry, Sophia. I don't believe that I heard you correctly. Did you just say that you could not accomplish some-thing on your own?"

His eyes glinted with sudden amusement. There he was, the Nicholas she liked best. Capricious. Irreverent. Clever. He was the only man who could always make her laugh, no matter the circumstances. "I missed you terribly while you were away in India. Do you know,

I believe I didn't laugh once while you were gone," Sophia countered, relief and an affectionate smile curving her mouth. "But I will not relent, Nicholas."

He crossed his arms over his expansive chest. "Do stop wasting my time, Sophia. Tell me what you've come for."

She peered down at the planked floor, wincing at his impatience. "Very well," she began, looking up and fixing him with a somber stare. "Now that Dash is married, someone will need to help you in the search for my mother's killer. And that someone, I believe, must be me."

Nicholas uncrossed his arms and propped his elbows on his knees, a menacing glint in his deep brown eyes. "No."

"I've valuable experience," she explained earnestly.

"Let me see if I understand: a bit of clerking at the Bow Street Office somehow qualifies you to hunt down a monster—who's ordered the killings of numerous people, one of whom, you just found out, was your mother," Nicholas lashed out, raking both hands through his hair until the rumpled black locks stood up on end. "Did you know that Smeade attacked Lady Carrington? Nearly choked the life from her because he'd been paid to do so. His superior will stop at nothing to preserve his anonymity. And you suggest I take you on—a woman, for Christ's sake—of all people?"

Sophia jumped up, kicking back and sending the chair skittering across the scarred floor. "You've no right . . ." she spat out before forcing herself to breathe deeply. "I understand the danger, Nicholas," she started again, her tone controlled. "It's precisely why I did not ask for Langdon's help. He never would have agreed to—"

"But you think I will? Am I that careless, then?" Nicholas interrupted bitterly.

Sophia reached out to him, flinching involuntarily

when Nicholas moved away to avoid her touch. "No, you misunderstand me," she begged, her restraint slipping. "Carelessness is not the issue here. I am asking you to do what you know is right."

"You cannot ask this of me," Nicholas shouted, standing up from the bed and roughly grabbing hold of her arms.

Sophia instinctively jerked back, the sensation of Nicholas so close troubling to her rattled mind and body. A raw, pleasing heat ignited where his fingers and palms touched her. Warmth traveled in rivers through her, her skin suddenly tingling with sensitivity and need. She fought the urge to lean forward, to experience more of the new, unsettling feeling that quickened her breath and sent her heart pounding. He loomed over her, too close, too male, and impossible to ignore. She willed herself to be still, refusing to retreat.

He loosened his grip on her bare skin and closed his eyes. "Please."

"We're alike, you and I," Sophia said with quiet conviction, though her heart raced with an aberrant thrill. "Somehow Dash managed to escape. And Langdon can see a future—in the distance, true, but it's there. As for the two of us? We can't let go of the past. And we'll never be able to until my mother's killer is captured."

Nicholas rubbed his thumbs over the sensitive bare skin of Sophia's inner arm. Her eyes fluttered closed, the scent of his spiced soap surrounding her. The slow, sensual drag of his thumb was intoxicating. She ached to feel his skin on hers in more intimate places. She angled her head slightly so that the slim column of her neck was exposed to him.

"Don't do this, Sophia."

Sophia forced her eyes open to find Nicholas staring at her, the potent mixture of anger and strong conviction that shadowed his face effectively weakening her will.

But not breaking it.

"I have to, Nicholas. You know that I do."

Nicholas let go of her arms and pointed to the door. "Go," he ordered, his voice raw.

The sudden release from his hold was disorienting. Her body mourned the loss of his touch, as if he had held her spellbound, enchanted, for those too brief moments. She trembled and her mind searched for an explanation that would provide a reason for her overwhelming response to him. Sophia found none that she could accept.

She stumbled backward, desperate to put distance between them. "You will return to London?" she asked, bracing herself for rejection. "I'll have your word."

Nicholas lifted his hands and began to methodically rub his temples as if in pain, barely nodding in agreement.

"Your word, Nicholas," Sophia pressed, regretting the childish demand the moment it flew from her lips.

"Go!" he roared, pointing savagely at the door.

Sophia started at the guttural cry and ran for the door, not pausing even once to look back.

# 3

"You look as if you've seen a wraith."

Sophia glanced nervously out the window of her carriage at the Primrose, then turned to her companion, Lettie Kirk. "Not a ghost, no. Perhaps a demon? Or a warlock of some sort."

The wheels of the carriage began to roll, stuttering briefly in the spring mud before settling into a slow, steady pace.

Lettie lowered her chin and looked pointedly at Sophia. "You speak of Mr. Bourne, I presume?"

Sophia held her still trembling hand aloft. "None other."

Lettie pursed her lips, her fifty-plus years on earth evident in the fine, feathery lines deepened by her disapproval. "He always did possess the tongue of a viper. What did he say to upset you this time?"

Sophia peered outside to the rutted road behind them. She was just able to make out the Primrose's tidy yard before a copse of yew trees obstructed her view. She appreciated Lettie's concern. More than that, she relied on it. For fourteen years the two had been inseparable, the nanny becoming her maid when Sophia grew too old for the nursery. Lettie was eventually assigned as a trusted companion when neither could bear to part. Lord Afton understood little of his own daughter, the heartbreak and mental anguish caused by his wife's death keeping him isolated on his estate in Wales. Lettie knew everything about Sophia. Better yet, she loved her all the more for it.

"It wasn't his verbal barbs as much as *him*," Sophia replied, lowering her hand though her troubled gaze remained fixed on her trembling fingers. "I'm not quite sure how to describe . . . His . . . Something has changed—no, he has changed. Nicholas is not the man I knew."

"Yes?"

Sophia looked up at the sound of Lettie's voice as if she'd been distracted. "I apologize. I don't know what, precisely, I expected his response to be. Oh, the yelling and carrying on was standard fare from him. And he used his usual weapons—sarcasm, self-loathing, volume."

"Well, that definitely sounds like the man I know," Lettie replied, softly taking Sophia's hand in hers.

"It does, doesn't it?" Sophia agreed. "Maybe I have it all wrong. Perhaps it wasn't Nicholas. Perhaps it was me?"

She'd never succeeded in giving up on Nicholas, and he'd offered her ample opportunity to do so. Throughout the years Sophia had held fast to the idea that she was acting in her mother's place, protecting the boy Lady Afton had often referred to as her young warrior with a heart of glass.

This latest round of feverish quarreling made Sophia angry. And aroused. Never before had her body betrayed her in such a demanding manner.

"No, my lady. I'm certain Mr. Bourne is to blame. You've always had a soft spot in your heart for that man," Lettie countered knowingly. "Either way, one thing is clear: you would do best to stay away from Nicholas Bourne. Let him continue the search for your mother's killer alone, as the viscountess requested."

"I cannot do that, Lettie," Sophia said, her heart pinching as the older woman's eyes brimmed with tears. "I have prepared for this moment my entire life. Nicholas's involvement cannot keep me from moving forward. You must understand."

Her companion's face fell as she struggled to accept Sophia's decision. "I see. And you are sure Lord Stonecliffe must not be told?"

Sophia had entrusted her companion with all that she knew, save for the Young Corinthians. It had been a burden, but one worth carrying; revealing their existence would have put Lettie's life in danger.

"As I explained during our ride to the Primrose, it is absolutely essential that Langdon remain unaware," Sophia replied, her fingers grasping hold of Lettie's. "There is Nicholas, though."

Lettie released Sophia's hand and eased her tall frame against the cushions. "Cold comfort, my dear."

❧

Nicholas waited impatiently in the common room of the Primrose. Mrs. Brimm was enthusiastically reprimanding a kitchen girl for burning the muffins.

He'd hurriedly packed his things and was prepared to leave. He simply could not remain another moment in the room. It reeked of Sophia's delicate floral soap. He'd found her shawl, a pale pink strip of fabric hardly useful against the cold, lying in a silken pool atop the rickety wood desk. And no matter where he fixed his gaze, she was there; leaning over his bed as she roused him, pity straining her beautiful face. Standing directly before him, her body shaking with the need to be anywhere else but in that room. And disappearing out the door, fear and disappointment fueling her escape.

Nicholas gritted his teeth in an effort to stave off the

humiliation. He had no need for her pity or disappointment, or his own self-loathing that would accompany it; he'd managed a lethal level of abhorrence for his very existence quite well over the years and saw no need to add to it.

Mrs. Brimm sent the young maid off with a vigorous shaking of her finger, and then turned to Nicholas. "Impossible to find good help these days, Mr. Bourne. Wouldn't you agree?"

He nodded in agreement, in no mood to converse.

Mrs. Brimm levered her sizable girth forward and looked over the oaken bar that separated them within the Primrose's common room. "Checking out, are we? Not like you to let a lover's spat get in the way of your fun."

Nicholas flinched as she dramatically winked not only one beady eye, but the entire left half of her pockmarked face. It was grotesque. And infuriating.

The woman assumed Sophia was his lover, come from London to demand his return.

*And why wouldn't she, you lackwit?* No more than an hour had passed since Sophia had gone. Yet here he was, bags packed, ready to settle up and be on his way.

The phrase "add insult to injury" appeared in Nicholas's mind. *Somewhere, most likely hell, the Roman writer Phaedrus is having a good laugh at my expense.*

Sophia had no information to go on; every last notation and detail concerning the case were neatly stowed away in the bag at his feet. His delayed return would give her time to reconsider her ridiculous request.

Moreover, it would afford Nicholas the opportunity to reclaim a portion of his manhood. Sophia was not his. She never would be. It was high time he accepted the fact and acted accordingly.

"Do you know, Mrs. Brimm, I've changed my mind. Put me down for one more night," Nicholas instructed the innkeeper. "And I would like a new room. The old one is far too full of quarrelsome spirits."

Mrs. Brimm cackled with delight. "You're a wicked man, Mr. Bourne."

"So they tell me."

# 4

*May 28*
The Albany
Piccadilly
London

Nicholas spent not one, but two additional nights at the Primrose Inn. He'd locked himself in his room and revisited the sheaf of papers concerning Lady Afton's murder, searching for something—anything—he may have missed.

And still, as his mare Guinevere jogged toward his London lodgings, a solution to the problem that Sophia presented was nowhere in sight. He slowed the mare to a stop in front of the Albany. Located just off Piccadilly, the elegant building was considered by the fashionable ton to be choice rooms for a bachelor uninterested in maintaining a larger house. Nicholas didn't care whether society approved the residence. He stayed at the Albany because it had been used by Langdon and therefore was ridiculously easy to secure.

"Thomas," he called out in greeting to the groom who'd appeared as if from thin air, ready to take Guinevere.

Thomas waited for Nicholas to jump down then took the reins from him. "Mr. Bourne, welcome home."

"I trust all is as it should be in the great city of London?" Nicholas asked, patting Guinevere on the neck.

"You could say that."

Thomas had always been a man of few words. But mysterious? Never.

"Should I be concerned?"

Thomas clucked to the mare and kindly urged her on. "Depends upon your outlook, I suppose."

Nicholas decided to ignore the groom's cryptic words. He'd slept very little the past two nights, his ass ached from the saddle, and really, he wasn't a terribly patient person to begin with.

"She's earned extra oats, Thomas," he said, slapping Guinevere's rump before mounting the steps of the Albany and stepping across its threshold.

He strode down the hall of the main floor, reaching his door and opening it. At once, he knew that something about the interior of the fashionable apartment was different from when he had last been there, though he didn't immediately perceive what it was.

Just to be safe, he pulled a slim stiletto knife from his boot, then stepped into the room and kicked the door closed. The thud was rather satisfying in his disgruntled mood. Tossing his beaver hat on a walnut side table, he crossed the entryway, entered the salon, and collapsed onto the soft gold sofa. If there was an intruder, he would have to come to Nicholas rather than the other way around.

The fading light slanting through the mullioned windows caught only the faintest trace of rising dust motes.

"Oh God," he muttered, closing his eyes with annoyance. Clearly, his housekeeper, Mrs. Fitzroy, had seen fit to take advantage of his absence from London, and *tidy up* his quarters. An impressive multitude of dust motes should have been leaping and dancing through the air at that very moment. And the sofa cushions, he noted with a frown, were rather plumper than they ought to be.

And then he smelled it. The rich, thick odor of champa incense that evoked instant memories of India. He knew of only one person who would have invaded his rooms and filled the air with the intoxicating sandalwood scent.

"Pavan Singh!" Nicholas yelled. "I warned you what would happen should you follow me to London, didn't I?"

"Breathe deeply." The melodic, accented words were spoken in an all-too-familiar calm, soothing tone.

Nicholas pushed up from the comfortable sofa, eyes narrowed as he searched the room.

Singh waited near the door to the hallway, his small frame swathed in the traditional loose white dhoti loin-cloth and a bright orange cotton overdress known as a kurta in his native India. "How could I forget, sahib Bourne? You threatened to disembowel me and leave me to the ravens."

"And yet, despite my threats," Nicholas commented as he crossed the carpeted floor, his curt tone hiding the surge of pleasure he felt at his old friend's presence, "you are here, in England, in my quarters at the Albany. And burning incense, no less," he added, looking at the small brass burner on the sideboard.

The older man raised both hands palms-up. "I had no choice, sahib Bourne. You saved my life and those of the villagers. I am bound by duty to serve you. And I do so happily." Beneath the snowy white of the turban cover-ing his black hair, his brown face held an expression of innocence. His black eyes, however, twinkled with amused affection.

Privately, Nicholas reluctantly agreed that Singh spoke the truth—at least the bit about how he'd saved the man's life. Work in India was easy enough to find—unscrupulous, ill-principled work, that is. Mercenaries were in high demand and Nicholas possessed all of the required traits: strength, intelligence, and the ability to not give a damn for his own safety.

Unfortunately, he also owned a conscience. And even more troubling, a moral code. Thankfully there had been men like Singh's village elder who found themselves in the unenviable position of doing battle not only with English interest in the form of the bloody East India Company, but also defending their people against bandits who saw the ruthless British taking what wasn't theirs and decided to follow suit.

The Maharajah of Amanphour had hired Nicholas to protect his people and their land; a land whose hills held a fortune in buried jewels. The task had proven to be the most challenging undertaking of all his Indian adventures. Still, Nicholas and his men subdued even the most powerful of the Maharajah's foes. In doing so, they saved countless lives and protected the ruler's precious jewels—including Singh.

Pavan Singh was a holy man, of sorts. Nicholas hadn't the patience for his own religion, never mind those of the rest of the world, so he could not be sure where Singh sat in the order of Hindu importance. But none of that had mattered. Singh's peaceful countenance and friendly nature had drawn Nicholas. When not fighting, he could be found in Singh's humble home, enjoying the benefits of the aromatic incense and listening to the man prattle on about destiny and other lofty ideas.

As luck would have it, that was exactly where he was when bandits surprised the village with a late night attack. Had Nicholas not been in the hut, Singh would have fallen to one particularly nasty soldier and his wicked tulwar knife.

So, in theory, yes, Nicholas had saved the man's life. Because it was his job. The jewels the Maharajah had given him as payment for service well done were quite enough, as far as he was concerned.

He'd earned a bloody fortune in India.

He hadn't any need for a holy man.

Clearly, Singh did not agree.

"England is a cold land, Singh—foggy, rainy, and miserable in winter months. You will never be able to bear it," Nicholas protested, reaching for a pitcher of water on the sideboard and dousing the incense.

Singh sighed, his gaze following Nicholas's movements with resignation.

He pressed his palms together as though he was readying to thank one of his gods. "I will wrap myself in the warmth of your friendship, sahib," he said solemnly.

"The food will not be to your liking—not at all."

Singh bowed his head. "Vishnu provides nourishment for my soul, and will surely do so for my body."

"It is all coming back to me now," Nicholas muttered, turning away from the irritatingly calm man and stalking back to the sofa. He lay down, stretching out until he was comfortably situated. "For a holy man, you are not terribly bright."

"Ah, sahib Bourne." A deep sigh managed to sound both patient and long-suffering. "You must remember: truth, contentment, forbearance, and mercy belong to great minds," Singh urged gently.

His beatific smile gleamed like some damn beacon in the night, Nicholas thought with irritation.

He closed his eyes and folded his arms across his chest. "Your wisdom will serve you very little here in London, Singh. This is not India. War does not rage on our streets in a traditional sense. Still, there is struggle, my friend. We humans cannot manage to breathe without destroying."

"Then I am doubly glad that I have come, sahib. It

sounds as though you need a holy man such as me now more than ever."

"Stop calling me sahib, will you?" Nicholas growled, chafing at the respectful form of address adopted by so many in colonial India.

The doorknob rattled as someone inserted a key. Nicholas released a roar of protest. "Mrs. Fitzroy, have mercy on me, I beg of you."

"I see you are alive—and as charming as ever."

Nicholas opened one eye and peered over the back of the sofa. "Langdon, is that you? I've only just arrived back in town."

Langdon sauntered toward him as he tossed a key up in the air and deftly caught it. "I was on my way to the club when I thought to check on you. Splendid bit of luck, wouldn't you agree?"

"That is one way of looking at it," Nicholas quipped, opening both eyes and glaring at his brother.

As usual, Langdon was dressed impeccably. A deep blue coat of light wool stretched over his broad shoulders with nary a wrinkle, his cravat and linen shirt were pristine white, and the black leather of his Hessian boots gleamed with polish.

Nicholas was abruptly reminded that his own boots were dull with dust. The ride from the Primrose to London had left his own black Weston-tailored coat and fawn breeches less than immaculate and imbued with the faint scent of horse and leather. And since he'd released his valet just prior to leaving for the Inn, he'd have to find a new man to care for his clothes and polish his boots. He nearly groaned aloud at the thought. He had little patience for fussy valets who moped and grew gloomy when his boots were dirty.

A polite but forced clearing of a throat reminded Nicholas why he'd collapsed on the sofa in the first place. "Oh yes. Langdon, say hello to Singh, a friend from India."

Singh padded to where Langdon leaned against the faded sofa and bowed. "Lord . . . ?"

"Blast," Nicholas uttered, already tired of polite society. "Lord Stonecliffe."

"A pleasure to meet you, Lord Stonecliffe."

"Langdon here is, as you've just learned, a lord," Nicholas informed Singh, sarcasm effortlessly lacing his voice. "And quite the lord he is, too. Responsible, kind, generous, honest—"

"In short, everything that my little brother is not," Langdon interrupted, playfully landing a punch to Nicholas's biceps. "Or so he'd have you believe."

Langdon offered his hand to Singh and smiled when the Indian took it. "Don't let him fool you, Singh. There's not a finer chap to be found."

"We are in agreement, then, Lord Stonecliffe," Singh replied enthusiastically.

Nicholas audibly groaned.

"I believe it is time for tea," Singh announced.

"Oh, splendid," Langdon said, smirking at Nicholas.

Nicholas closed his eyes. "I would groan in response if I did not recall doing so only moments ago."

"Indeed, you did, sahib," Singh confirmed with a complete lack of guile, and then quit the room.

"I like him," Langdon said with conviction.

Nicholas frowned. "You would," he answered. "Very much alike, you two. So full of *goodness* and all."

"Come now, Nicholas," Langdon chided. "Must you always be so hard on yourself?"

Nicholas folded both arms across his chest. "Simply doing the dead lord proud."

Langdon sighed, as he always did whenever Nicholas referred to their father by the disrespectful sobriquet.

Not that he held the man in any more lofty esteem.

It was the principle of the matter; and to Langdon, that meant everything.

Nicholas could let principle hang, and often did. Especially as it pertained to his father. The late Earl of Stonecliffe was not a violent man. Nor was he irresponsible, dissolute, or particularly unlikable. No, he was simply uninterested in his second son. Until Nicholas decided he'd *make* his father notice him. He could not do everything right—Langdon had already claimed that role—but he could do everything wrong, and rather fabulously.

He captured his father's attention, all right. And the man's quiet contempt and disappointment.

Which only hurt more. And, in turn, encouraged Nicholas to push harder. Even now, with the man dead and buried in the ground, Nicholas continued to hone his debauchery.

He couldn't say why. It was simply what he did; or, to be more precise, who he was.

"Now, dear brother." Nicholas opened his eyes and pushed upright. "Care to tell me why you're really here?"

Langdon's angelic smile did not fool Nicholas for one moment.

"Your club is nowhere near the Albany, unless one was blind, drunk, and in possession of a terribly misleading map." Nicholas perused Langdon's person skeptically. "None of which applies to you."

Langdon stretched out his legs and crossed his boots at the ankles. "I needed to see for myself that you were well."

"Is this to do with Carrington's wedding?" Nicholas asked, shame bubbling to life low in his belly. "I'd fully intended on being there. I must have misremembered the date."

"I do not doubt you, Nicholas," Langdon assured

him. "But he is your dearest friend. I knew that something was wrong. If not for Corinthian business I would have collected you myself."

The shame began to boil in earnest. It was always worse when it came to Langdon because his brother truly cared; judgment was never an ulterior motive with him.

Nicholas wished it were. Especially now.

"Look at you, though—back in London of your own accord. That's something, brother. Wouldn't you agree?"

Nicholas could taste the bitter, familiar tang of self-loathing fill his mouth.

He nodded in agreement, earning a hopeful grin from Langdon for his efforts.

"Now, where is Singh with the bloody tea?"

*The Fabersham Residence*
GROSVENOR SQUARE
LONDON

Nearly three days after leaving Nicholas at the Primrose Inn, Sophia accompanied her friend Mrs. Mason to a charity event at the home of one of fashionable London's leading hostesses.

They were a study in contrasts. Sophia wore a fashionable, deep yellow gown of fine silk with a cream shawl draped gracefully around her shoulders. The toes of her matching embroidered slippers peeped from beneath her skirt. Her hair was caught up in a bright sunshine-colored ribbon, held in place with amethyst clips, and a delicate amethyst pendant hung from a filigree gold chain about her throat. Mrs. Mason was clad in a more serviceable gown of dark blue wool, her slippers sturdy black leather, and she'd pinned her hair up in a restrained knot atop her head. Their attire spoke clearly of the gap between their stations in life and yet there was an ease between the two that could not go unnoticed by even the most casual of observers.

"Are you enjoying yourself, Mrs. Mason?" Sophia asked her companion. The two women stood near the back of Lady Fabersham's drawing room, where a tea was well under way.

Mrs. Mason forced a smile in response. The founder of the Halcyon Society was clearly uncomfortable amongst the ladies of the ton.

"I know this is not precisely within your bailiwick," Sophia replied with sympathy. "Still, think of the good we can do," she added, hopeful the distraction would ease the woman's nerves.

The Halcyon Society offered women in desperate situations a safe haven. Beyond shelter, food, and clothing, Mrs. Mason supplied training and moral support for all who came seeking assistance, ensuring that no one would fall back into the bad habits or heartbreaking realities that had landed them on her doorstep in the first place.

Dash's wife, Elena, was intent on establishing a sister institution in her home village of Verwood. Such an undertaking required money. And lots of it. Which was where Lady Fabersham and the other well-intentioned ladies of her acquaintance entered the equation.

Mrs. Mason fingered the modest neckline of her dark blue morning gown. "Of course. And please don't think me ungrateful."

"I would never, Mrs. Mason," Sophia assured her. "And believe me, I know all too well the toll such events can take on a person."

Mrs. Mason's brow furrowed, causing her glasses to slip.

"Just because a person is born into a life with certain expectations does not guarantee they have any real talent for the task. Never mind an inclination," Sophia added. "Our circumstances do not dictate our fate. Wouldn't you agree?"

Mrs. Mason's lips softened into a curve of understanding. "Of course. But if I may say so, one would never know it to look at you. The Furies' work?"

"Yes," Sophia confirmed, a fond smile blooming.

Everyone in London knew the Furies—or at the very least, knew *of* them. Three well-connected sisters with minds like wire traps and the wills to match. They'd been friends of her mother's and had willingly taken Sophia under their wings after Lady Afton's death.

"I thought so," Mrs. Mason replied approvingly.

Lady Fabersham approached, anticipation coloring her full, round cheeks. "Lady Sophia, Mrs. Mason. I believe we are ready."

"Are you prepared then?" Sophia whispered to Mrs. Mason, whose face showed nothing more now than polite interest. The small nod the older woman gave her before turning to their hostess was answer enough.

"Excellent," Mrs. Mason answered, a nearly imperceptible tremble in her voice.

"Please, come with me," Lady Fabersham beckoned to her. "I will provide a brief introduction, after which the floor will be yours."

Mrs. Mason nodded and allowed her hostess to lead the way.

Sophia slipped into an empty chair near the doorway. The ladies clapped politely after Lady Fabersham's remarks, and then the room quieted. Mrs. Mason took her place behind an ornate mahogany podium and looked out at the audience. Her simple dress was a stark contrast to the deep rose of the sumptuous silk drapes framing the window behind her, which looked out at a riot of spring blooms swaying on the breeze. She paused for a moment to smooth gloved fingers over her already tidy hair. "My ladies, I fear what I am about to tell you will be difficult to hear, for my life has not been an easy one. Still, without my story, there would be no Halcyon Society. And that is more terrifying to me than anything I have lived through."

Sophia felt a surge of pride at the sound of the brave woman's voice, now strong and clear as she laid the foundation for her powerful tale. That very morning, she'd listened to Mrs. Mason practicing her speech. The sorrow and despair of the woman's former life juxtaposed against the hope and healing of Halcyon House had moved Sophia to tears; she felt sure the ladies in attendance would respond in a similar fashion.

Which was exactly why Mrs. Mason's presence was so important. In her position as mistress of Halcyon House, she possessed something that the other women in this room did not: real life experience.

Sophia did not mean to be cruel. In fact, she very much envied her peers. If life had been kinder, she would be amongst them now, sipping her tea and listening to Mrs. Mason's tale until her heart ached and her reticule felt far too heavy for its own good.

It was true enough that Sophia held a position in elegant society that her family's title commanded. She spoke the ton's language. Behaved in the prescribed manner decreed by good breeding. Attended all the right balls and soirees.

And yet she knew in her soul that it was all a sham.

She was not one of them.

Bearing the awareness of life's darker side, indeed the very possibility of such a thing, was a heavy burden and one Sophia would not wish on her greatest enemy. Just enough insight so as to induce a charitable heart was noble, at least to her way of thinking. Too much, and you risked injuring the organ beyond repair.

Mrs. Mason had reached the point in her story where

her redemption appeared to be an impossible goal. Sophia blinked back tears and surveyed the room. Dainty handkerchiefs were earning their keep, almost every last woman in attendance physically moved by the harrowing account.

Sophia had seen tragedy up close. Her mother's death had robbed her world of light and joy and left her feeling helpless. Alone. Her work with the Runners and the Halcyon Society had done *something*. And now, with Nicholas's help, she would find the man responsible for ruining so many lives.

Sophia joined in the rousing chorus of applause when Mrs. Mason concluded, a tentative smile forming on her lips. Was it possible she, too, might one day live nothing more than a normal life, free from her past and its constant presence?

There was only one way to find out. It had been three days since her trip to the Primrose Inn, and still not a word from Nicholas. She'd waited long enough.

## 5

*Seven Dials District*
St. Giles Parish
London

Nicholas had spent three hours attempting to convince Singh that he should return to India. The man's help had proven invaluable when Nicholas had been a foreigner thrust into danger in exotic, lethal surroundings. As a thank you, he'd settled a small fortune on the man, intended to provide retirement for Singh in familiar, safe surroundings.

The possibility that the holy man would join him in yet another dangerous endeavor was not acceptable.

But Singh was obstinate in his determination. Which is why Nicholas found himself with Singh, standing in the center of the notorious Seven Dials, taking in the frenetic pace of the people who traversed the seven roads that branched off from the centralized point.

"Why is everyone in such a hurry, sahib?" Singh asked, quickly darting out of the way of a woman busily dragging her three children toward White Lion Street.

The last child in the procession, a little urchin with dirt-stained cheeks and grubby clothes, stuck out his tongue and crossed his eyes at the men. His mother tugged harder, urging the three youngsters on at an impossibly fast clip.

Amused, Nicholas grinned at the child and moved forward as though to follow.

The boy squawked in fear and rushed around to bump against his mother's side, earning a clout on the head for his efforts.

"One does not want to be caught in the streets when night descends on St. Giles, Singh," Nicholas explained, watching as the family disappeared in the growing dusk.

Singh looked around at the decaying buildings that lined each of the seven streets. "Then this is not the prosperous section of London, sahib?"

Nicholas was tempted to disagree. It was his plan to show Singh all of the worst that London had to offer in an attempt to encourage him to return home. Though India boasted many of the world's most disturbing slums, Singh had grown up in the lush and beautiful countryside and never traveled far from his village. If the St. Giles rookery was not enough to convince Singh to go home, Nicholas did not know what would.

"No, not precisely," he answered, unable to look into Singh's trusting eyes and lie. "Still, I thought it best to acquaint you with the area, as it is important you know the entire city before deciding to stay in London."

"But I have already decided to stay, sahib," Singh answered simply. "Nothing will change my mind."

Nicholas sighed deeply. "Surely you miss your village, Singh. This," he paused, gesturing at the tavern behind them. The faded sign hung drunkenly from one chain and the lamplight was barely visible through dirty windows. As they watched, a man in filthy, torn clothing staggered out the doorway and reeled away, down the street. "This is hell itself—especially when compared to the beauty of your home."

Singh tilted his face up and pondered the darkening sky above the Seven Dials, then looked again at Nicholas.

"Sahib, it is said the most beautiful things in the universe are the starry heavens above us and the feeling of duty within us. My duty is to you, so here I am. And the stars that fill your London sky are the very same ones that watch over my beautiful valley in India."

"You've a saying for every instance, don't you?" Nicholas asked begrudgingly, knowing very well that the smoke-smudged air over the city would hide any glimpse of Singh's stars. Nevertheless, he too tipped his head back to look at the expanse of soot-stained sky that seemed to hang heavily above the rookery.

"Sahib, it is said—"

"It was a yes or no question, Singh," Nicholas interrupted, placing his thumb and middle finger over the bridge of his nose and firmly pressing.

"Ah," Singh uttered calmly. "Then, yes, sahib. My answer is yes."

"Well then, in that case, let us discover what your gods and wise men might have to say about the bowels of St. Giles, shall we?" Nicholas lowered his hand and turned in a slow circle. "I believe we'll begin with Queen Street."

"Surely your monarch does not reside here?" Singh asked disbelievingly.

Nicholas stepped down from the circular road junction and gestured for Singh to follow. "No, my good man. I am afraid the queens to be found on this particular street have nothing of the royal about them. Now pay attention, Singh. St. Giles is infamous for its thieves and other, more dangerous, criminals."

He looked behind him, hoping to see the back of Singh as he ran for his life. What met him was the man's damnably serene smile. "Murderers, Singh," he said with emphasis. "I refer to murderers—and worse."

"Yes, sahib, I understand." Singh nodded, gingerly stepping over a stream of raw sewage. "Though I think you may be mistaken. For what could be worse than robbing a man of his life?"

Nicholas waved off a beckoning prostitute and swore in exasperation. "Bloody hell, Singh. You seem to be missing the point. If we continue into the depths of St. Giles, there is every possibility that we will be attacked. A criminal in this part of London prays for men such as us to wander into their web. In this world, they are the spiders and we are the flies."

"That reminds me of a very well-known saying in my country . . ."

Nicholas felt his frustration grow. He'd never intended to actually enter the heart of the rookery; he'd have to be a lunatic to do such a thing. St. Giles was dangerous enough during the day, its narrow lanes seemingly designed for crime.

And yet, here he was, with night threatening to fall, walking down Queen Street with Singh at his side. Duty was all well and good, but Nicholas had not rescued the village wise man only to have him murdered in St. Giles.

He stopped abruptly and turned to face his companion. "Are you not afraid, Singh?"

"Are you, sahib?" the man countered in his annoyingly wise way.

Nicholas sized up the distance between them and the Seven Dials. Other than the prostitute, no one else looked to be standing between Singh, himself, and safety. "Well, frankly, yes. I could hold my own, I've no doubt of that. But I never intended for us to go this far."

"Why are we here, then?" Singh asked, his eyebrows drawing together into one perplexed line below his turban.

"I don't remember you asking so many questions in India," Nicholas replied, cracking his knuckles in frustration.

"Then I will give you an answer, sahib. Yes, I am

frightened of this dark place. Less so, I think, than the boy there, though. He looks to be running for his life, which would be frightening indeed." Singh pointed past Nicholas's shoulder and up the street behind him.

Nicholas turned, his gaze following Singh's finger. An urchin was running toward them as fast as his spindly legs would allow, two burly men following close behind. The child nearly knocked Singh down before taking a quick right and disappearing into the rookery's labyrinth of lanes.

There had been only a moment when his eyes met the lad's, still Nicholas suspected that he knew him—had in fact employed the urchin to gather information concerning Lady Afton's killer, Francis Smeade. "Was that Mouse?" he asked, staring after the boy.

The two men chasing the boy came roaring down Queen Street, short lengths of wood held like clubs in their beefy hands. "You go that way. I'll cut 'im off at Bowl Yard," one of them yelled as they passed Nicholas and Singh. The bigger of the two peeled away and followed the boy while the one who'd given the order continued straight on.

"I cannot say if this boy is your Mouse," Singh answered, his voice remarkably calm.

"For the love of God," Nicholas swore, beginning to run. "Retrace your steps to the Seven Dials and secure a hackney. I will see you at the Albany," he yelled.

He turned down the alley where the boy had disappeared, picking up speed as his blood heated with the familiar feel of danger racing through his veins. He had nothing more than the sound of feet slapping against pavers to guide him, the waning light in the narrow lane hiding any view of his quarry.

He reached Shorts Garden Road and stopped, listening intently. The fast thud of footfalls was more muted here, telling him he'd either gone the wrong way or the two he chased were simply too far ahead.

A dim light shone through the grimy windows of an apothecary just up the street and on his left. Nicholas ran toward the building, so intent on identifying his whereabouts that he nearly missed a street sign affixed to a tall post just beyond. Jolting to a stop, he narrowed his eyes and read it. "Bowl Yard."

He raced down the lane, the sound of pounding footsteps growing louder once again, accompanied now by a roar of angry slurs and violent threats. Nicholas could not be sure that he'd found Mouse and his pursuers. Children being chased by armed men were not unusual here in the rookery. Really, anyone could be chased by armed men in St. Giles without raising eyebrows.

But it was all that he had. He followed the sounds down Bowl Yard, narrowly missing stepping on a terrier who'd wandered out from one of the shops to bark at the passersby. The small dog yipped as Nicholas raced past, then finished his complaint with a low growl.

The spotty lighting from the lane's shops and taverns was suddenly overwhelmed by another source close ahead. Nicholas saw Mouse, followed closely by the large man, burst into the pool of light briefly, then disappear. He pushed himself to run faster and soon discovered they'd reached the end of Bowl Yard and exited onto Belton Road. A lamppost illuminated the cobbled stretch, where Singh stood over one of the men, lying prone on the lane's grimy surface. Mouse crouched behind the Indian, gulping down air, while the second pursuer paced back and forth in front of his partner's apparently lifeless body.

"Sahib, there you are," Singh said by way of greeting. "Do not be concerned. He is not dead."

Nicholas gave the second man a wide berth as he

strode across the cobblestones to join Singh and the boy. "I told you to go."

"Yes, you did, sahib."

Nicholas eyed the unconscious man on the ground. "Did he fall?"

Singh shook his head.

"Suffer some sort of fit?"

"No, sahib."

"I don't give a bloody ha'penny how he found his way to the ground," the second man spat out, pulling a knife from his waistband. "Hand over the boy or you'll be suffering yourself."

Singh reached back and protectively wrapped one arm around Mouse. "I am afraid I cannot do as you ask. And should you insist, I will be forced to stop you."

"There are two of us and only one of you," Nicholas pointed out coolly, prepared to defend his friend and the boy.

"You're out of your bloomin' mind," the ruffian replied, ignoring Nicholas to step over his partner's prone body and leer at Singh. "The boy is more of a challenge than your man here."

Nicholas palmed the haft of the razor-sharp stiletto stowed in his boot and with one smooth, practiced motion drew the knife. "That may be so, but you still have me to—"

He didn't have the opportunity to finish his sentence. Singh cocked his elbow back, then his hand moved at lightning speed, his fingers striking the man's right inner thigh.

The brute crumpled to the ground, landing sprawled on top of his partner.

"Singh." Nicholas stared down at the incapacitated thugs. "What in God's name just happened?"

Singh bowed his head humbly. "I do apologize for interrupting you, sahib. But I felt it would be in our best interest to remove ourselves as quickly as possible. The night is nearly fully upon us."

Nicholas could not argue with the man's logic. And besides, he was out of breath and completely lacking in patience. "Come along. We will take Mercer Street to Long Acre and hire a hackney there. You too, Mouse," he ordered. "Oh, and say hello to Mr. Singh here. He did, after all, just save your life."

Singh and Mouse obligingly fell into step next to Nicholas and the trio set off for the eastern end of the rookery, moving quickly.

"How does a Hindu wise man know anything of hand-to-hand combat?" Nicholas asked pointedly.

Singh put his arm about Mouse's shoulder and urged him to walk faster. "Wisdom must be earned, sahib, through much experience and struggle. And I am a very wise man. Very wise, indeed."

## THE ALBANY

Picking the lock on Nicholas's front door had been as effortless as the felon Roger Rollins had always assured Sophia breaking and entering would be. A chatty and extremely dexterous burglar who worked the Hyde Park mansions, Rollins had taken a particular liking to Sophia when they'd met by chance at the Bow Street Office. He'd claimed her hands were made for thieving, and proceeded to prove it, schooling her in the ways of silent entry.

Sophia blew out a breath in frustration, sending an errant lock of her hair fluttering. Yes, gaining entry had been easy. However, reading her mother's case notes had proved to be the opposite.

She sat in Nicholas's study, mindlessly drawing on a piece of discarded foolscap while she reviewed the official papers. She'd begun, sensibly enough, at the beginning. Dash's father and Lord Carmichael had supervised the efforts, the notes written in the agent's loopy scroll. Most of the details were ones Sophia already knew from Dash. They included a list of people in attendance at the house party where her mother had been murdered, as well as servants and anyone else connected to the Afton estate, and their comments when they'd been questioned over the following two days. In addition, there were drawings of the nursery where her mother had been found, including the exact location of the body.

Sophia turned the disturbing sketch over onto the growing pile, and then skipped ahead to where Nicholas's notes began. There was a summary of the information provided in Lord Carrington's journal of his encounter with the prostitute—though the journal itself was nowhere in sight.

And finally, Nicholas and Dash's investigation began in earnest. "The Bishop" was printed in dark, bold letters on the page; someone had clearly traced and retraced the strokes until the paper was nearly torn. References to the Bishop's appearance within Carmichael's original report were called out beneath the ominous headline, including notations concerning several similar murders that took place in the years following her mother's death.

Sophia licked her fingertip and turned the page. A crude map of the Seven Dials district followed, with a handful of nefarious businesses circled on the sketch. She pondered what significance the infamous area held for the case before setting the map aside.

Mr. Smeade's profile appeared next. According to Nicholas's careful notes, the man had killed in order to fund his lavish lifestyle and taste for the extravagant.

*My mother was murdered for cheroots and coats by Bond Street tailors.*

Both outrage and sadness washed over her. She pushed

on, though, aware that she couldn't afford to become distracted. After all, there would never be a reason that made sense, Sophia silently acknowledged as she continued to leaf through the bundle of bills of sale and specialty orders.

Still, there was something particularly demoralizing about the bill from Fribourg & Treyer: a two weeks' supply of the highest quality snuff.

Sophia forced herself to return the bill to the stack, and her gaze was caught by the drawing on the small sheet of foolscap.

The shape of a Catholic bishop's hat occupied most of the page, with a small chess piece roughly sketched in the bottom right corner.

*The Bishop.*

Could the church be part of this? Sophia had been raised to believe in God and His holy rule. But even she had to admit that not all church officials were saints on earth.

As to the chess piece? Sophia had less luck imagining a situation in which a game took center stage.

The slamming of a door made her jump. She listened closely, Nicholas's deep voice reaching her through the closed study door.

Sophia wanted to stay there, safe in the study, where she could sort through the papers again. She'd failed to take any notes of her own and surely the sketches deserved more of her attention.

She folded her arms on the desk and pressed her forehead down. *Safe.* As if to say she wasn't so when she was with Nicholas. It was ludicrous. Still, her response to him at the Primrose continued to weigh heavily on her mind. Sophia could not explain why she'd acted in such a manner. And even more worrisome, she could not guarantee it would not happen again.

Even now she could feel his hands on her bare arms.

Her skin still pulsed with the memory of that moment when heat had poured into her from him.

She dreaded facing him, afraid her countenance would reflect all the confusion and turmoil she felt toward him. She was unaccountably vulnerable as never before in the presence of a man. It wasn't a circumstance she welcomed.

Perhaps she should slip out of his apartment as silently as she had entered, and return tomorrow?

"Stop making excuses," she said aloud to herself, lifting her head and purposely squaring her shoulders. She'd held her own against Nicholas many times before, and would do so many times again.

There was no need to be afraid.

# 6

"I ain't never seen nothin' like it," Mouse exclaimed around a bite of stew. "You poked him just like one of those thugs Miss May pays to beat up customers when they won't let loose of their money."

Confused, Nicholas and Singh stared at Mouse as they sat around the scrubbed kitchen table. The boy had not uttered a word during the hansom ride from the rookery to the Albany, nor at any time since they'd arrived home, not until that moment.

"Perhaps young Mouse does not know what he is saying?" Singh offered, ladling more stew into the youth's bowl. Mouse's gaze followed the transfer of carrot chunks, potatoes, onions, and beef, all swimming in thick gravy, with an expression of awe and greedy anticipation.

Nicholas swallowed his spoonful of stew, flavored with the faint bite of Singh's curry spice, and pushed his bowl away. "He is speaking of you, Singh."

"And perhaps sahib is confused as well?" Singh's perplexed brown gaze fastened on Nicholas's face, his dark eyebrows lifted in inquiry.

"Miss May is the proprietor of a local opium den," Nicholas explained, leaning back against the thick oak slats of his sturdy chair. "The thugs are Miss May's family and also in her employ. She brought them into her business for their fighting technique skills—which come in handy when dealing with customers who are reluctant to pay her fees."

Singh's brow cleared and he nodded in understanding. "Ah, I see. And these men, they are quite adept at their craft?"

Mouse's spoon scraped the bottom of his bowl and he shoveled the last bit of stew into his mouth. "No one messes with Miss May's boys if they know what's good for 'em."

Singh's face lit with pride and approval. "Then I am glad for the comparison, young Mouse. And I would very much like to meet these accomplished men."

"No, you would not, Singh, nor they you," Nicholas told him in no uncertain terms. "Now, Mouse, tell us why those men—"

"Good evening." The melodic feminine tone and unexpected greeting startled all three males.

Nicholas looked over his shoulder and found Sophia poised in the doorway.

She was dressed simply in a pale yellow gown with a modest neckline, no jewelry or adornments visible.

He would have bet the last shilling he possessed that Sophia thought she presented a plain appearance. She was wrong. Her skin glowed against the delicate yellow of the gown and her dark hair shone in the candle's glow. She was a slim, vibrant female presence who subtly demanded the attention of all three males in the room.

She glanced at him through half-lowered lashes. There was a flash of uncertainty in her green eyes and Nicholas suddenly realized that he'd been staring at her, silently, for far too long.

He shoved his chair back and rose. "Well, this is a surprise."

A broad smile broke out across Singh's lips. "Sahib, will you *properly* greet the beautiful lady or should I? It is not polite to keep her waiting, you understand."

"Well, of course I know it is not," Nicholas began, recovering from the impact of Sophia's sudden appearance. "And she is no beautiful lady, Singh. That is, she is . . ."

Nicholas looked to Sophia for help.

"Please, do finish your thought," she said wryly. Her eyes gleamed with amusement, her soft, plush lips curving in what surely was an unconsciously tempting smile.

Nicholas nearly groaned aloud.

"Singh, take Mouse upstairs and find a bed for him."

Singh's bright smile slowly dimmed until his disappointment was unmistakable. "If that is what you wish, sahib. Then I will obey."

"Obey? I am not your master, Singh," Nicholas countered.

"But you are, sahib."

"I am not." Nicholas felt his jaw clench.

"I mean no disrespect, but you are."

"I am not, and that is final!" Nicholas roared, slamming his hand on the table. "Bloody hell," he muttered. "That sounded like someone's master, did it not?"

Singh and Mouse nodded in unison.

Sophia merely dipped her chin in quiet agreement, which was far worse.

Nicholas rubbed his fingertips over his temples, where a headache had begun to pound in time with his pulse. "You will remain silent. Do I make myself clear?"

Singh nodded in understanding.

Mouse peered longingly at Nicholas's bowl of stew. "Of course, my lord."

"He is not a lord, young Mouse," Singh corrected. "He is the second son, you see—"

"The particulars of the peerage may be addressed at a later time, Singh," Nicholas broke in, pushing his bowl across the table to Mouse.

"If you would make the introductions," Sophia suggested leadingly.

"I wonder if we might simply avoid those two altogether and move on to the reason for your visit?" Nicholas posed hopefully.

Sophia looked at him as though he were mad. "I believe the gentlemen are as curious to know more of me as I am of them."

" 'Gentlemen' is rather stretching it," Nicholas said under his breath, the headache beginning to pulse harder. "But yes, by all means, let us be polite. Singh, Mouse, stand up." Chairs scraped back as the two obeyed with alacrity.

Nicholas waved a hand at his turbaned friend. "This is Singh."

Sophia glared at Nicholas.

"Mr. Singh," Nicholas amended begrudgingly.

"I am glad to properly make your acquaintance, Mr. Singh," Sophia said graciously, giving Singh an enchanting smile.

The man bowed before the woman as if born to do so. "My lady, you are too kind."

"And you? You are not afraid to face me, are you?" Sophia asked warmly, turning her attention to Mouse.

Mouse's eyes widened and he backed up until his thin shoulders hit the wall. "Gov said I was to be quiet. And that's what I'm doin', you see."

This statement earned Nicholas a second glare from Sophia.

"Do you know my head is pounding—harder by the moment, if you were at all wondering," Nicholas said to no one in particular. "But by all means, let us not forget our manners. Mouse, do step forward and meet the nice lady," he instructed impatiently when the boy seemed to hesitate.

The lad jumped to attention and stepped forward

three steps, hesitating before taking a fourth. "I'm not prepared for meetin' no ladies," he explained, glaring down at his torn and dirty clothing. "Never met no lady before."

"Well, Mouse, may I tell you something?" Sophia asked, leaning forward with friendly intent. "You are the absolute first person I have ever met with the name Mouse. So this is a day of firsts for us both."

"Is that right, then? Well, I s'pose there's no need for names like mine where you come from," Mouse confided, his inhibitions fading. "In the rookery? I've mates named Hook, Badger, Knuckles, Penny Pete—"

"Thank you, Mouse. That will be quite enough," Nicholas assured the boy, gesturing for him to rejoin Singh.

"Sahib, I do not mean to interrupt," Singh whispered loud enough for the whole of London to hear. "But you've forgotten the beautiful lady's name."

"My apologies," Nicholas groused. "May I introduce . . ."

He paused, garnering a look of confusion from each of the three.

He didn't know why, precisely, Sophia was in his house, nor how she'd secured entry, come to think of it.

And while it could be said that Mouse was somewhat endearing—if one were partial to filthy, thieving children—the fact remained that Nicholas knew very little about him. It simply was not safe to reveal Sophia's true identity.

"Might I be of assistance?" Sophia offered helpfully.

Rather too helpfully, if Nicholas was being honest. God, he needed a drink.

"No, that's quite all right, Sophia . . ." He paused again, reaching for a suitable surname. Nothing too regal, nor too plain. His gaze landed on a serving spoon lying next to the steaming pot of stew and inspiration struck.

"Sophia Spoon."

To her credit, Sophia merely blinked at the sound of her new name, and then smiled with friendly interest at Singh and Mouse. "That's right. You may call me Miss Spoon."

"Never heard of such a name for a doxie. I like it. Simple. Not too flow'ry," Mouse commented before returning to his stew.

Singh cleared his throat. "I'm afraid I am not familiar with this word 'doxie.' Miss Spoon, please, if you would be so kind as to elaborate—"

"You're quite mistaken, I'm afraid," Sophia interrupted, her placid demeanor intact though her cheeks were pink with embarrassment. "While my presence here—and at such a late hour—certainly does appear improper, I assure you I am no light-skirt. I am, in fact, Mr. Bourne's secretary."

Now Nicholas needed to sit down.

"Mr. Bourne's extended stay abroad made quite a tangle of his affairs here at home," she continued, the fanciful tale flowing from her lips with ease. "It will take no small effort on my part to tidy up, but it is what my father would have wanted."

"Your father?" Singh asked, thoroughly engrossed in Miss Spoon's history.

"Didn't you know?" Sophia countered, as if *everyone* knew the Spoon family's business. "He was Mr. Bourne's secretary. When Papa became ill, I promised to continue on in his place."

Singh nodded in understanding.

"Yes, it is all rather touching, I'll give you that," Nicholas offered sarcastically, "still I believe it is time for Mouse to be abed."

"I don't have no bed. Don't have no curfew, either,"

Mouse protested, picking up his bowl and tipping the last of the stew into his mouth.

Nicholas would have roared with irritation if not for the damage the noise would do to his head and growing headache. "Singh, if you would, please help the boy to the guest room."

"I would be most happy to assist young Mouse," Singh agreed, holding out his hand. "Come along."

Mouse set the bowl down and stood, a scowl pinching his pale lips. "All right, then. I'm tired, anyway." He refused Singh's hand and instead fell behind him, the sound of his reluctant footfalls echoing on the polished floor.

Nicholas emitted a deep, weary sigh. "All right, Miss Spoon. It is time to pay the piper."

❧ ❧

Sophia's gaze followed Singh as he quit the room with Mouse in tow before she took the seat opposite Nicholas. A subtle sense of panic at being left alone with him settled in her chest. She smoothed her skirts, folded her hands in her lap, and contemplated him as he eased back in the wooden chair and negligently crossed one leg over the other.

An illustration of a black panther she'd once seen in a book came to mind as his strong, muscular form effortlessly settled into the space while his intense gaze remained fixed on her. It was always so with Nicholas; he projected an air of uninterest and ease while beneath the casual façade, his mind worked swiftly, all at once dissecting, analyzing, and understanding whatever problem lay before him.

This time, that problem was Sophia.

"First, let me apologize for my behavior at the Primrose," Sophia began, hopeful that taking the reins of the conversation would ease her nerves.

He continued to stare at her silently for a moment, then, finally, he spoke. "You broke into my home to apologize? Really, Sophia. A letter would have sufficed."

"Nicholas, please," Sophia sighed. "I'm asking you to forgive me. I shouldn't have pushed you. It was childish and rash."

"Is *that* what happened?" Nicholas asked, his gaze sharp.

"Do you forgive me?" Sophia pressed, avoiding his question.

"Will doing so move this conversation along?" Nicholas teased, one eyebrow lifting in sardonic inquiry.

Annoyed—and oddly comforted to be so—Sophia pursed her lips in disdain and narrowed her eyes at him. It was now her turn to remain stubbornly silent.

"Yes, I forgive you," he shrugged dismissively, continuing to watch her with unwavering intensity. "Now, why are you here?"

"I could wait no longer, Nicholas," she answered, shaking her head in frustration. "I know I've only just apologized for invading your privacy. But I needed to move forward, and familiarizing myself with the case seemed the logical first step."

Nicholas went still, his eyes sharpening with disbelief. "Do you mean to tell me—"

"That I broke into your home, located your notes in the study, and proceeded to read them?" Sophia interrupted, realizing as she listed her offenses just how serious they sounded. She cringed with chagrin. "Yes, that is precisely what I am telling you."

He leaned forward in his chair. "How the hell did you even know they existed?" he growled.

A buzzing sounded in Sophia's ears and heat gathered at her temples. The pulse at the base of her throat pounded faster. "I saw them in your room at the Primrose. I did not read one line then, I promise you."

"What does that matter now?" he jeered.

"It has been three days, Nicholas," Sophia explained, her arms now prickled with perspiration. "Why would you make me wait three days? Did you believe I would relent, even after I expressly told you otherwise?"

Nicholas chuckled low in his throat. "I know you too well to believe you would be reasonable. Still, I had hoped."

Sophia glared at him, her palms itching with the urge to punch him squarely on the chin.

"No response?" Nicholas asked.

She was overheated and anxious. Her head felt filled with angry bees, her stomach captured by butterflies. And she was tired. So very tired—physically, mentally, and more important, emotionally. "I do not want to fight with you anymore."

Nicholas closed his eyes. "But you've given me no choice."

Sophia stared at him, noting the angular cheekbones so much like Langdon's, and yet his sun-kissed skin was so very different from his brother's.

The undeniable sense that she was seeing him for the very first time returned. When she'd informed Lettie that he was no longer the Nicholas she'd known she'd felt confused. Now she was curious. And dangerously so.

He opened his eyes, his gaze unreadable.

"There never was a choice," Sophia finally whispered, captivated by the minute gold flecks within the sea of umber of his irises. His thick black lashes half lowered and she felt the force of his gaze as he stared at her mouth for one long, torturous moment. When his glance lifted to meet hers again, the heat in his eyes seared her sensitive skin.

But then he blinked and it was gone. Bewildered,

she wondered if she'd imagined the flash of desire. She struggled to speak, relieved when her voice sounded reasonably normal. "My involvement was a foregone conclusion. The question was whether you would help me or not."

He lowered his arms to the table, brushing her wrist with his hand. Sophia pressed her fingertips against the hard wood though she wanted nothing more than to touch him back—to experience the delicious thrill his nearness afforded.

She held her breath and waited.

## 7

He wanted to kiss her. Badly. The embarrassment over their altercation at the Primrose lifted from his obstinate heart as she searched his face. He could see his reflection in the depths of her emerald eyes, and he liked the view this time around. He was not the depraved, pathetic soul she'd encountered at the inn. No, he was soul-weary, but sober.

He lowered his forearms to the table. His hand brushed torturously against the inside of Sophia's wrist.

"How can I say no?" Nicholas asked, his throat suddenly parched.

Sophia licked her lips.

He watched as the tip of her tongue dampened her full bottom lip, and then lightly stroked the top lip until it glistened.

"You can't."

He should have been angry. Enraged, even.

Instead, he was aroused.

A loud crash rang out above, followed by a cry of distress.

Sophia blinked quickly, as if awoken from a dream. "Was that Mouse?"

Nicholas ran his hands through his hair until his scalp tingled. "It could've been Singh. I suppose we should check on them?"

Sophia nodded as she pushed her chair out and stood.

She rounded the table before Nicholas could secure his bearings, and quit the room in a swirl of flying skirts.

Nicholas hit the table hard with his fist, biting off a curse as he stood and followed after her, feeding his speed with frustration.

The muffled sound of voices grew more distinct as they turned down the hall. By the time they neared the open guest-room doorway, there was a second crash, followed by Singh's abrupt wail of protest.

The two paused just across the threshold, staring in disbelief at the chaos.

His thin face determined, Mouse stood with his back to the wall on the far side of the fireplace. He held a poker upright, gripping it with both hands as he threatened Singh.

Singh stood across the room, eyeing the boy.

The remains of a porcelain pitcher and bowl lay scattered in pieces on the floor between them.

"What happened?" Sophia asked.

The two turned to look at Sophia and Nicholas. Mouse's expression took on a faint edge of fear; Singh's face one of bewilderment.

"I suggested to young Mouse that he might be more comfortable if he washed." He gestured at Mouse's appearance, covered with grime. "And he broke the bowl. And the pitcher. Have I offended him in some way?"

"He's right," Nicholas told the boy, attempting to hide his amusement. "You're filthy."

"No." The boy shook his head, a stubborn light in his blue eyes. "I'll catch my death, I will. I never wash. My mum warned me not to."

Sophia moved farther into the room, closer to Mouse, and nodded in understanding. "While I'm sure that's true, I think your mother would approve of a quick wash-up. The soap and water will do you good."

Mouse continued to look skeptical about the whole undertaking and held his ground.

Nicholas tapped his hand on his thigh and readied to strong-arm the boy into surrender.

"The men will help you undress, Mouse, while I fetch a second bowl and pitcher. I'll be back shortly," Sophia said with calm command.

All three males watched with varying degrees of astonishment as she confidently strode from the room.

"Christ's blood," Mouse swore, leaning the poker against the brick then letting out a weary sigh. "I'd forgotten what women were like."

Surprised, Nicholas laughed, the lingering tension of his time in the kitchen with Sophia melting away. He beckoned the boy to come forward. "We've our orders."

The boy moved slowly, dragging his feet the entire width of the room to underscore his unwillingness.

Singh took a length of linen from a sideboard and joined Nicholas. "Perhaps you would hold this up in front of young Mouse while I assist with his clothing?"

"I don't need no help," Mouse grumbled, bending over to untie his boots.

"Are we ready?" Sophia asked a moment later as she swept back into the room. She set a bowl full of soapy water and a pitcher for rinsing on the floor near Mouse's feet then handed Singh several clean rags.

Mouse stood up and kicked off his boots, a grim set to his lips. "S'pose so." He peeled off a threadbare coat and cotton shirt, dropping both on the floor.

"And your breeches," Singh mentioned helpfully.

"Those will stay right where they are, Mr. Singh. Even Miss Spoon won't change my mind." Mouse's chin set stubbornly, a militant gleam in his eyes.

Singh looked at Nicholas.

Nicholas looked at Sophia.

Sophia narrowed her eyes at the boy, her disappointment clear. "That will do—for tonight, that is. Tomorrow you will have a proper bath, in a tub, without a stitch of clothing on."

She bent down to retrieve the pile of rags and pair of street-worn boots and carried them to the door, tossing them into the hall.

"She stole my clothes!" Mouse cried out.

"If she hadn't, I would have," Nicholas replied. "Now clean yourself before my arms grow too tired to hold this up any longer."

He looked meaningfully at the length of fabric that concealed the boy's quantity of bare skin from Sophia.

"You wouldn't," Mouse squeaked, grabbing a rag from Singh and lunging for the bowl.

"No, he would not," Sophia answered, glaring at Nicholas. "Still, I will turn around all the same."

The boy squeezed his eyes shut and covered his matted hair with the soaked rag. He rubbed vigorously, the soapy water stripping dirt away to reveal a surprisingly light shade of hair. Water ran down his face and over his thin chest, making slim paths of cleanliness through the layer of grime.

His collarbones protruded like chicken wings beneath his pale skin, each one of his ribs all too visible.

Nicholas winced at the swift sympathy that pinched his heart. He looked away and grunted deep in his throat. "Turn about, Mouse. Let Singh attend to your back."

The boy let out a suffering sigh. "If you must. But I'm ticklish, so watch yourself."

He turned around. Singh dunked and wrung out a clean rag. Nicholas returned his attention to the boy and caught sight of something on Mouse's right shoulder. He squinted in order to make it out beneath the soapsuds. It looked to be a brand of sorts, in the shape of a chess piece.

"Young Mouse, tell me," Singh said, rinsing the boy's back with clean water from the pitcher. "Why do you have a tattoo of a chess piece on your shoulder? Is this customary for young English boys?"

Mouse threw himself forward, tripping on the edge of the wool carpet and falling face-first onto the bed. "That's none of your business is what it is," he yelled. He rose on all fours and scrabbled across the mattress, dropping off the opposite side and disappearing underneath the frame.

Singh looked at Nicholas in disbelief. "What have I done now?"

"I've no idea," Nicholas replied, slapping his friend on the back reassuringly before rounding the bed to reach for the frightened boy. "Mouse, come out from under there and tell us what is wrong."

The boy began to sob, the rough, scratchy sounds loud in the quiet room.

"Then I will have to fetch you," Nicholas announced, a growing concern making him impatient. He crouched down and reached for Mouse.

The boy jerked back and Nicholas's fingertips only grazed bare skin. He swore under his breath and stood just as Mouse rolled out from under the far side of the bed and ran for the door.

Singh lunged for him. Mouse darted to the left, his bare feet slipping on the wet floor. He lost his balance and fell to his knees.

"Enough," Sophia commanded, wrapping her arms protectively around the frightened boy.

Nicholas moved to help her with the child, but Sophia warned him away with a hurried flick of her hand. He halted, close enough to intervene if needed.

"You are safe, Mouse," she said firmly, her tone calm and soothing as he struggled for release. "You are safe."

The boy's terror was obvious and Nicholas had no idea how to help. "What can I do?"

Before Sophia could reply, Mouse stilled and allowed her to rock him soothingly back and forth. The sobbing began once more, giant gulps of air punctuating the agonizing sound.

"Mr. Singh, please bring me a tumbler of brandy," Sophia instructed as she stroked the boy's pale blond hair. "And Mr. Bourne, I will see to Mouse while you review my notes concerning your accounts. You'll find them on the desk in your study. The sketch as relates to the men in question should be of particular interest, I would think."

Nicholas knew she referred to the Afton file. He just didn't know why.

※ ⚘

The door hinge creaked, drawing Sophia's attention.

"Under the bed again?" Nicholas asked softly, stepping inside and closing the door to Mouse's room behind him.

Sophia rose from the wing-back chair and took the candlestick in hand. "Follow me," she whispered.

She pointed to the farthest corner and moved ahead of him across the Aubusson carpet, tiptoeing around the bed. "There," she said quietly, pointing to where Mouse lay on his stomach, the bed linens pushed to his waist. The featherbed pillows were lined up in a row, forming a barricade between him and the room.

"Why?"

Sophia shooed Nicholas back toward the fireplace and motioned for him to sit. She couldn't be bothered to return the chair she'd moved nearer the door should Mouse attempt an escape. So she'd followed Nicholas's tall form and sank to the carpet in front of the hearth.

Nicholas instantly stood up.

"Do sit down," Sophia urged, halfheartedly arranging her skirts about her. "I'm too tired to stand up, so you're wasting your time."

His eyes narrowed with displeasure and he lowered to the floor, backing up until the velvet upholstered chair supported him.

"He's never slept in a bed." Sophia rubbed the back of her skull where a wayward hairpin had been poking and worrying the spot all day. "Even after swallowing the entire tumbler of brandy, he would not yield and climb beneath the covers. So we moved the blankets to the floor. The pillows, I suspect, are for protection."

She expected Nicholas to respond with a caustic remark. Instead, he nodded in agreement.

"As ridiculous as it sounds, I believe you're correct," he said. "With his back in the corner, two sides are safe. That left two more to guard. Sleeping in the rookery must have presented a dangerous proposition."

Sophia wanted to cry. Instead, she allowed her fingers to fumble once more through her hair. Despite her efforts, the menacing pin remained at large. She bit her lip in frustration.

"It's all right if you need to cry."

Her breath caught. His voice was soothing, considerate, and tempered with concern. "Who are you?"

Nicholas's eyes flared in surprise. "Do you mean to tell me I'm responsible for your tears, not Mouse's insufferable existence?"

"No," Sophia replied, swiping at her wet cheeks. "That is, yes. Oh, Nicholas, I don't know. I cannot bear to think of his life before this," she added, looking around the beautiful room. "But there's more; there's you. India changed you, I believe. Your affection for Mouse and Mr. Singh is quite revealing."

"Affection?" Nicholas parroted as if to deny any such

silly notion. "I am hoarse from trying to convince Singh to return to his village. And as for Mouse, the boy fell into my lap. I had no other choice."

Sophia watched as he averted his eyes, knowing every word was a lie. "You care for them, Nicholas. There is tenderness beneath your bluster. You cannot deny it. I've seen it for myself now—and, to be entirely honest, it is befuddling. I feel unsure of where I stand with you. Does that make any sense?"

He dismissed her claim with a subtle shrug of his shoulders.

"Don't," she added, the tears she'd valiantly fought off up to that point threatening again. "Please don't hide from me."

Nicholas yanked the knot in his neckcloth free and pulled the linen off. He leaned forward, one big hand cupping her chin while he carefully dried her tears with the cloth.

Sophia's breath caught. His lashes were lowered over his eyes as he concentrated on the task, and she could study him unobserved. A faint shadow of beard darkened the line of his jaw. She badly wanted to test it with her fingertips. Would it be rough against her sensitive skin? His mouth was a firm line, echoing the concern in the faint frown that drew his dark brows lower.

He looked up, his gaze meeting hers, and went still. Sophia was instantly mesmerized by the depth of emotion that blazed in his dark eyes.

The backs of his fingers brushed over her heated skin in a sensual caress, fingertips tracing the line of her jaw before his hand cradled her cheek.

"I don't know that anything would make sense at a quarter past three o'clock in the morning," he answered gently. He bent by slow degrees until his lips nearly brushed hers.

No biting remark or cutting comment. He'd remained

in plain sight, revealing a part of himself Sophia had only ever imagined was real. The distance between a kiss was no more than one foolish flex of her muscles and a monumental leap in judgment.

"Yes, I suppose you're right. It has been a rather trying day," she murmured, her gaze fixed on his full, sensuous mouth.

"A rather trying number of years, Sophia," Nicholas corrected. "There will be time to make sense of all that has happened, once you've rested."

She closed the small expanse that separated them and placed her lips against his. The contact did nothing to lessen the perplexing need growing within her. She pressed into him harder, her lips seeking relief from the turmoil he'd inspired.

He lifted a fraction, his breath ghosting over her damp, parted lips as he tilted his head to press his mouth against hers at a slightly different angle. The dizzying flick of his tongue as he opened her mouth and tasted her communicated his own primal need.

Sophia's nipples hardened at the sensation and she instinctively grabbed at his shoulders, pulling him in closer.

Nicholas suddenly stopped and tore his mouth from hers, his eyes flashing with anger. "Christ, Sophia. Here you are, exhausted, vulnerable. In need of nothing more than comfort. And what do I do? I take advantage of you."

He sat back against the chair and brought his knees into his chest.

Sophia felt foolish. Exposed. Confused. Grasping for a reprieve, she adopted a calmness not one measure of her body nor mind felt and shook her head. "It is all right, Nicholas. A moment of weakness on both of our parts—a very human need, I would think, in such a situation. Let us agree to forget this moment altogether, shall we?"

Nicholas nodded in agreement, though he looked loath to do so.

Sophia cleared her throat. "Did you find the sketches I left with your case notes?"

Nicholas hesitated, the cravat dangling from his fingers in the space between them. "I did," he finally answered. He dropped the neck cloth on the floor. "Quite remarkable on your part."

"Not really," Sophia said, picking up the linen and folding it as she consciously slowed her breathing. "A bit of mindless drawing, really. And it could still be sheer happenstance and not connected to Mouse's brand. Still, I think it's worth looking into." She offered the neat square to Nicholas, smiling nervously when he accepted it.

"I agree." He laid the cravat on the chair cushion behind him and looked at Mouse. "We'll not question him—not yet."

"Not ever. I would never forgive myself if we caused the boy more anguish. We'll need to find another way to secure the answers we seek," Sophia countered firmly with a worried shake of her head, glad for the distraction of conversation. "What you witnessed was only the beginning; Mouse slipped into some sort of waking nightmare, as if fear had consumed him. He wasn't the same boy, not even after drinking the brandy. Calmer, yes, but still altered. I won't willingly put him through that again."

Nicholas turned back toward Sophia and nodded, his gaze grim. "Perhaps we won't have to. I'll see what I can find out through my street contacts."

"As will I," Sophia answered. "Mrs. Mason is very familiar with the St. Giles gangs."

He frowned and looked as if he would protest.

Sophia pushed to her knees and rose before he had the chance to speak. "It's too late to do anything further tonight, and I confess, I am exhausted. Please call a hackney for me, won't you?"

"Don't be ridiculous. I'll see you home."

Sophia could not bear to be alone with him any longer. "That won't be necessary."

"If you'll not allow me to accompany you, then I insist Mr. Singh go in my place," Nicholas pressed. "I trust the man as I do Langdon. And I've told him the truth—he knows who you are and will keep our secret from Mouse, so there is no need to be concerned in his presence."

Sophia nodded, unable to argue anymore.

# 8

*The Queen's Head Tavern*
SEVEN DIALS
ST. GILES PARISH
LONDON

"What do you mean, the boy got away?"

Robby Filchum didn't like it much when he had to talk to the master. For one, the boss went by "the Bishop" instead of his real name. True, everyone in the gang had themselves a nickname. Robby himself was known on the streets as Stonehenge for his thick, massive build and what he could do to a man with his fists. That didn't mean he'd given up his Christian name. Would he want a doxie crying out "Stonehenge" with him on top of her?

"I'm waiting for your answer," the Bishop pressed, not bothering to look up from the papers he'd been examining when Robby had arrived in his office.

"Rex and I had him run down—nearly, anyway," Robby began, pushing all thoughts of doxies—and him on top of doxies—from his mind as best he could. "We split up before hitting the Seven Dials with plans to catch 'em on Bowl Yard. I was on his heels, ya see, as we hit the Litchfield. So was one of the gents. And—"

"Gents?" the Bishop asked, interrupting Robby's exciting tale. "Not from St. Giles, then?"

"Not from the looks of him. Fancy clothes and all. And when he talked, it was all proper and such. And the other weren't from around here. He had an accent—a foreign accent. Indian, I think. He wore an odd white hat and had dark skin."

The Bishop looked up from his work, a spark of interest in his eyes. "You talked with the gents? And how did that opportunity present itself, considering you were meant to be capturing Mouse—not making conversation?"

"Didn't have no choice," Robby replied simply. "The foreigner knocked Rex to the ground. Done more than that, come to think of it. Rex was alive. He just couldn't move nothing. Not his arms nor legs. The foreign fella with the odd hat said he'd done something having to do with a snake."

"A snake?" the Bishop repeated disbelievingly.

Robby had never gotten to know the master well, but he knew enough not to test the man's patience. "Not a real snake, no. Like a punch, only not—something what Miss May's boys do. You know, the oriental arts? That fancy fighting instead of what works best; plain old punches and jabs what does the trick."

The man never lost his temper with no one, Robby thought. No, he stewed all quiet like when he was angry, then had someone else do his dirty work.

And the master was looking a might too calm for Robby. "The foreign fella did the same thing to me that he'd done to Rex. No matter what I tried, I couldn't move. I could hear, though. The three of them talked a bit before running off. From the sounds of it, the posh one knew Mouse. Called him by name even."

Robby felt a tug of regret for adding that last bit, not sure if the master would be happy with the idea of Mouse working for a man outside the Kingsmen. Either way, the boy was already dead in the Bishop's eyes. Nothing Robby could do about that. And it was Mouse's own fault he was in such a mess.

If the boy had followed orders and not gone poking about in the man's private business, Robby and Rex never would have been sent after him in the first place. But Mouse had to be clever. And fast. Two things the master found useful. He should've just stuck to the tasks he was best at doing.

"And how do you plan to retrieve Mouse?" the Bishop asked, his voice controlled and quiet.

Robby didn't like quiet. He'd never been anywhere that wasn't filled with screaming and fighting. It wasn't natural, to his way of thinking.

Nor was it natural for him to do his own planning. He wasn't ever asked to think. Only do.

He wasn't sure he liked it. There wasn't nothing to be done about it now, though. "Well, there can't be too many gents with foreigners for friends wandering about St. Giles, now, can there?"

"And?" the master pressed, turning his attention back to the papers on his desk.

"And we'll find them. Once we do, I've my ways of convincing people to give me what I want. We'll get Mouse, don't you worry."

The Bishop dipped his quill into an ink pot and tapped it efficiently. "Oh, I'm not worried. Because you'll have Topper along with you. Rex will be busy elsewhere."

Robby did his best to hide his disappointment, though his bulbous nose wrinkled at the mention of Topper. He was smart enough, that Topper, but mean as a baited bear. Some said he was in league with the devil. Robby figured if anyone was working hand in hand with the Old Scratch, it would surely be Topper.

"All due respect, sir. But Rex and I can take care of things."

"You're mistaken, Stonehenge," the Bishop said, his

pen scratching as he wrote on the paper before him. "If you did, Mouse would not be lost. Surely even you can see the sense in that."

God, but Robby got tired of thems with brains reminding him that he was dim, he thought. As far as he was concerned, smarts only got you in trouble. Look at Mouse, for crying out loud. Besides, the saddest people Robby knew were those who thought too much. A curse, intelligence.

"Suppose so," Robby reluctantly agreed. "Still, Topper's a mean 'un. You sure you want him chasing after Mouse?"

Rumor said Mouse was a favorite of the Bishop's. Some claimed the boy was being groomed to take over the master's job when he eventually moved up the ladder of the Kingsmen.

"We all have our talents, Stonehenge," the boss answered. "Topper's on the north side, taking care of something for me. I'll let him know to find you once he returns."

Whatever Mouse had seen, it was worse than Robby ever could have imagined. Either that, or being the man's favorite didn't pay.

"Right," Robby replied, a sinking feeling settling in his gut. "I'll be waiting at the—"

"He'll find you, Stone. No worries on that regard."

Robby envied Rex. Why was it him, Robby, who'd been sent for by the master? Rex had as much to do with the shambles they'd made of the situation as he did. Maybe even more, if one thought about it hard.

Robby wasn't one to hold a grudge, though. Never had been, and never would be, he thought staunchly. He liked Rex well enough and wished him no harm. Hell, they'd had the same chance to be standing where Robby stood now. It wasn't Rex's fault he'd come up lucky.

"That's all for now." The man's voice was its usual chilly and calm tone.

Robby turned around and made for the door, closing it quietly behind him. No, it wasn't nobody's fault that he was in the master's black books and stuck working with Topper. But it sure was a crying shame.

May 29
THE HALCYON SOCIETY
BLOOMSBURY SQUARE
LONDON

"Shall I see to the bed linens now, Lady Sophia?"

Sophia ceased running the quill along the seam of her still-sensitive lips and laid the writing instrument down. "Yes, Milly, thank you." She smiled at the young woman's perfectly executed curtsy and turned her thoughts of last night's regrettable kiss to focus on the charming girl. Her rough cotton skirt was caught up at precisely the right angle, the gray material and white apron lifted just enough to clear the top of serviceable black boots without exposing her stockings. She lifted her head, color flushing her round cheeks as she peered at Sophia in inquiry.

Milly was one of the less heartbreaking cases at Halcyon, if such a term could be applied. Milly's sickly mother, once in service to the Duke of Marley, had sent her illegitimate child to Mrs. Mason in the hope that she could learn the skills necessary to one day secure a place for herself in one of the grand households.

And though Mrs. Mason did not typically take on such girls, Milly's cheery attitude and dimpled smile stole the woman's heart and she'd agreed.

"Lovely," said Sophia.

"Thank you, my lady, you are too kind," Milly answered, bobbing again in an abundance of exuberance, her face flushed with pride. Then she dropped another curtsy, once more for good measure.

"Milly, your curtsy is coming along quite nicely," Langdon commented as he entered the small study at the back of the house.

The girl emitted a cheep of embarrassment. "Lord Stonecliffe," she uttered before dipping a low, final show of respect and quitting the room.

Sophia gave Langdon an amused look and shook her head, hopeful her sudden unease at his appearance was not noticeable. Would he sense her growing guilt over the altogether foolish kiss?

"It was a compliment," he argued, clearly mystified—both with Milly's predicament as well as Sophia's.

"From a lord—and a handsome one at that. She's terrified of you," Sophia explained with mock censure, relief easing her nerves. She took in the gleam of his polished boots, his perfectly fitted coat, his intricately tied cravat, and smiled. "Surely you're aware of just how intimidating you really are, aren't you?"

Langdon's brow furrowed as he feigned serious consideration of Sophia's accusation. "Hmm, is that right? Is it the 'lord' part or the 'handsome' bit?"

"Both," Sophia replied, laughing as an endearing grin broke out across his face.

Langdon leaned casually against the door frame and folded both arms across his chest. "Really? And yet, I've failed to convince you to give up your work with the Halcyon Society. I cannot be as scary as all that, then."

Sophia sighed. Langdon meant well; he always did. And if Sophia would simply live in a heavily fortified castle with a moat full of crocodiles and her own personal dragon? Well, such conversations as the one they were about to engage in, for the 221st time, would not be needed.

Sophia found castles drafty, crocodiles bad company, and dragons hard to come by.

And more important, she valued her independence— and craved more by the minute. The sketch of Mouse's brand called to her from its concealment beneath the record book on the desk.

"I know you only want to guarantee my safety." Sophia tried her best to sound appreciative rather than provoked.

"Only?" Langdon countered diplomatically. "There is nothing more important to me than your safety, Sophia. You know that I respect and admire Mrs. Mason's work. Still, you must admit that keeping such company as you do here is not necessarily in your best interests."

Actually, it was, Sophia thought instantly. The Halcyon Society made Sophia feel useful; as if, somehow, saving one woman from her mother's fate could explain, in part, why Sophia lived. Surely Langdon realized this?

"I will not live in hiding," Sophia replied, "and there is no point in asking me to do so."

Langdon pushed off from the door frame and walked nearer, frustration gleaming in his eyes. "Very well. If you'll not lock yourself away, then perhaps you'll accompany me to Gunter's?"

Mrs. Mason appeared in the open doorway, stopping abruptly at the sight of Langdon.

A corner of the sketch peeked out from under the record book as if calling to Sophia.

She beckoned for Mrs. Mason to enter. "I would like nothing more," she told Langdon. But I fear there are still a number of tasks I must accomplish before this evening's ball."

It wasn't a lie. At least not entirely. Still, the disappointment in his eyes matched what Sophia felt for her increasingly troublesome behavior.

Langdon acknowledged Mrs. Mason with a nod, and

then bowed before Sophia. "I'll leave you to your work, then. I'll see you this evening."

"Thank you, my lord," Sophia said, watching as he turned and walked from the room.

"Work, my lady?" Mrs. Mason asked. "Is there anything I might help you with?"

"No, not as concerns Halcyon. I wonder, Mrs. Mason, would you mind answering a few questions about London gangs? It would take only a moment of your time," Sophia asked, worrying the edge of the drawing with her finger.

Mrs. Mason sat down in the chair opposite Sophia, her eyes lit with curiosity. "Not at all, my lady."

Sophia slipped the piece of foolscap from beneath the book, revealing the crude drawing of the chess piece. "Do you recognize this?" she asked, holding the paper up.

"Where did you get that?" Mrs. Mason asked. Her voice held a faint echo of shock and her lips pinched with nervousness. She edged abruptly back in her chair, seeming to shrink away from the paper.

"I made the sketch. I recently saw the figure branded on a boy's shoulder," Sophia explained. The delicate hairs on her nape and arms lifted in warning as Mrs. Mason attempted to school her features into an expression of calm.

"Why would you have reason to see a young scamp's bare shoulder?" The older woman's fingers trembled and she folded them tightly together in her lap. "Did he come by while you were here? Was he begging for food or clothes? Did he threaten you? If this should happen again, Lady Sophia—"

Sophia ignored the flurry of questions and focused on Mrs. Mason's first reference. "Why do you assume he was a scamp?"

Mrs. Mason stared at Sophia. For the first time in

their acquaintance, her gaze was hard and unreadable, and Sophia glimpsed the woman she had been during the years she'd spent as a prostitute.

Then the moment passed and Mrs. Mason's gaze slid from Sophia's.

She stared at her lap, where her hands were gripped tightly together. "Perhaps you've been spending too much time with the Runners," she suggested, her voice once again returned to her normal easy tone. "The word 'scamp' is hardly cause for alarm."

The Runners always seemed to come up whenever someone was trying to evade a question. Sophia had come to view the recurring references with amusement, although she could not find the humor in Mrs. Mason's obvious discomfort.

The woman was frightened, that much was clear. And trying to hide her fear.

"Mrs. Mason," Sophia began in a purposefully calm, soft tone, "do you recognize this mark from your time spent in the brothel?"

"No," she answered, looking up to answer Sophia. "That is not a mark that would be used on a girl working at Le Maison Bleu, that much I can tell you."

Sophia laid the drawing on the desk and traced her fingertip over the penciled lines that made up the outline of the chess piece. "Then where, Mrs. Mason?"

The woman lowered her chin, her gaze fastened on the slow progress of Sophia's finger over the drawing. "Do you have wish to die, Lady Sophia?" she asked starkly.

Her question surprised Sophia. "Why do you ask that?"

"Because questions about such things as what you have there," she nodded significantly at the drawing, "will get you killed."

Sophia abruptly stopped tracing the symbol. "Tell me, Mrs. Mason, do you think me lacking in intelligence?"

"You are the most intelligent person I know, my lady," Mrs. Mason answered, lifting her chin and meeting Sophia's gaze once more. "But the people connected to that symbol couldn't care less if you've Yorkshire pudding for brains. By the time they're done with you, you won't be needing to think at all."

Excitement crackled, lifting the fine hairs on Sophia's nape. Still, she remained calm, knowing that to do anything else might convince Mrs. Mason to keep her own counsel.

"If you do indeed believe that I am intelligent, then you must trust me, Mrs. Mason," Sophia said plainly, hoping that common sense was on her side.

The other woman unclenched her hands and reached across the desk. Picking up the drawing, she brought it nearer to inspect it more closely, frowning as she did so. "Did you know, Lady Sophia, that some of the London gangs like to brand their members?"

"I had no idea. What could possibly be the point?"

"To protect their property, should any go missing," Mrs. Mason answered, folding the paper carefully in half to effectively hide the drawing, laying it back down on the desk. "Much the same as farmers do with their cattle."

"Then this is the mark of a gang in the vicinity of Bleu Maison?" Sophia pressed on, willing herself not to think about the process required to complete the barbaric act.

"No, I was not lying when I told you I'd not seen this mark during my years in the brothel," Mrs. Mason reminded Sophia, then sat back in her chair, her spine poker stiff. "No, my lady, this is the mark of a St. Giles gang."

Sophia mentally reviewed the information she had read in Nicholas's study. The Rambling Rose, where Mr. Smeade's connection to the Bishop was discovered, stood in St. Giles. "Are you absolutely sure?"

"Yes, my lady," Mrs. Mason gravely confirmed. "Do you remember Mary Riley? A fellow prostitute contacted Halcyon after Mary was beaten and left for dead."

"I know the name, but did not have the opportunity to meet her," Sophia replied, suddenly finding it very hard to sit still.

Mrs. Mason nodded knowingly. "Does not surprise me. Mary was with us for two days before she succumbed to her injuries. We talked, her and I, about her life. And about the brand of a chess piece on her back. She was worried for me. And for all of the women here. She said that if the gang she belonged to discovered she was alive, they'd track her down and make sure she died the second time around. And then they'd see to those who had taken her in."

"Do you know where Mary lived? Is it possible that someone in the area around her home may know something more of these men?" Sophia picked up the drawing.

Mrs. Mason pushed her spectacles farther up on the bridge of her nose. "Did you not hear what I said, my lady? Mary is dead because of her involvement with this gang. Will you not heed a warning from beyond the grave?"

Mary Riley's warning meant nothing to Sophia. She knew that it should. Such indifference more than likely meant that her need for revenge had overwhelmed any sense of right, wrong, or otherwise.

Still, she did not care. She couldn't.

"Mrs. Mason, do you know where Mary Riley lived?"

"St. Giles, my lady," the woman answered, getting up from her chair. "I filed a report with the Runners. They'll have the address in their notes."

Sophia nodded somberly. "Thank you, Mrs. Mason."

"You've nothing to thank me for," she replied, then quit the room.

## 9

Bow Street Offices
COVENT GARDEN
WESTMINSTER
LONDON

"Lady Sophia, good afternoon. We were not expecting to see you today."

Though Sophia liked Mr. Royce and would normally enjoy chatting with him, she was pressed for time. She'd left for the Bow Street Offices the moment Mrs. Mason had told her about Mary Riley's tattoo. Still, there was a ball that evening that she'd promised Langdon she would attend. If she had any hope of returning home in time to prepare for the engagement, she needed to find Mary Riley's file and be gone within the hour.

"Mr. Royce, good afternoon to you," she replied politely, slowing her progression but not stopping to invite a lengthy conversation. "You are correct—I would not normally be in the office today. A notation in one of the cases I recently reviewed kept me awake all night. I simply must read through it again, to be certain I didn't miss something."

The Runner pushed back his chair and half rose. "I'll fetch the file, Lady Sophia. Which one is it?"

"No, Mr. Royce, that is quite all right," she said quickly. She scanned the man's desk, her glance alighting upon a steaming cup of tea. "I would not want your tea to grow cold. If you'll just give me the key?"

Sophia knew from past experience that Mr. Royce was a man who could not abide lukewarm tea. He eyed the cup with pleasure and smiled his thanks for her thoughtfulness. "Here you are, my lady. You'll let me know if you need anything?"

"Of course, Mr. Royce," Sophia replied. Her smile held both charm and relief as she accepted the key and left him, hurrying toward the file room located at the back of the office.

She placed the key in the lock and turned it, exactly as she'd done a thousand times before. Nervously, she glanced over her shoulder at Mr. Royce and felt a wash of relief when she saw he'd clearly already forgotten her and he'd taken up his tea, a file in his hand.

Sophia pushed the door open. Careful to leave it ajar so that she might hear if someone approached, she stepped inside.

Mary Riley had died barely three weeks earlier. Sophia walked to the first bookshelf, where the most recent cases awaited sorting. She lifted a large wooden box from the shelf and carried it to a table pushed up against the west wall of the room. Removing the lid, she began to flip through the papers, which were organized according to date. She discovered Mary's file a third of the way through the stack and pulled it free from the rest.

Her fingers shook as she quickly paged through the report, briefly stopping at the crude sketch detailing Mary's injuries before scanning the remaining documents. The address wasn't there. Sophia forced herself to breathe deeply and went back to the beginning, finding the information on the fourth page.

She took a piece of foolscap from the stack sitting on the table and a stub of lead left there by one of the

Runners. "Number Four Upper St. Martin's Lane," she said aloud as she took down the address then set the pencil back in its place.

Stuffing the scrap of paper into her reticule, Sophia returned the file to the box and secured the top once again.

"Find what you were looking for?" Mr. Royce called from his desk.

Sophia hastily placed the box on the shelf and walked from the room, locking the door after her. "Exactly what I was looking for, Mr. Royce."

*Afton House*
MAYFAIR
LONDON

Sophia sat still as her companion deftly pinned up her long hair. "Lettie, have you ever done something you shouldn't have?"

The woman selected a ruby encrusted pin from the side table and secured a curl into place. "Yes. Hasn't everyone?"

"Well, that was rather easier than I thought it would be," Sophia countered, surprised at her companion's response.

Lettie took up a second pin and moved to the opposite side of Sophia, looking into the mirror to check her handiwork. "You must remember: there are actions one undertakes, and then there are *actions*."

Sophia supposed her dear friend's statement was true enough, though her guilty conscience was having difficulty deciding where the line should be drawn between the two.

"Tell me what you've done, my lady."

Sophia cringed. "I believe I'll list my transgressions in chronological order—much more organized, you see."

Her companion raised one eyebrow in reaction, remaining silent.

"Very well," Sophia announced with more phlegmatic fortitude than she felt. "Last night, when I told you I had a headache? I did not; it was an excuse. I snuck out and made my way to the Albany—where I broke into Nicholas's apartment. Then I lied to Mr. Singh and Mouse concerning my identity. And finally, I convinced Mr. Royce of the Runners that a nagging detail was the reason I required access to the file room. When, in fact, I needed to gain entry in order to steal information. Which I did, obviously."

Lettie reached for the final pin and secured the last curl, stepping back to admire her work.

"You haven't said anything," Sophia pointed out, painfully aware that she'd failed to include the kiss, arguably the most important action of all.

The older woman lifted a glittering ruby and diamond necklace that had belonged to Lady Afton from the lacquered jewel box atop the dressing table. "I'm thinking."

Sophia admired Lettie's control and thoughtfulness. She'd been an admirable mentor while Sophia was young, daily exhibiting such qualities.

Now Sophia wished she'd simply spit out something— *anything*.

Lettie fastened the clasp and adjusted the ruby drop until it was centered precisely above the sapphire silk gown's low-cut bodice. "First, not every action was criminal, correct?"

"Correct, though—"

Lettie raised one finger and began to pace. "Now, what was your reason for visiting Mr. Bourne?"

"Four days have passed since we returned to London

from the Primrose," Sophia answered. "I was worried that Nicholas would proceed without me. He made it absolutely clear that was his preference."

Her dear friend nodded and clasped her hands behind her back. "A reasonable concern, I'll give you that. And this Mr. Singh and Mouse? Why did you deceive them?"

Sophia considered mentioning Nicholas's part in the charade, but thought better of it. "Nicholas and Mr. Singh were acquaintances in India, and thus he knows the loyalty and self-control of the man. But the boy Mouse's discretion is a mystery to both of us. It seemed best if my position in society was kept hidden for now."

Lettie nodded and continued to walk back and forth, her lips set in a grim line.

"A second reasonable concern, wouldn't you agree?" Sophia pressed.

Lettie finally ceased pacing, stopping in front of Sophia. "If you will not give up this dangerous pursuit, at the very least I beg you to be more careful. The ton's gossipmongers like nothing better than embroidering tales about a lady such as yourself and a man with Mr. Bourne's questionable reputation."

Sophia considered her companion's words. "You're right. Of course you're right," she replied. "Somehow it is all too easy to become caught up in the theatrics and excitement of it all, even though I know the danger is real."

"I imagine your mind needs some sort of distraction from the dangerous circumstances; otherwise, fear might overtake you. Still, Lord Stonecliffe is not a stupid man. If there are whispers amongst your set suggesting indiscreet behavior involving you and his brother, he'll hear them."

Sophia rose from the tapestry-covered stool. "The last thing I wish to do is hurt Langdon," she replied honestly.

Langdon had been kind, patient, and understanding with Sophia. He could have bowed out of the gentleman's agreement their fathers had made and looked elsewhere for a wife. Lord knew scores of the ton's ladies had tripped over themselves, and one another, in an attempt to gain his favor. Langdon had politely declined their many efforts. And, she thought with remorse, for far longer than any other man of his standing would.

*Or should.*

Lettie's words had greatly diminished the guilt Sophia suffered for her actions, with the exception of the kiss. Her companion's insight only underscored her rash and dangerous behavior. Nicholas may have revealed something within himself that spoke to her soul, but that did not change her obligation to Langdon.

"Then be very careful, my lady," Lettie advised. "Or Lord Stonecliffe will become a casualty in this war you and Mr. Bourne are waging. And he'll have never seen it coming."

## 10

### The Clifton Residence
### Grosvenor Square

"Do stop staring." Nicholas continued to peruse the crowded ballroom, feeling the weight of his brother's gaze as if Langdon were touching him. The two stood with their backs to the gold, silk-covered wall, well out of the stream of strolling guests circling the edge of the dance floor.

"What makes you think I'm doing anything of the sort?" Langdon countered mildly.

His ridiculous denial drew Nicholas's pointed attention. "Because every last person here is doing it. And while you, dear brother, are truly one of a kind, I believe even you cannot resist such entertainment."

He'd woken up in a strange mood that morning; like a tiger who'd consumed more than he should and knew it; foolish, greedy, and galled by his own stupidity.

Nicholas could not help himself last night; he'd willingly given in to the pull Sophia's presence always exerted. Was he delusional enough to believe her behavior indicated she needed him for anything more than temporary comfort? Perhaps; but more than likely, no.

Still, he'd had her all to himself. And Nicholas wanted more. The need for her pulsed just beneath his skin, even while his brother stood beside him.

He'd never hated himself as much as he did right at that moment.

"You can't blame them for being curious." Langdon nodded at the throng, many of whom were casting sidelong, interested glances at Nicholas. "You've been back in London for weeks and this is the first social event you've attended. No doubt they all want to get a look at the man who's reputed to have returned from India with crates of jewels and gold. Plus," his eyes glinted with amusement, "there's also the fact that even before you left London for India, you rarely attended balls. So tonight all the ladies wish to dance with you and all the men want to hear tales of tiger hunts and harem girls."

"There aren't harem girls in India and I didn't bring back crates of jewels," Nicholas bit out.

"They don't know that," Langdon said mildly. "You can stop most of the speculation by dancing with a few women. They would be sure to spread whatever tale you tell them within moments of the music's ending."

"I don't feel like dancing," Nicholas growled.

Langdon chuckled. "Then why are you here? Clearly, it's not because you wish to socialize with friends and family."

"Fetch me a drink and we will see if I cannot be persuaded to behave otherwise," Nicholas countered dryly. He waited for his brother's witty retort, disappointed when none came. "Are you so easily bored by me that you cannot be bothered to keep up?"

Langdon frowned, his eyes somber. "It is not boredom, Nicholas. Actually, I have been meaning to speak with you for some time."

"Oh bloody hell." Nicholas groaned, more irritated than surprised by his brother's concern.

A trace of disappointment flickered across Langdon's expression. "You are lucky that none of your brandy binges have resulted in something worse than an aching head. It was one thing to live in such a manner when you were younger. Now, you have more responsibility. You created quite a business in India; you now have the means to settle down and build a proper life."

Nicholas steeled himself against the flood of guilt, remorse, hope, pain—a cacophony of emotions roused by his brother's words.

"Did you say 'proper'?" Nicholas asked, feigning indifference as he cupped his left ear. "Because I am almost sure you did; which would beg the question, what in the goddamn world would make you think I've any interest in a proper life?"

Langdon did not match Nicholas's caustic tone, nor did he adopt a defensive stance. Instead, he patted Nicholas on the shoulder as a father would his son. "I have upset you. And for that, I apologize."

Nicholas wanted Langdon to fight back. Some part of him always had. But his brother would do no such thing; Langdon was an honorable man. And honorable men were not provoked by the likes of Nicholas.

"No, it is I who should apologize," he muttered, tamping down the flames of self-loathing that licked at his heart. "You did nothing more than what a brother should do."

Langdon smiled in appreciation, which almost made everything worse. "Let us leave such maudlin talk for the evening. Sophia has arrived."

Instantly diverted, Nicholas followed his brother's gaze across the ballroom floor. Ladies and their lords continued to arrive, their ascent down the grand staircase marked by the thump of the majordomo's wooden staff. Just behind a reed-thin woman in gold stood Sophia and her companion for the evening, Lady Charlotte Grey.

He couldn't look away from Sophia. She wore a sapphire silk gown that clung to her curves, her hair piled atop her head in tousled curls. A delicate necklace encircled her slim neck and drew the eye downward to its largest ruby, nestled just above the upper swell of her breasts.

Langdon too continued to watch as Sophia and Lady Charlotte were announced. "I think it's time I married her. Don't you?"

Nicholas tore his gaze from Sophia and stared at Langdon. "That depends."

"On what, exactly?" Langdon asked distractedly as he continued to watch Sophia.

Nicholas snapped his fingers directly in front of Langdon's face. "Why do you wish to marry her *now*?"

"I'd think that rather obvious," Langdon answered, batting Nicholas's hand away. "She's my fiancée."

"And has been for years—which begs the question, what is your hurry?" Nicholas pressed, desperation clawing at his skin. "Specifically, why now?"

"Carrington," Langdon answered, smiling politely at Lady Trinbull and her pasty-faced daughter as they trundled past. "To be more precise, Carrington's marriage. He looked so happy at his wedding—as if nothing else in the world mattered to him now. I wouldn't mind giving that a go. Besides, Sophia will not leave off with her charity work. I paid her a visit at the Halcyon Society earlier today. She looked utterly exhausted and was a tad cross with me—which is unusual for Sophia. And then there is that Bow Street business. I need to secure her safety. And that will not be accomplished until she's living under my roof."

Nicholas doubted Sophia would agree to abandon her interest in either the Runners or her charity work. And, he realized, he'd be disappointed if she did. Before he could comment, Langdon spoke.

"Come now, tell me you're happy—for myself and

for Carrington," Langdon urged Nicholas, gesturing for him to walk with him. "Leg-shackled at last."

"And why would I not be?" Nicholas answered sarcastically, flashing an appreciative smile at Lady Simmons and her friend, each displaying a scandalous show of bountiful cleavage.

Langdon ignored the women. "You would not be human if you failed to feel envy over Carrington's luck. I know I did—and I am rather glad for it; Lord knows how much longer I would have waited to ask Sophia to set the date."

God, Langdon was so bloody kind and understanding. Not for the first time, Nicholas puzzled over how, precisely, they sprang from the same line.

"And now that Carrington is settled, with me soon to follow his example, surely you see that there is hope for you," his brother continued cheerfully.

Nicholas wanted to punch him. He knew that he should not. Nor, in all likelihood, would he do so if given the opportunity.

Still.

"There is a woman out there for you, Nicholas."

Langdon's assurance left his lips just as Sophia turned about and saw them. Her warm smile lit her features as her gaze swept across the brothers.

Nicholas flinched inwardly from the stab of sheer pain at her timing.

*Yes, there is a woman out there for me. And she is closer than you could possibly imagine.*

Langdon made a perfect bow and the ladies reciprocated with charming curtsies.

When both Sophia and Langdon looked expectantly at Nicholas, he sighed, offering a polite, if brief, bow. "Really, you two, it is not as if we do not know one another."

Langdon sighed with disapproval. "Have they no manners in India?"

"Come now," Lady Charlotte offered in her quiet, intelligent way. "Mr. Bourne has been abroad for some time. Have some patience with him."

"You always have been my favorite of the Furies," Nicholas said with approval.

"I know," Lady Charlotte replied, a small, satisfied smile curving her lips. "Not that my two sisters do not have their admirers," she added diplomatically.

Sophia tapped her fan against the fingers of her opposite hand. "I always think of the three of you as one—a united front, if you will."

"Or an indestructible force. Perhaps the three horsemen of the—"

"There were four horsemen of the apocalypse, Nicholas." Lady Charlotte's dimples flashed and her eyes twinkled, her amused comment interrupting the pair as politely as one could. "If you should ever wish assistance with your daily Bible devotionals, I would be more than happy to come to your aid."

"May we go back to the kissing bit?" Nicholas asked with a wink at the stylishly elegant older woman.

"Of course, dear boy," Lady Charlotte answered, holding out her hand.

Nicholas took it gently in his and placed a small kiss on her knuckles.

"Rather like kissing the king's ring," he grumbled.

❧

Sophia watched with feigned amusement as Nicholas kissed Lady Charlotte's hand, chuckling at his dry observation while her mind spun with concern.

Sophia had never deceived Langdon, not even about the extent of her work with Bow Street. There had been no need to hide any aspect of her life from him. Until last night. She feared it was only the beginning.

"Fancy a dance?" Langdon bent to murmur in her ear, his hand closing over her arm just above her elbow.

Sophia flinched when he unexpectedly brushed his thumb across the bare skin.

"Are you quite well?"

Sophia silently cursed her reaction and made herself stand calmly under his hand. "Of course. Perhaps you might escort Lady Charlotte onto the dance floor and save the next one for me?"

"Of course," Langdon replied, easy acceptance in his voice. "Lady Charlotte, would you do me the honor of partnering me in a dance?"

"Certainly, Lord Stonecliffe," the older woman answered, offering Langdon her hand. "Though I feel I must warn you, I am not as quick as I used to be."

"I don't know about that," Nicholas countered dryly.

Lady Charlotte arched one silver eyebrow in laughing response and allowed Langdon to steer her toward the crowd gathered on the dance floor. "He will require some looking after, Sophia," she added over her shoulder before she and Langdon joined the throng.

"How is it possible that the Furies somehow never seem to age?" Nicholas said, watching his brother and Lady Charlotte join a set of other couples. "Rather, their power only grows. Would you not agree?"

Sophia wanted to reply to his humorous observation, but found it impossible to do so.

Nicholas turned to look at her, his head cocked slightly to the side as he studied her. "Come now, Sophia. Light repartee is a specialty of yours, is it not?"

"It would seem the act of deception comes quite naturally to me," she began, startled by his pert comment. "Rather like putting on a play, really."

He grinned in understanding. "I suppose you're right; 'all the world's a stage' and whatnot, *Miss Spoon*."

"*Having* lied and deceived?" Sophia continued. "That is a bit more challenging."

Nicholas narrowed his gaze. "In what way?"

"The guilt, Nicholas," Sophia explained. "How does one make it go away?"

"Impossible. There is always guilt," Nicholas warned, his gaze unsympathetic.

"I was afraid of that," Sophia replied, searching his eyes for a hint of empathy.

Nicholas shook his head. "As well you should be. Exacting revenge on your mother's killer will change everything, Sophia—most likely it already has begun."

"I'm doing this for all of us, don't you see?" Sophia countered, her hackles rising in response to his distant behavior. "Once my mother's killer is captured we'll be free, Nicholas."

"Of what?"

"Everything that has plagued us for the last twenty years," Sophia explained, an urgency growing in her throat. "Surely Langdon will understand *that*."

Nicholas's piercing gaze captured hers. "Then why do you feel guilty?"

"Because I should," Sophia replied, the inexplicable premonition of an approaching storm coloring her tone with apprehension. "Because it is Langdon. Because I am the last person he would ever suspect of lying to him."

"You have choices, Sophia," Nicholas reminded her. "One week in and already you are in shambles. If you would leave the investigation to me . . ."

Sophia forced herself to look away from his handsome, compelling face. She inhaled deeply and exhaled in equal measure. The act seemed to shore up and stabilize her shaken nerves. "I've given you my reasons,

Nicholas. And they've not changed. Besides, I've already made some progress. Mrs. Mason was of use, after all. I'm in possession of an address that should help in finding the Kingsmen."

Nicholas took a step back, visibly distancing himself. "But *you* have changed. And soon enough, everything else will follow suit. No bloody address will help then."

Sophia's eyes widened with alarm. "What do you mean?"

"Langdon is intent on a wedding, Sophia," Nicholas answered curtly. "Your wedding, to be exact."

"Why now?" she asked, her hands beginning to tremble.

"Why now?" Nicholas repeated her question, confusion reflected in his countenance. "Because you have been engaged for nearly twenty years—"

"Please, do not exaggerate, Nicholas," Sophia chided, taking yet another deep breath and attempting to relax taut muscles.

"All right, then," he replied, his tone menacing. "What about the fact that he loves you? And you love him? Is that not enough reason to marry?"

"Please don't be cruel," Sophia whispered, forcing a smile in response to Lady Bascombe's nod as she strolled by.

"What, precisely, is cruel in reminding you of your approaching marriage?"

Sophia fixed her gaze on a wall sconce to the right of Nicholas's head and concentrated on her body, attempting to ease the tense muscles first in her temples, then her neck, and still lower, until she reached her toes.

She closed her eyes briefly before looking up at Nicholas. "Why are you doing this?"

Sophia caught sight of Langdon and Lady Charlotte from the corner of her eye. The dance had ended and they were returning, Langdon's hand atop Lady Charlotte's on his bent arm. He smiled at Sophia, his familiar, fond show of affection so stark in contrast to Nicholas's enigmatic glance.

"You did not answer my question," Nicholas said, turning to look at the returning couple. "Is it cruel to mention your love for my brother?"

"I do not know if it is cruel. It is pointless, though. Of that much I am certain."

❧

How long Nicholas had been at the faro table was a mystery not even the empty bottle of brandy next to his cards could reveal.

He looked around the room at his fellow players, noting the numbers had thinned considerably. "Are we the only ones left with money to wager, then?" Nicholas asked no one in particular.

Three gentlemen seated with him at the table stood, one retrieving a small amount of bank notes and coins from in front of him. Then all three walked from the room, leaving only Nicholas, and one other gentleman sipping brandy at a nearby table.

"Come, Braxton," Nicholas urged the man, nearly falling out of his chair from the effort. "We could use another player. Or rather, I could."

Lord Charles Braxton, Baron Maplethorpe, had also been born the second child. Fortunately in his case, the firstborn had possessed the decency to come into the world a girl. There had never been any question what he would do with his life.

Nicholas had not been so fortunate.

He was vaguely aware of the thread of sheer meanness running through his thoughts—often a sign that he'd had too much to drink.

Or, looked at in a different light, a sign that he'd not had enough.

"My good man," Nicholas called to a footman. "Fetch another bottle for me."

"Of course, sir," the young man replied, bowing before leaving the room.

"Don't you think you've had enough, Bourne?"

Nicholas was not sure who had addressed him, then realized there was only himself, Braxton, and two footmen present. He stood up and attempted to walk toward Braxton.

The table he'd been seated behind had the audacity to not spontaneously move of its own accord, catching Nicholas's left hip and sending him crashing to the floor.

"I believe you just answered my question." Braxton bent over Nicholas, his features somewhat fuzzy, while his intentions were crystal clear. "Let me help you, Bourne." He held out his hand and waited.

Nicholas batted the man's hand away. "I do not need your help, Braxton," he spat out, rolling onto his stomach.

"That is arguable. Still, suit yourself," Braxton replied.

Nicholas snapped. There was no other way to describe his reaction to Braxton's words. As if the man possessed any right to judge him! It was unthinkable. Absolutely ridiculous. And deserving of retribution.

Nicholas shoved himself up off the floor, grabbing the table to steady himself. "Turn around, Braxton, or you might not live to regret it."

Braxton slowly turned and faced Nicholas, his expression dubious. "You can't be serious, Bourne. I'll not fight a man in his cups."

"Why, because your honor won't allow it?" Nicholas countered. "I've always thought it too convenient when cowardice masqueraded as honor."

"Does he not have any friends with him?" Braxton asked the footman, who only shook his head in response. "I've no quarrel with you, Bourne. Let me find your brother. Perhaps he can talk some sense into you."

Nicholas watched Braxton turn toward the door and begin to walk away. A sickening sense of urgency coursed through him. "Afraid, are you? Then run away. You'd only lose—but then, you clearly already knew that."

The tinkling of crystal caught Nicholas's attention. He looked over his shoulder and watched as the footman discreetly picked up a tray full of empty glasses and backed away.

"I don't know that such precautions will be necessary, my good man," Nicholas said loudly, resettling his gaze on Braxton. "It appears young Lord Maplethorpe will not be defending his honor today."

Braxton stopped in the doorway and spun about. "I warned you, Bourne."

Nicholas braced himself as the man stalked toward him.

"And you do know, after what you've said here in front of these witnesses, I could kill you and no one would question my actions," Braxton added, folding one hand over the other and cracking his knuckles.

Nicholas smiled with evil intent and put his fists up in preparation for the fight. "Oh, I know it only too well, Braxton. Only too well."

The man shook his head in disgust and Nicholas nearly felt sorry for him. Then Braxton landed a stinging blow to his right cheek and Nicholas forgot all about such a ridiculous notion.

And instead focused every last ounce of shame and remorse, bitterness and regret on his opponent.

He staggered at first, widening his stance in order to

recapture his balance. Braxton's fist connected a second time, grazing Nicholas's ribs on the right side.

"There now, Braxton. You do have a bit of life in you." Nicholas ducked to avoid a punch to the eye.

"Wouldn't want to disappoint you, Bourne," Braxton replied, grunting when Nicholas hit him square in the stomach.

He doubled over and Nicholas took the opportunity to catch his breath. "Impossible, Braxton. The moment you turned back I knew I would not be disappointed."

"You're insane," Braxton muttered, standing upright once again.

Nicholas raised his fists. "Now you're beginning to understand."

"I am tired and would like to go home to my bed. Let's finish this, shall we?"

Nicholas nodded in agreement. "A capital idea, Braxton. Absolutely cap—"

Braxton launched himself at Nicholas, clearly intending on following through with the plan. The two crashed against a table, sending a deck of playing cards flying. Braxton grabbed Nicholas's lapels and toppled him over onto the floor, landing squarely on top of him.

Nicholas writhed in an attempt to free himself, swinging wildly with his fists. Braxton avoided his hits by ducking and leaning back, the shifting of his weight forcing the air from Nicholas's lungs.

And then he set to pounding the life out of Nicholas. There was a certain rhythm to it, Nicholas realized, admiring the man's steady, determined efforts. Surely Braxton had boxed before. His technique was polished. His punches clean and to the point.

Perhaps Braxton would kill him, after all.

A small part of Nicholas's brain realized what he was admitting; he had, in fact, goaded Braxton into fighting him, with his goal being death.

It sounded a touch too dramatic for Nicholas, but he would not rule it out.

The pain had gone from excruciating to a somewhat duller throb and burn, leaving Nicholas to wonder if the man had managed to sever every last nerve ending in his face.

"All right, my lords. Time to end this."

Nicholas opened his eyes as best he could and attempted to look over Braxton's shoulder, the shape of a face hovering there. "I'm afraid you're mistaken. Braxton here is the only one with a useless title."

Suddenly Braxton's fists stopped and the man lurched forward, collapsing in a heap atop Nicholas.

Over his shoulder, Nicholas had a clear view of a footman, wincing as he shook his right hand. Must be the fist he hit Braxton with, Nicholas thought with oddly detached calm.

"I warned him," the footman announced, resignation in his tone. "More than likely be dismissed regardless."

"I suppose so," Nicholas answered, then blacked out.

# 11

*May 30*
BOAR'S NEST TAVERN
SEVEN DIALS
ST. GILES

"It is truly a blessing that you bore such a beating last evening, sahib. For your injuries make you look like any other ruffian here."

Nicholas stared at Singh with his one good eye. They sat at a corner table at the Boar's Nest, the fifth tavern they'd visited that day. Mary Riley's address was exactly the break he'd been waiting for. Now it was a matter of finding someone who was not afraid to speak of the gang.

So far, that was proving to be a difficult task.

They had started with establishments closest to the prostitute's former lodgings. No one had been willing to talk, although instantly paling faces, nervous tics, and brief answers had indicated that some of those questioned knew more than they admitted.

"Yes, Singh, you have mentioned my bruises a dozen times now," Nicholas answered with impatience.

They were some twenty streets from their starting point now, with little more information than they'd possessed that morning.

Singh, however, had managed to acquire a low level of inebriation during their travels.

"Tell me, how do you find our English ale?" Nicholas inquired, taking a deep drink from his own tankard.

Singh adopted an air of comical indifference. "I must be honest with you, sahib: it is not to my liking. Our Feni wine is far superior to your ale. But do not think on my suffering. For it is necessary to the search, is it not?"

He reached out to grasp his tankard and missed, frowning at his fingers as if they'd failed him.

"Well, no, Singh," Nicholas replied, pushing the tankard even farther out of the man's reach. "You've done your duty."

Singh nodded gravely, and then turned his attention to a fight near the back of the tavern. The man always appeared serene. Calm. Perfectly happy to wait.

If Nicholas did not hold great affection for Singh, he would have beaten the hell out of him by now. And if they did not find someone with information on the gang soon, his ridiculously tender feelings for the wise Indian might not be enough to save him.

The barmaid approached, a large tray balanced in her right hand as she wiped away spilled ale and swept food crumbs from neighboring tables with the other. She tossed the soiled rag onto the tray and stopped in front of Nicholas. "Another pint for you and your friend?"

Singh opened his mouth, ready to agree, and Nicholas cut him off. "That won't be necessary. But if you have a moment, I would like to ask a question."

"I'm a barmaid, sir, and happy to be so. If you're looking for companionship, best be talking to Madeline over there," the woman replied, pointing to the corner where the fight had now ended. A garishly dressed woman, her face painted bright enough that they could make out her features even in the poor lighting of the pub, stood next to the winner of the round, wiping blood from his face with a dirty handkerchief.

Nicholas turned back to the barmaid and smiled. "No, it is not companionship I seek. I'm looking for information concerning a young boy. He goes by the name Mouse. Do you know him?"

The barmaid's smile faded. She looked quickly, fearfully, over her shoulder before she reached out and grabbed Nicholas's tankard, dropping it inelegantly on her tray before snatching up Singh's as well. "Can't say that I do, no. And I believe it's time for you to go."

Nicholas reached into his vest pocket and retrieved enough coins to pay for the ale and then some. "Are you quite sure you don't remember anything about the boy?"

The barmaid eyed his hand with greedy interest. Nicholas reached out and she took the coins, tucking them into her neckline before stepping back. "Yes. *Quite*," she hissed. "Now go. Your money's enough to pay for the ale and a warning—don't come back if you know what's good for you."

She spun on her heel and left, her homespun dress flouncing about her booted feet as she moved quickly toward the bar and kitchens beyond.

"She is lying, sahib," Singh informed Nicholas. The woman's rudeness and grim warning apparently had a sobering effect on him. "Much like all the others we've spoken with today."

"Obviously," Nicholas muttered, drumming his fingers on the surface of the rough wooden table. "Is it too much to expect that one single person could rise above their selfish greed and fear in the interest of doing what is right?"

"No, sahib." Singh slid out from the bench and stood. "It is not. Believing in the inherent good of your fellow man is all that we—"

Nicholas raised his hand to silence Singh as he too stood. "Not now, Singh." He was too frustrated to listen to his friend's wise words.

Singh acquiesced with a nod and fell into step behind Nicholas, remaining silent as they walked the width of the tavern and left the Boar's Nest.

Nicholas stopped to get his bearings. "I'm afraid abject failure has dampened my appetite for today's hunt. We will return to the Albany for the evening. A good meal and generous glasses of brandy should help—or at the very least, wipe this frustrating day from our memories. After you." Nicholas pointed up the street toward the Seven Dials and set off with Singh on his left. He'd not taken more than five strides when a chunk of wood struck him on his right shoulder.

Nicholas crouched and spun to face the threat. An alley ran between the Boar's Nest and a brothel next door. A man stood in the shadows, staring at him.

He welcomed the excuse to vent the day's frustration. "You chose the wrong man to harass this evening."

In a few long strides, he was in the alley.

"Sahib!" Singh yelled. "Wait!"

Nicholas ignored Singh, blocked a blow, and sank his fist into the man's midriff. The man grunted, grappling as he fell against the outer wall of the Boar's Nest, taking Nicholas down with him.

"You bloody bastard." Nicholas punched his opponent in the ribs and grabbed a fistful of his shirt when he sagged. "Why the hell are you provoking strangers? That's a boy's trick."

"I needed to get your attention." The man threw his weight to the right, forcing both of them to roll. "To ask about Mouse."

Before Nicholas could react to the unexpected words, something connected with his skull, and stars flashed and spun before his eyes. He let go of his assailant and rolled onto his back.

"Did you not hear the man?" Singh said from above him.

Nicholas gingerly touched the back of his head, expecting to find the slippery wetness of blood. "Of course I did. How could I not, with him literally in my face while uttering the words? The blow to my head wasn't necessary." He was surprised to find his hand dry.

Singh offered his hand to Nicholas. "I could not let you kill the man, sahib," he explained.

"So instead you thought to kill *me*. What did you hit me with?" Nicholas grasped Singh's hand and let the man pull him to his feet.

Singh dusted off the back of Nicholas's coat. "The Bear Paw—it would not have killed you, sahib. It is meant to disarm, not destroy."

"Well, that is a comfort," Nicholas growled, his irritation ebbing.

Singh turned away and slowly approached the other man, who appeared dazed. "May I apologize for sahib? It has been a very trying day, you see."

The stranger waved off Singh's help, rolling onto his hands and knees before staggering upright. "I tried to not draw attention, you fool. Now we'll be lucky if half the cutthroats in St. Giles don't know of our meeting."

Nicholas raked his fingers through his hair and shrugged his coat into place. "Mr. Singh is correct. It has been a difficult day. What is it you want of us, Mr. . . . ?" He paused, waiting for the name.

"Boyle. You can call me Boyle," the burly man replied, brushing at the smears of dirt on his vest and shirtsleeves. "Owner of the Boar's Nest."

"Boyle." Nicholas nodded an abrupt acknowledgment and waved his hand at Singh. "This is—"

"Don't go telling me your names," Boyle interrupted,

wincing as he gingerly rubbed his ribs where Nicholas's fist had caught him. "You'll likely lie, no doubt. And I've no need for the truth, anyway. Other than when it comes to Mouse."

Yells and raucous laughter erupted from the street as a group of men left the Boar's Nest, a randy rendition of a bawdy song filling the air in the gathering dark.

Nicholas gestured for Singh and Mr. Boyle to follow him deeper down the alley. They ducked into the dense shadows of a shed near the southern corner of the pub.

Nicholas waited until the revelers' whoops and drunken singing grew fainter. "What do you know about the boy?"

"Can you promise me he's safe?" Boyle asked pointedly.

"Would you believe me if I told you he was?" Nicholas countered.

Boyle shrugged with pragmatism. "You're not one of them, that's for sure. I'd be dead by now if you were."

"One of *them*?" Nicholas said swiftly.

Boyle stiffened and offered no information. "I just want to know if Mouse is safe."

"And how can I be sure that you are worth trusting?" Nicholas asked, curious as to what else Boyle might accidentally let drop.

"That's the thing—you can't."

Nicholas couldn't deny the blunt truth of the man's statement. "Well, when you put it that way . . ." he remarked dryly, leaning a shoulder against the brick wall of the Boar's Nest. "In answer to your question, yes, the boy is safe. For now."

Relief flooded the pub owner's ruddy face. "Thanks be to God for that."

"You do know him, then?" Nicholas asked.

Mr. Boyle nodded. "Aye, I know him. Mouse's mother worked the district. She'd leave him here at the pub while she entertained clients—which was often, as you can imagine. The lad helped around the pub and in return I looked out for him. A bright boy, our Mouse. I did my best to keep him out of the gang's path. They got their claws into him, anyway."

Nicholas could hear the regret in Boyle's voice. And a touch of sorrow. "An impossible task, Mr. Boyle, from what I understand of the St. Giles gangs. And the boy's mother?"

"Caroline disappeared some time back," Mr. Boyle replied, shaking his head. "She wasn't ever much of a mother to Mouse. Still, the boy missed her something fierce."

"A victim of the same gang that's after Mouse?" Nicholas asked. He knew prostitutes were fair game for gangs, as well as any number of other nefarious individuals.

Boyle scratched his bald head. "Hard to say, really. No one wants to be found on the wrong side of those men, that much I know."

"'Those men'?" Nicholas said, his gaze sharpening. "Who are they—what's the name of the gang?"

"What's it to you?" Boyle countered, stepping back to put distance between himself and Nicholas. "It's best you don't know. And don't be bringing Mouse back here. They'll hunt him down and kill him. So there's no need for you to be worrying about such things."

"I want the name of the gang." Nicholas's voice held steel. "And I'll do whatever is necessary to get it."

Boyle pointed his index finger level with Nicholas's heart. "Is that it, then? You'd sacrifice the boy, knowing he'd be dead within the week?"

"Nothing could be further from my mind," Nicholas replied. "I have every intention of keeping Mouse safe."

"Sahib speaks the truth, Mr. Boyle," Singh chimed in.

"Young Mouse will never see the inside of your rookery again."

"Then why are you here?" Boyle jabbed his finger at Nicholas once more before lowering his arm. "No sensible man goes snooping about St. Giles unless he's got something to gain."

"Well," Nicholas sighed with feigned regret, "human nature being what it is, you are absolutely correct, Mr. Boyle. You see, I believe the gang who tried to capture Mouse is responsible for a string of murders committed some time ago. Women died with their throats slit from ear to ear, and the killer was never found."

"A common occurrence here, sir."

"One of those women was my concern. If you were me, Boyle, what would you do?"

The tavern owner crossed his arms over his chest, his raspy voice begrudgingly acknowledging Nicholas's right to revenge. "I'd be doing just what you are—looking for the name of the man who'd done the killing. Even if it meant I might get myself killed in the process."

"Then you know I won't stop searching and asking questions," Nicholas replied.

"I'd be endangering myself if I talked," Boyle said pointedly. "If they found out it was me what told you . . ." He paused, looking down and shaking his head. "St. Giles gangs aren't known for their forgivin' nature. I'd be a marked man."

Nicholas could have lied to make himself look more sympathetic. He could have pretended that he knew little of how gangs operated or denied the chances of Boyle's betrayal would likely get back to the gang.

He lied every day. To himself. To others. Even those he cared most for—especially those he cared most for.

For some unknown reason, he did not want to lie to Boyle.

"I know what I'm asking of you," Nicholas answered

soberly, "but I need the information. I'm willing to fight for it. If that makes me a bad man, so be it."

"It does not make you a bad man. It makes you an honest one."

Nicholas couldn't remember a time when he had been called an honest man. It made what he was asking of Boyle even worse. "The name, Boyle."

"You'll keep Mouse safe?" Boyle pressed. "Provide for him and make sure he don't ever end up back in the rookeries?"

"I will."

Boyle's big frame shifted from foot to foot, the weight of the decision clearly hard to bear. He unfolded his stout arms and scrubbed at his face with both hands, looking up at the shed roof as though seeking divine guidance.

He muttered a curse under his breath, and then looked back at Nicholas. "The gang you're looking for is called the Kingsmen. They're the ones that owned Mouse."

*May 31*
BOW STREET OFFICES

"If I may, you seem distracted today, Lady Sophia. Is there anything I might do to help?"

Sophia looked up from her notes, the sheets of paper spread out on the table in front of her. Mr. Thomas Bean, the man in charge of the Bow Street Runners, sat at his desk across the sparsely furnished room, eyeing her with concern. Lettie's words of warning had kept her up for much of the night thinking. There were many reasons to involve Bow Street in her mother's case, and only one not to: Nicholas. She felt sure he would be very angry with her if she was to tell Mr. Bean about the Bishop.

Beneath the covering of her green muslin gown and the fine cotton of her corset and chemise, Sophia felt her heart beat faster as she considered Mr. Bean's question. She could hardly make decisions based on Nicholas's moods.

"As it so happens, there is," she said gravely.

A bear of a man, Mr. Bean pulled a wooden chair over from his own desk and settled it into place next to Sophia. "Then I'm glad I asked."

Sophia folded her hands together in her lap and looked directly into Mr. Bean's kind eyes. "There is a lead in my mother's case."

"Is that so?" Mr. Bean asked, the instant, keen interest in his voice layered with surprise. "I've heard nothing of such things."

"The information was gathered from other sources. It is reliable," she assured him. She couldn't reveal her knowledge of the Young Corinthians and fervently hoped he would not demand the details.

Mr. Bean's broad brow furrowed in concern. "Lady Sophia, I know you have engaged the services of several individuals over the years to investigate your mother's death. Is this information from such a source?"

"No, Mr. Bean," she replied, wanting to put his mind at ease—at least on that point. The "individuals" that he referred to had been no more than well-intentioned novices at best and charlatans at worst. The work of detection to solve long-cold crimes was still a relatively mysterious undertaking in and of itself, so the men's failure to find any useful information was not that unexpected. But Sophia had been disappointed all the same. "I have not sought help from yet another investigator."

"Naturally, I am curious as to the identity of your source, both for your safety and my own interest as a Runner. I will not demand such information from you, however, even though it is within my authority to do so."

"Thank you, Mr. Bean." Sophia smiled at him, deeply appreciative of his restraint. She had witnessed for herself just how persuasive he could be when he wanted information. His size alone had intimidated and compelled answers from scores of criminals he'd interviewed over the years. "Although I would prefer to reveal the source of my information, I cannot. I am, as ever, glad for your consideration and kindness."

Mr. Bean's features reddened and he cleared his throat with a harrumph of embarrassment, waving his hand dismissively. "Ah well, you cannot blame a man for being curious, and I trust you will confide in me when you can. Now, let us get to the heart of things. Tell me what you've found."

"Of course," Sophia agreed, aware that Mr. Bean would persist in his curiosity, but glad for the reprieve. "Now, where to begin. Let me see . . ." She paused, sorting out what was absolutely necessary to share with her mentor. "By the time I was made aware of the renewed effort to find my mother's killer, the individual who committed the act had been identified."

"And that would be whom?" Mr. Bean asked.

Sophia could not see the harm in giving the name. In fact, not doing so might hinder Mr. Bean's ability to help. "Mr. Francis Smeade."

"A gentleman?" Mr. Bean wondered aloud, tapping one beefy finger on the deep dent in his chin.

"You are aware of Mr. Smeade?" Sophia asked.

"In a manner of speaking, yes," Mr. Bean replied. "His death was as suspicious as they come—'course, a gunshot wound to the chest always is. And his being a gentleman, plus the location of the shooting . . . We do not find many corpses in the middle of Tower Bridge.

Everything having to do with the case was odd. Or is odd, I should say . . ."

Mr. Bean's voice trailed off, as though he did not want to continue. "Not to imply any wrongdoing, of course, Lady Sophia . . ."

"I know what you are wondering," Sophia offered mercifully. "And the answer is no, I do not know the identity of his killer, nor does my source. But I believe there may possibly be a way to find out."

Mr. Bean's relief over not having to accuse Sophia of a crime was tempered by his obvious desire to know more. "Is that so?"

"Yes, indeed, Mr. Bean. It seems Mr. Smeade was employed by a gang of thieves and murderers head-quartered in St. Giles."

"You'll have to be more specific, Lady Sophia," Mr. Bean urged. "As you know, there are numerous gangs in that section of the city."

Sophia took a stack of papers from her table and paged through it until arriving at the drawing of Mouse's brand. "Unfortunately, there is very little information to be found regarding the gang. We have this, though." She handed the drawing to him and waited for his response.

"Where did you get this?" Mr. Bean asked. He studied the sketch intently before quickly folding the paper into fourths and tucking it into his inner vest pocket.

Taken aback by his action, Sophia scooted to the edge of her seat. "Mr. Bean, why did you take the drawing?"

"Answer my question, Lady Sophia," he commanded, his voice polite but firm.

"It was burned—branded, actually—on the back of a young boy," Sophia replied, glancing at the corner of the drawing that peeked out from Mr. Bean's dark blue coat. "And now it is your turn to answer my question."

Mr. Bean looked about the room, clearly checking the location of the other Runners and clerks to make certain he would not be overheard. "I took the drawing for your safety, Lady Sophia," his voice rumbled, pitched lower so only she could hear.

"But it is nothing more than a crude sketch. How could such a thing be dangerous?"

"You say you found the likeness on a young boy's back?" Mr. Bean asked. "Was the boy alive or dead?"

"Quite alive, I assure you," Sophia replied, "and on the run from the Kingsmen."

Mr. Bean nodded in understanding, crossing his substantial arms over his equally broad chest. "Lady Sophia, I must urge you to turn the matter over to the Runners."

"You know I want to be involved in the investigation. If I give everything over, you'll cut me out."

"You cannot assume such a thing," Mr. Bean countered, his mouth settling into a determined line.

"You stole a drawing right out of my hands, Mr. Bean. Because it could, in some unknown way, put me in danger. If I am not allowed to possess a simple sketch, how can I believe your men will allow me to be involved in an investigation involving the drawing?"

Mr. Bean's dark eyebrows lowered until they appeared to form almost one continuous line of irritation. "You've put me in a difficult position. I am honor-bound to reveal any information that pertains to an open case to my superiors."

"And I am sorry for that, Mr. Bean," Sophia admitted apologetically. "Still, it does not have to be true. If you would tell me what you know of this gang, without any more questions, then the only information you have is their connection to Smeade's death. Surely you can't lie about what you *don't* know?"

Before Mr. Bean could answer, a loud crash sounded from the hall, followed by a heavy thud, startling Sophia.

"Let me see to whatever is going on in the outer chamber, and then we will continue our conversation," Mr. Bean said. His level gaze promised Sophia he meant every word, then he stood and strode across the room.

He shoved against the partially open door and stepped out.

And Sophia heard a deep, familiar voice say dryly, "He's only a Runner, Mouse, not God. There is no need to be frightened."

## 12

"What is all this?" Mr. Bean demanded.

Nicholas turned to the large man who stepped out from behind a partially opened door. "I am afraid your Mr. Connelly frightened young Mouse here."

The Runner looked first at Mr. Connelly, inspecting his co-worker's slight build and undeniably pleasant face, then turned his attention to Mouse, who had taken up residence behind a cabinet near the front door of the office.

"Mr. Bourne?" Sophia peered around the Runner, who seemed to be in charge. "And Mouse? Is that you?"

Nicholas barely had time to register the surprise of her lovely features. Her slim figure, clad in a fashionable gown trimmed in cream ribbon, moved with swift grace as she slipped out from behind the Runner's broad bulk and hurried past him to the boy. "Whatever happened? What are you doing here?"

"As I just told Mr. . . . ?" Nicholas paused to look inquiringly at the bulky man, noting with admiration that the Runner stood a full head taller than him. He held out his hand and waited for the man to take it.

"Bean," the older man replied, accepting the friendly gesture and shaking Nicholas's hand politely.

"Mr. Bean?" Nicholas repeated, curious as to whether he might take the opportunity to underscore just how delightfully the man's name failed to describe him. He looked first at Sophia, whose patience appeared to be waning, then back to Mr. Bean. The Runner hardly looked in the mood for pleasantries, either.

"Very well," Nicholas continued, releasing Mr. Bean's paw. "As I was just telling Mr. Bean, Mouse found Mr. Connelly's attack to be quite frightful."

"Your attack?" Sophia asked the young Runner accusingly.

Mr. Connelly's mouth gaped at the question. "I swear I did nothing of the sort."

"Then what did you do?" Sophia pressed, reaching for Mouse and pulling him upright.

"I said hello to the lad. That is all. I promise."

Sophia led Mouse around the cabinet and gently tugged him after her until they joined Nicholas. "Mr. Bourne, are you indulging your habit of stretching the truth?"

Nicholas looked down at Mouse, who was watching Mr. Connelly and Mr. Bean with fierce yet frantic eyes.

"Oh, all right. The jig is up, as they say," Nicholas replied, patting Mouse on the back. "Mr. Connelly is not to blame for the boy's reaction—not directly, anyway. It seems young Mouse has a bit of an aversion to the Runners, don't you, Mouse?"

The boy kept looking back and forth at the men as if his life depended on it. "You could say that."

"Mr. Bourne?"

Nicholas turned to the doorway. Mrs. Kirk stood on the threshold, holding a tea tray and eyeing him with calm inquiry.

"What an unexpected delight, finding you here, Mrs. Kirk."

"I could say the same to you, Mr. Bourne," she replied, turning to set the tray down on the cabinet vacated by Mouse only moments before.

Sophia cleared her throat and looked at Nicholas with

a disconcerting gleam in her eye. "I believe we will take tea in Mr. Bean's office today, Mrs. Kirk."

"Of course." The older woman lifted the tray once more and walked toward them.

Sophia intercepted Mrs. Kirk just as she reached Mr. Bean's door. "Thank you, Lettie. I will see to the tea. If you would be so kind as to assist Mr. Connelly and entertain young Mouse while Mr. Bourne and I speak with Mr. Bean, I would be ever so grateful."

Mrs. Kirk smiled knowingly and gestured for Mouse to follow. "Come along, Mouse."

The boy peered up again at Nicholas, uncertainty and fear written on his worry-pinched features.

"It will be all right," Nicholas assured him. "I'll just be in there," he added, nodding toward Mr. Bean's office, "taking tea with a Runner." He gave the boy an exaggerated wink, then efficiently nudged him in the general direction of Mrs. Kirk.

In truth, he felt a similar sort of apprehension. What the devil was Sophia up to?

"Shall we?"

Nicholas responded to Sophia's prompting and followed her into the office, Mr. Bean bringing up the rear and closing the door behind them.

"I called at your home first. Clyde told me you'd gone to the Bow Street Offices," Nicholas began, taking a seat in a serviceable straight-backed chair near Bean's desk. "I was hoping you might agree to a trip to Gunter's—an apology for my foul mood at the ball, you see."

Sophia moved to the table and lifted the teapot lid, then, satisfied, began to pour. "A bit of luck on my part that you did so."

"Luck?" Mr. Bean asked, taking his seat behind the desk.

Mr. Bean's confusion over the purpose of the conversation did little to clear up Nicholas's questions. "Yes," he said, "what about this luck?"

Sophia turned and gracefully handed Nicholas a cup and saucer. "I was just now speaking with Mr. Bean about the case."

Nicholas's fingers tightened on the saucer and the cup wobbled, nearly spilling his tea. "And what case might that—"

"I see no reason to involve Mr. Bourne," Mr. Bean interrupted, aiming a clipped smile at Nicholas. "Bow Street business is best kept within the walls of this building—and not one step beyond."

Nicholas agreed with the man, as long as the case Sophia had been discussing with Mr. Bean was not Lady Afton's. "I have no intention of prying any particulars regarding Bow Street business from either of you."

Sophia prepared a second cup and offered it to Mr. Bean, then readied her own. She joined the men, taking the seat next to Nicholas. "Mr. Bean has been apprised of the recent developments in the Afton case."

"God Almighty," Nicholas hissed, setting his cup and saucer down on Bean's desk with controlled force.

Mr. Bean did the same, sloshing most of the contents of his cup into the saucer, where it immediately overflowed onto the desktop. "I have to agree with Mr. Bourne."

"Well, I do not," Sophia replied before taking a small sip of tea. "There are many reasons why such a partnership is advisable, not the least of which is Lord Stonecliffe. When he discovers my part in all of this, his anger will be greatly diminished by Bow Street's involvement. I must take the necessary precautions, you see."

"Lord Stonecliffe has not been apprised of the situation?" Mr. Bean asked. He began to tap his index finger against his chin once again, frowning at her.

"No one was to be 'apprised' of it," Nicholas ground out, "especially not the likes of you."

"Nicholas," Sophia admonished. "I would trust Mr. Bean with my life."

"I wish I could say the same."

*  *

"Ain't never had no ice," Mouse informed Sophia and Nicholas for the fifth time since they'd departed the Bow Street Office. "What's it like?"

"Cold," Nicholas answered the boy before reaching into his vest pocket. "Here, take this and fetch a posy for Miss Spoon, won't you?"

Mouse caught the coin in mid-air and grinned cheekily at the two. "Don't need a coin for such things."

"You do if you don't want to answer to me," Nicholas replied sternly. "Now, go."

Mouse took off at a trot for the flower cart farther up the block. He easily dodged around clusters of ladies and gentlemen that strolled in chattering groups, the maids with baskets over their arms who hurried purposefully along, and the occasional governess shepherding her young charges with militant ease.

"How did you explain Miss Spoon's tie to the Runners?" Sophia asked, genuinely curious. "You took quite a risk bringing him to Bow Street."

"Singh was nowhere to be found and I could not leave Mouse alone," Nicholas explained in a curt, clipped tone. "I convinced the boy that you were acting on my behalf in a rather delicate situation. He absolutely devoured the story, if you must know. Now, tell me, did my comments at the ball convince you to speak with Mr. Bean?"

On the street behind them, carriage wheels rattled over pavings, the creak and groan of moving vehicles discordant background music to the city scene. Suddenly, drivers called out, shouting warnings as a heavy dray lumbered too close to the lighter conveyances. The resulting noisy confusion benefited Sophia and Nicholas, assuring no chance passersby could overhear their conversation.

Sophia gripped her reticule with both hands, the silk drawstring tightening about her wrist. "You think me so petty that I would seek retaliation for . . . what? Words? Your uncivil mood? Really, Nicholas. If that were the case, I would not have enough time in the day for my machinations."

"Stop walking and pretend to inspect the hats," Nicholas commanded, tipping his head toward Pensington's Millinery.

Sophia obeyed, halting in front of the shop's large glass window and looking closely at a puce chip bonnet within. "Mr. Bean has access to information that we do not, and a staff of men to help, should we find ourselves in a difficult situation," she explained, watching Nicholas closely as he stared with complete disinterest at a display of the latest spools of ribbon artfully arranged in the shop window. "Besides, he was the only one to take the idea of criminal psychology seriously—still is, unfortunately."

Nicholas looked at Sophia, clearly puzzled. "Criminal psychology?"

She hesitated, not sure that she could bear it if he ridiculed her work.

"Sophia, I am aging right before your eyes," Nicholas said dryly, looking up the street toward the flower cart. "And Mouse will be returning soon."

Sophia's gaze followed his and she smiled at the sight of Mouse as he stood proudly next to the cart, a charming bouquet grasped with both hands. "Are you familiar with the science of criminal psychology?"

"Not in the slightest," Nicholas answered, one eyebrow lifting in inquiry. "Should I be?"

"Preferably not," Sophia said sternly. "Criminal psychology is concerned with understanding how a criminal thinks. If you can enter their mind and see things as they do, then you have an opportunity to not only understand why they commit crimes, but how to treat them so that, hopefully, they will stop."

Nicholas held up his hand and gestured for Mouse to wait. "And how would one go about learning such methods?"

"There are books by authorities in the field. Also case notes, personal interviews," Sophia replied, her natural confidence returning as she warmed to her subject. "Access to the crime scene is vastly informative."

"Cavorting with criminals? Is that what Mr. Bean has allowed you to do?" Nicholas remarked snidely.

"Look at me," she demanded quietly, standing absolutely still as he obeyed. "Now tell me, Nicholas, when did you last have a drink?"

"I fail to see what relevance that information could possibly have to our conversation. Still, if you must know, I enjoyed a bit of brandy after dinner last night."

Sophia looked into his eyes, watching as his pupils dilated to twice their normal size. Then she looked down at his hands where they rested at his sides. "Nicholas, you're lying. You cannot go more than eight hours without a drink. If you do, you develop a tremor in your hands—which is absent at present. Also, your pupils are the size of saucers. This is the body's natural response to the stress placed upon it by deceit."

Nicholas folded his arms across his chest. "This is what you've learned? A bit of sly gypsy magic, then?"

"Am I right?" Sophia pressed, gazing at his strong chin.

A muscle flexed along his jawline. "Mr. Bean taught you how to detect such things?" he asked quietly.

"No, he did not," Sophia answered. "But he believes in my methods and will do whatever is within his considerable power to help. I would say that makes him a valuable partner, wouldn't you?"

Nicholas nodded, his broad shoulders shrugging in acceptance.

Sophia nodded curtly and made to step around him, only to have Nicholas block her path.

"I want to apologize," he said grimly. "Actually, that's a lie. I don't want to. I need to. It is why I sought you out today. I've no good reason for the way I treated you at the ball—nor for the rude comments I just made. I don't know why I tend to take my feelings out on those I care for; it is just what I've always done, I suppose. A ridiculous reason, really."

Sophia returned her gaze to the shop window and feigned a deep interest in the hats while absorbing the weight of Nicholas's confession. "You never should have been as kind and understanding as you were to me in Mouse's room. Do you know, you'd convinced me that there was some small measure of hope for you."

"God, Sophia, that was cruel—and wholly deserved," Nicholas muttered as he looked to the ground.

Sophia studied him from the corner of her eye, the raw quality of his response doing her in. "And now I must apologize. I'm afraid this was all so much more clear when your dislike for me was on permanent display. Why are you letting me in—and, rather more importantly, shutting me out all at once?"

"Please, haven't we talked about our feelings enough for one day?" he asked, flattening his palm against the brick exterior of the shop.

Did Sophia, as she suspected, sense there was more? Or did she simply want there to be? "I knew you. For one brief moment, you revealed yourself to me when we kissed. And then you eviscerated me at the ball as though nothing had changed between us. Help me understand, Nicholas."

He returned his gaze to the window. "Stop, Sophia."

"All I want is the truth—"

"The truth is that you are to be my brother's wife," Nicholas snapped. "A fact that has eaten away at my heart all of these years until there's very little of it left. That is the truth, Sophia."

Sophia felt the very ground beneath her feet violently shift. In an attempt to maintain her questionable balance, she turned to face his profile, steadying herself against the window. "You disliked me . . ." Her tongue struggled to form an intelligent response. "You burned my dollhouse, attempted to drown me in the pond. Even fled for India because of me, if Dash is to be believed."

He continued to stare at the bonnets in the window, his jaw flexing with tension. "I was a stupid boy, Sophia—and I've grown up to be a stupid man," he answered, a weariness in his voice. "It was far easier to pretend to hate you than to accept that you would never love me."

Sophia repeated the sentence in her head, turning it this way and that in an effort to draw out any facets she may have missed. "Why didn't I understand?"

"There was never a need on your part. You have Langdon."

*You have Langdon.*

Sophia knew herself to be an intelligent woman. Still, she was struggling to absorb what Nicholas was telling her.

"What if I do not—"

"For the lady," Mouse interrupted, suddenly shoving the posy into Sophia's hand.

"I don't know what to say," Sophia whispered, unaware she'd said anything at all.

"You say 'thank you,'" Nicholas answered, his mouth slanted into a small, sad smile. "And move on."

*Dear Lady Fabersham,*
  *It is with profound gratitude that I write to you today.*

Sophia rested her quill on the mahogany writing desk in her bedroom and folded the unfinished missive in half. The Halcyon tea hosted by Lady Fabersham had been the single most successful event for the charity to date, no fewer than fourteen ladies pledging their support.

The woman deserved more than "profound gratitude," surely?

Situating a fresh piece of paper in front of her, Sophia reclaimed the quill with determination and began again.

*Dear Lady Fabersham,*
  *On behalf of the Halcyon Society, I would like to extend a sincere thank you for hosting*

"Sincere?" Sophia complained out loud. She ran the feathered end of the quill back and forth across her forehead in an attempt to unearth some measure of inspiration. Perhaps Mrs. Mason would be better suited to writing the thank you letters?

Sophia dismissed the idea immediately. Mrs. Mason had far more important matters to see to.

Besides, wasn't such a task meant to be something every lady of the ton performed without issue? Sophia realized with acute irritation that the revelation did little to help.

*Dear Lady Fabersham,*

*I wonder, might you be able to help me? The man I've loved for lo these many years—the very man I am to marry—no longer holds my heart. Actually, I'm not sure he ever did. He is kind and responsible. An honorable man whom all admire. He possesses every last quality that a woman could ever possibly desire in a husband. And I do love him.*

Sophia looked up from the letter and stared out the window into the approaching night. She did love Langdon—it would be impossible not to love the man. Then why was she suddenly struggling to make sense of something she'd hardly ever considered before?

*But he does not challenge me. Quite the opposite, really. He does not encourage me to see the world from a different perspective, nor expect I will ever grow beyond the staid, solid environs of my existence.*

She scribbled mindlessly while rereading the list of complaints. A lady could do much worse than to suffer such, of course.

*And then there is his brother. He is reckless and unreliable. Not one measure of his heart is free from torment. Those who see him approach run the other way. He cannot rest until I am overwrought and undone. And yet . . .*

Sophia dropped the quill and savagely blew out one of the two candles lighting the room. She allowed the gloaming to settle about her and soothe her contradictory mind.

*And yet, one revelation on his part and I am sitting in the darkness of my room, writing a letter that I will most assuredly never send.*

*~~He loves me. And always has. And I have to wonder, have I loved him all along as well? Was that what drew me to him time and time again? Or are my feelings for him entirely new, born from our shared experience and encouraged to grow by his dem~~*

*I apologize, Lady . . . Blast, I cannot even remember your name now. I am thinking too much. Pondering the quality of love when greater minds than mine have failed to define it time and time again. I am overwrought, you see. Undone as well. I am promised to one man I do not love. And in love with another, whom I cannot marry.*

*I am in love.*

*I am in love.*

*I am in love?*

*~~Or am I simply frightened by the prospect of my future finally arriving?~~*

*Or am I simply frightened?*

*No matter my decision, love will be lost. By one or by two, but lost all the same.*

*Your immediate and insightful response is requested.*

*With the utmost sincerity,*
*Lady Sophia Afton*

Sophia set down the quill and took up the letter, folding the paper until it was no bigger than a quail's egg.

"And yet," she repeated out loud, pulling open the small drawer of the desk that housed her unused quills and depositing the letter within.

Such a silly turn of phrase—as if one could forget ev-

ery truth that had been before in favor of newly unearthed findings.

Sophia slowly closed the drawer, watching the letter
disappear into the desk.

Truths were far more complex. Hardly the sort of information to be sorted out according to one's wishes.

# 13

"You cannot be serious."

Nicholas stopped just inside the door of his apartment and stared with stunned disbelief at the transformation before him.

Mouse bumped into him. "Beggin' your pardon, Mr. Bourne," he apologized, circling around Nicholas's still figure to stand next to him. "Whoa, looks like something from a story my mother used to tell me. 'Arabian Nights' it was."

"It does, doesn't it?" Nicholas asked absentmindedly, distracted as he continued to stare at the changes to what was once his comfortably shabby home.

"Singh," he called out, a growing irritation adding to his already tense nerves.

Mr. Singh appeared from behind a flowing orange silk drape that now divided the entryway from the rooms beyond, Langdon at his side. "Welcome home, sahib. And to you as well, young Mouse."

He was dressed in a deep umber tunic and loose breeches that were decidedly not British. His turban was snowy white and exactly matched the impressive teeth displayed in his ear-to-ear smile.

"Perhaps you would tell me what the hell happened to my apartment," Nicholas snarled, looking about at the elaborate paintings of Hindu gods that now adorned the walls before walking in the general direction of the drawing room. "Should I be wary of elephants? A monkey or two, perhaps? Did you have something to do with this, brother?"

Nicholas realized he was only marginally joking about the animals and stepped lightly as he made his way to the drawing room. He tossed his hat on a new and overly bright settee before pouring himself a drink from the crystal decanter on the side table.

"I'm afraid I cannot take any of the credit," Langdon replied, settling easily on one end of the settee.

"Sahib, do not be foolish," Singh answered as he and Mouse followed. "There are no monkeys to be found in London."

Nicholas considered asking Singh if he'd actually gone looking, but decided it was best not to know the answer. "All right, then, no monkeys—thank God. That leaves the rest of this." He gestured at the room.

"Surely it is obvious, sahib," Singh replied, removing Nicholas's discarded hat from the settee and crossing the room to place it on an ornate goddess hat rack. "If you would like, though, I would be most pleased to explain."

"Yes, I would like," Nicholas said, carrying his drink to the settee and sitting down next to his brother. "Blast, Singh, this sofa is overstuffed. And it does not bear the imprint of my body as the other did."

"I believe you meant to say it is stuffed, as the previous sofa appeared to have been stripped of any padding necessary for it to be comfortable," Langdon interjected, taking Nicholas's glass from his hand and pouring the brandy into a potted plant near his end of the sofa.

Singh crossed the room to join Mouse. The boy was apparently struck speechless. He stared wide-eyed at the colorful, sumptuous, exotic splendor of the room's furnishings. "But you are correct, sahib. It is very unlike its predecessor.

"Now, young Mouse," Singh continued, turning his attention to the boy. "You may go downstairs and assist Mrs. Clark, the new cook, with preparations for the evening meal. And I believe you will find sweet sugar biscuits. Ask before taking one. Cook has a temper," the man warned, then shooed the boy from the room.

"Cook?" Nicholas wondered aloud, absentmindedly accepting the now empty glass from Langdon. "I have a cook?"

Mr. Singh nodded pleasantly. "Ah yes, sahib. You see, when I asked whether the maid knew how to prepare curry, she became very offended and informed me that she neither knew how to cook curry nor anything else. I apologized profusely for the misunderstanding, upon which she was kind enough to explain the English servant system."

"Maid?" Nicholas snarled.

"Oh yes, sahib. Her name is Molly," Singh continued. "A very pleasant young woman—though I find it odd that your English servants appear to be rather limited in their abilities. Still, I did not think it wise to attempt any alterations of the current accepted practices. And so you have a cook."

"All because of curry?" Nicholas asked.

"Precisely."

Nicholas held the glass out and waited for Singh to take it. "And does this cook know how to prepare the dish?"

"No," Singh admitted with patent disappointment. "Once she has settled in, I will teach her. As I mentioned, she has a temper . . ."

"Most cooks do," Langdon offered sotto voce, earning a brotherly punch to the arm.

"And the redecorating? Was that done in the name of curry as well?"

"Sahib, have you forgotten everything of your time in India?"

"Yes, brother, tell us—"

Nicholas held up a hand in warning to Langdon. "Singh, I have talked more in the last week than I did the whole of last year. Please, just explain all of this."

"Very well, sahib," the man replied simply, then took a seat across from Nicholas and Langdon. "One cannot reside in a home that does not nurture the soul and revitalize the spirit."

"And my old furniture did not accomplish this nurturing business?"

"No, sahib," Singh answered, shaking his head slowly. "It was old and neglected. Sad and in ill-repair. Such things cannot feed the soul nor the body."

Nicholas could not shake the sense that Singh was drawing parallels between him and the shabby former contents of the apartment. "Well, there is little to be done about it now. Let us renew and revitalize—or whatever the hell this is meant to do. How did you pay for all . . ." he waved a hand in a gesture that encompassed the room ". . . this?"

"Oh, that was quite simple, sahib—more so than I thought it would be. The maid told me to procure the cook using your name. When that proved successful, I did the same at the shops where I found the wares you see before you."

Langdon chuckled.

"Of course you did," Nicholas answered dryly. "And my room? You left it untouched, yes?"

"Oh yes, sahib," Singh said, disappointment in his voice. "The finery for your chamber will not be delivered until the end of the week. I apologize, sahib, but we must be patient."

"That is one way of looking at things, Singh," Nicholas replied. "Not necessarily what immediately comes to mind. Still, an option."

His friend smoothly rose from the sofa as if levitating by the power of goodness and well intentions alone. "Now I will go and see how our young Mouse is coming along."

Nicholas watched Singh float from the room, then turned his attention to his brother. "And you? Making a habit of dropping in, are we?"

"Should I concoct an elaborate story," Langdon asked, "or simply start with the truth?"

Nicholas scrubbed at his jaw. "Do save me the time."

"It's to do with Maplethorpe."

"Of course it is," Nicholas groaned. It wasn't enough that he'd poured out his bloody heart to Sophia on the street an hour before. Now he was expected to endure a tongue-lashing from Langdon.

And one he rightly deserved.

"I understand you were inebriated," Langdon began with caution.

"I believe I might save us both a bit of time," Nicholas announced, standing and stalking to the side table. "Let me see, where were we . . . Ah yes, I was inebriated—bloody good and inebriated, in fact. I started the quarrel with Maplethorpe and he did everything within his power to end it peaceably."

Nicholas paused to pour himself a large glass from the decanter and took a drink. "I wasn't having any of it, you see."

"And what was the quarrel about?" Langdon asked, settling back onto the comfortable cushions of the sofa.

Nicholas took a second drink and thought for a moment. "Do you know, I've no idea. Doesn't matter, really. There are times when a man simply needs to fight for no good reason."

Langdon furrowed his brows. "What do you mean?"

"You would not understand, Langdon," Nicholas replied, tossing back the rest of the brandy. "Because we're not alike—not at all. And the sooner you stop trying to reform me, the better."

He'd relented earlier, on the street with Sophia. He'd given in and been honest because he wanted to think it would mean something to her.

He poured himself another brandy and finished it in one swallow.

"Is that what you're doing now?" Langdon asked in a somber tone. "Are you in need of a fight?"

Nicholas picked up his glass and the decanter, then moved to quit the room. "Stop being so damn insightful, brother. It makes the rest of us rather pale in comparison."

※　♪

Sophia dreamed of her mother that night.

She was a child once more at Petworth Manor.

She skipped every other stair on her way to the nursery, buoyed by her excitement at having successfully avoided Mr. Reynolds. The butler would be outraged if he knew she'd managed to sneak into the house without his knowledge.

Which only made the accomplishment that much more enjoyable.

As did the boys' loss of their race from the lake to the manor. Langdon, Dash, and Nicholas would be irate when they learned she'd reached the nursery before them.

Sophia let out a giggle, clapping her hand over her mouth to hold back laughter as she gained the fourth floor and ran for the nursery.

The summer heat made her skin sticky with sweat, but she continued her fast pace until she reached the nursery door. Glancing up and down the hall, she made sure the boys were nowhere in sight, then grasped the brass doorknob and turned it guardedly, pushing on the paneled oak and walking into the room.

Her mother sat in a Sheridan chair placed in the center of the cheery rose-patterned rug. She beckoned Sophia to come closer, the faint scent of her rosewater eau de cologne drifting across the space between them.

Sophia closed the door behind her and stood still, staring at her mother, unease making her pulse quicken.

"Whatever is the matter?" her mother asked, uncrossing her ankles and moving forward to the edge of the chair cushion.

Sophia did not want to answer. Would remaining silent be rude? Or did she believe that perhaps, this time, her mother would stay—if only Sophia could keep the truth from her?

"You can tell me, Sophia," Lady Afton urged, warm concern filling her lovely voice. "Do not be afraid."

"I'm not afraid, Mama," Sophia assured her, taking a step closer.

Her mother folded her hands in her lap and smiled sweetly. "Are you fearful because I am alive?"

"Mama," Sophia urged quietly, taking another step and then another. "Please, do not ask."

"It is all right, my darling. You'll not change the course of my life, nor yours, by being truthful," her mother answered, beckoning her nearer. "But I do have something to tell you, and we've not much time."

Sophia took a hesitant, final step that brought her within reach of her mother. She slowly extended her arm and felt her mother's cool, soft fingers interlace with her own. "I can feel you, Mama," she murmured in amazed delight, pulling until their interlocked hands pressed against her forehead.

"I need you to pay attention, Sophia."

Sophia knelt on the carpet and rested her head on Lady Afton's lap. "Please, Mama. I only want to be with you. Do not ask anything of me."

"I know, my dear, sweet girl," her mother crooned, running her fingers through Sophia's tangled brown curls.

Sophia closed her eyes and reveled in the soothing sensation. "Mama, you've never spoken to me in my dreams before. Why are you doing so now?"

"You were not ready to hear me."

"That's not true. I've wanted nothing more than to speak with you," Sophia protested.

Lady Afton lifted her fingers from the crown of Sophia's head to cradle her chin and gaze into her eyes. "You were not prepared. And now you are," she said simply.

Sophia sat back on her heels. "Because of Nicholas?"

"In part, yes," her mother replied, folding her hands in her lap. "But it is far more complicated than that. And now I may tell you what is required of you."

Sophia felt an odd sense of injustice. "Required of me? Ma—"

"I know how you've sacrificed, my Sophia," Lady Afton delicately interrupted. "And you are so close to reaching your goal. But it cannot be done without you returning to Petworth Manor."

The name of her family's summer home made Sophia's heart skip a beat; the rhythm when it resumed, shaky and unpredictable. "There must be another way, Mama."

Her mother slid from the chair to join her on the carpet. "I wish there were, Sophia. But there are memories there that require retrieval."

"I remember everything of that day, Mama—more than I care to, if you must know," Sophia answered, staring at the rose-patterned rug. "I haven't returned to the house since you died. And I don't want to—ever."

Lady Afton wrapped her arms about Sophia and pulled her into a loving embrace. "That's just it, my darling. There are things you do not remember—details you've pushed so far from your mind that they are nearly impossible to find. But they're there. Returning to Petworth Manor will help to unearth them."

Sophia buried her head against her mother's shoulder and began to cry. "I cannot, Mama. You must understand. It is impossible. Please don't make me go there."

"I do understand, Sophia," Lady Afton whispered into her ear. "Better than anyone else. Be brave, my dear, sweet girl. Be brave."

Sophia wrapped her arms tightly about her mother's waist and let the tears wash away her fear until all she was able to feel was acceptance. Bitter, but necessary acceptance.

Suddenly someone was pulling her away from her mother. Sophia fought to escape the person's grip, begging Lady Afton to hold on to her.

"Lady Sophia!" a voice cried out.

Sophia opened her eyes, expecting to find she'd been dragged across the nursery and away from her mother. Instead, her companion's worried face met her gaze.

"Lettie?" she asked.

Her trusted companion released Sophia's wrist and looked down at her. "I heard you moaning and came to see what was wrong. I believe you've had a nightmare."

Sophia scooted upright and pulled her hair back, her fingers damp from the tiny beads of perspiration at her temples.

"Was it the same dream, my lady? Was it about your mother?"

Sophia squeezed her eyes shut and tried to remember every last second she'd spent in her mother's presence.

"Yes, Lettie, my mother was there, but this one was different. She spoke to me of Nicholas, and of what I must do," Sophia replied, the linen sheets bunching in her fists. "I must return to Petworth Manor at once."

"I'll have a message sent to Mr. Bourne and ask that he come straightaway," Lettie answered, concern coloring her voice.

Sophia opened her eyes and grabbed for Lettie's hand. "No! Do not send for Nicholas. Just you and I will go."

"Do you think that is wise, my lady?" her companion asked.

"Trust me, Lettie. It is better that we go alone."

## 14

*June 2*
### THE ALBANY

"I do not believe it." Nicholas stared at the brief note, unable to accept the contents.

His words elicited a deep sigh from the maid. "Well, I don't either, sir. Without a proper footman to answer the door, deliver posts, and other such duties, they all fall to me—apparently."

Distracted, Nicholas looked up from the missive and shook his head in confusion. "I'm sorry, what was that?"

"You need a footman, sir," the maid replied matter-of-factly.

Nicholas could not see the connection between the maid and the necessity of a footman at the moment, but needed the woman gone. "Speak to Singh. Tell him I gave my permission."

The maid curtsied, beaming with delight. "I'll go find him now—that is if there's nothing else you require?"

He shooed her away with a wave of the letter and walked to the windows at the back of the apartment. Staring out at a small garden situated between the Albany and the neighboring building, Nicholas realized that he'd never bothered to look out this particular set of windows. He hadn't even known of the garden's existence.

He tapped the note against his palm, unsure of what he should do. For reasons Nicholas was not privy to, Sophia was clearly set on traveling to Petworth Manor. Alone.

Barely realizing he did so, Nicholas began to count a tidy row of tulips near the middle of the display below. He did not want to go to Petworth Manor. As far as he knew, not one of the four friends, including Sophia, had ever set foot in the summer home after Lady Afton's death.

"Why on earth would we?" he muttered aloud, aware of a growing unease that tightened his nerves and settled heavily between his shoulder blades.

There was nothing left for them on the sprawling estate—nothing that they needed, anyway.

He pulled an engraved silver pocket watch from his vest—arguably the only thoughtful gift his father had ever given him—and checked the time.

Sophia would have departed for Sussex by now.

Nicholas slipped the watch back into his pocket and gazed out the window again, absentmindedly taking up where he'd left off with counting the row of tulips.

What if Sophia was right about returning to Petworth Manor? Was there something, or someone, within the house or about the grounds that had crucial information the Young Corinthians had missed? Lord Carmichael had overseen the investigation himself. Nicholas knew the man well enough to trust he'd made damn sure it was carried out exactly to his specifications.

Nicholas lost his place in the row of colorful blooms and moved his attention to the next one, his irritation piqued.

Then what of Smeade? The Corinthians had not discovered his connection to Lady Afton's death. It was Carrington who'd unearthed the man's part in the scheme.

It would be the right thing to follow Sophia, even if she did not want him there. And after yesterday's run-in with his brother, Nicholas could do with a dose of karma.

"Sahib, Molly has informed me of your wish to employ a footman," Singh's voice interrupted his musings.

"Really, Singh, and just as I was nearly finished counting the flowers," Nicholas answered, suddenly resolute as to his next move.

"You see, sahib, already the changes I have made to your home are beginning to help," Singh replied, joining Nicholas at the window. "Ah, yes. A world of beauty in one single flower."

"You said something about a footman?" Nicholas asked.

Singh continued to gaze out the window, enraptured by what Nicholas could only assume was an overwhelming amount of happiness. "Yes, sahib. The footman. I will arrange for several candidates to be sent over right away so that you might choose."

"I'm afraid that will not be possible, Singh."

Nicholas's response pulled the man from his happy contemplation of the bucolic scene outside the window. "And why is that, sahib?"

"Because I will be leaving very shortly for the country-side, Singh," Nicholas answered, only just realizing that he still held Sophia's letter in his hand.


*The Star Pub*
PETWORTH
SUSSEX


Nicholas stood outside the Star pub in Petworth, the bands of reds, golds, and orange in the dazzling sunset a charming backdrop to the whitewashed building and the surrounding village.

Unfortunately, the scene was one he couldn't appreciate at the moment. He'd ridden hard from London, wanting to arrive at the manor before Sophia and Mrs. Kirk. Stopping only for food and to rest Guinevere, he was now filthy, exhausted, and barely able to stand upright without his legs bowing out in the shape of his horse's mid-section.

All his complaints could have easily been borne, however, if his destination was not Petworth. Even with the blazing sunset and gloriously fresh air, Nicholas had already begun to count the hours until he could leave.

His reluctance to remain in Sussex could be managed, of course. He simply needed to stay on task and not allow himself to be distracted by memories—fond or otherwise.

Difficult to do when the very sight of the pub catapulted him backward in time to his childhood, when Langdon, Dash, and he would creep from the manor house and run for their very lives across the shadowed grounds to the pub. They could not go in, being so young. Still, they did steal longing looks through the leaded windows, desperate for their chance to join the laughing patrons inside.

Two men, looking fresh from the fields, dusty and thirsty, walked around Nicholas and into the pub, the bells on the front door ringing merrily as they pushed it open. He caught a bit of raucous conversation and a burst of the tantalizing aroma of simmering beef and potatoes before the door thudded closed behind the two.

He looked in the direction of the manor house but it wasn't visible from where he stood. The sprawling grounds that surrounded it kept the estate separated from the town and its inhabitants. He could feel its presence, though. The almost overwhelming awareness threatened to send him riding back to London.

Nicholas felt like a coward. And a fool. If Sophia's assumptions were incorrect, they'd have both made the trip to Petworth for no gain and a very high emotional cost.

A couple emerged from the door of the Star, both smiling kindly at Nicholas as they turned and strolled arm in arm up the high street.

He was even more of a fool for standing in the middle of the street, Nicholas realized, swearing under his breath.

He raked his fingers through his windblown hair and strode quickly to the pub's door. Turning the brass knob, he stepped inside. The mouthwatering smell of hearty food once again teased his nostrils as he entered, and he looked about for an available table. Finding none, Nicholas continued on to the bar at the back of the low-ceilinged room and settled in next to an elderly man. The man's dog, a handsome black and white border collie, lay dozing at his feet, his paws muddy from what had probably been a good, long walk.

"What'll you have, sir?" the barkeep asked as he refilled the farmer's tankard. The thick, foamy ale poured into the glass and nearly spilled over the rim.

"I'll have what he's having and a plate of whatever your cook has prepared," Nicholas replied.

The barkeep nodded and reached for a tankard, filling it to the brim and setting it down on the polished bar in front of Nicholas. "I'll be right back with your stew."

He disappeared through a door, presumably where the kitchen and fragrant stew were kept.

"The best stew you'll have in all of Sussex," the man beside him offered in a gravelly voice, turning stiffly to face Nicholas. He winced and rubbed at his right shoulder, letting out a soft grunt of pain.

The dog sat up and nosed his master with concern. "Ah, it's all right now, Pilot. Only my achy bones."

"Pilot, is it?" Nicholas asked, holding out his hand for the dog to sniff. "He's a handsome one, your Pilot."

The dog sniffed warily at Nicholas's hand, then licked his palm, tail wagging.

"Sweet talk always works with good ol' Pilot," the man remarked, smiling widely and revealing a mouthful of chipped and worn teeth.

Nicholas returned the smile, glad to be distracted. "I'm Nicholas. Nicholas Bourne." He held out his hand and waited.

The man stopped rubbing his shoulder and gripped Nicholas's hand with surprising strength in his gnarled, calloused hand. "Joseph Wends. And 'tis a pleasure to meet you."

The barkeep returned with a steaming bowl of stew and a plate holding a crusty round of fresh brown bread.

"Join me, Joseph," Nicholas suggested.

The man waved his hand dismissively. "I better not. Pilot would have nothing to do with me if I ate stew and he didn't."

"Barkeep," Nicholas said to the young man just as he started to turn away. "Bring us two more bowls of stew, won't you? One for my friend Joseph, and one for Pilot."

"Perfectly good stew for a dog?" the barkeep protested. "Well, it's your money, I suppose." He shrugged his shoulders as if to suggest Nicholas was mad, and then returned to the kitchen.

Joseph clapped Nicholas on the back. "Aye, you'll have a friend for life now—and not just the dog."

Nicholas laughed and saluted the old man with his tankard. "I should hope so."

The barkeep returned with the bowls of stew and

plates of bread, setting them in front of Joseph. "I'll not be serving your dog, Joseph Wends. And that's that."

Nicholas chuckled, joined this time by Joseph.

"I suppose he wouldn't like it if I gave Pilot a stool to sit on and let him eat at the bar, then?" Joseph asked, grinning.

The nagging unease that had plagued Nicholas since he left London calmed with the easy banter and he took a pull of ale. "No, I suppose not." He reached for the third steaming bowl and bent down, setting the stew in front of Pilot.

"Here's to ye," Joseph said, picking up his tankard and raising it in salute.

Nicholas joined him and the two tossed down a healthy amount of ale, wiping the foam from their upper lips with the back of their hands before moving on to their stew.

"Now, seeing as you've done me the kindness of buying me a meal, I feel it's only proper that you tell me about yourself, Mr. Bourne."

The unease returned as Nicholas scrambled to compose a suitable story. "I'm afraid there's little to tell, really. I'm just up from London and passing through Petworth on my way to visit a great-aunt in Fernhurst."

"So you've never visited our fine part of the country, then?" Joseph asked as he forked a chunk of beef covered with gravy into his mouth.

"Never," Nicholas confirmed effortlessly, glancing down at Pilot.

"Well, you must stay a few days before traveling on," Joseph said, taking a quick swig of ale. "If only to see the manor house."

Nicholas nearly choked on a bite of carrot and coughed, swallowing hard. "Is that right?"

"Oh yes. It's a grand house, it is. And the estate has the biggest herd of red deer in all of England," Joseph explained, poking about the stew with his fork. "I worked at the manor house from the time I was a boy until ten years ago when I retired. Still live on the property. Well, the edge of the property, anyway."

Nicholas did not have to do the calculations to know that Joseph would have been employed by the Aftons at the time of her ladyship's death. "Surely the family would rather be left alone than have a bachelor poking about their home."

Joseph set down his fork and reached for a piece of bread, his infectious smile replaced by a somber frown. "Oh, Mr. Bourne, the family hasn't been in residence for more years than I can count. A tragedy, there was, at the manor. The lady of the house was murdered—right under her own roof, if you can believe it. After that, well," he paused, slathering creamy butter on a thick slice of bread, "I suppose her husband and the girl couldn't bear to stay there."

"That is a tragedy," Nicholas replied truthfully. "And the murderer?"

"Never caught," Joseph said with finality, then ripped the bread in half and threw a chunk to Pilot. "And now some say the lady of the house haunts Petworth Manor, on account of never being avenged. I've not seen her myself, but if it were me, I'd be raising a ruckus. She was a fair and decent woman, her ladyship—more than I can say for some of the people who visited the manor. She always treated the help with kindness; made us feel appreciated, you see."

Nicholas watched Pilot devour the bread in one bite then wait expectantly for his master to throw more. "I do, Joseph. That I do."

# 15

*June 3*

PETWORTH MANOR

The Afton traveling coach rolled along the bumpy lane leading to Petworth Manor, and with each revolution of the wheels, Sophia grew increasingly apprehensive.

She'd been able to dismiss her nerves up until the coachman turned the four gray horses down the Petworth high street. Long rides in a carriage on country roads were notorious for causing fatigue. Nights spent in posting inns could hardly be considered restful. And eating at odd times wreaked havoc with one's system. It was all perfectly understandable.

And perfectly false.

She stared out the window at the familiar grounds. It looked exactly as she remembered from childhood. Ancient chestnut trees dotted the land, their trunks so thick that even her father's land steward could not stretch his long, brawny arms around their girth and make his hands meet. Nonetheless, Sophia had never tired of begging him to try.

The Afton estate's renowned herd of red deer was grazing on the grassy expanse just in front of the classic Greek folly. Their numbers seemed to have grown since she'd last seen them, their distinctive reddish-brown coats and delicate features duplicated until she could hardly distinguish one from the other.

As a child, Sophia had tried time and time again to befriend the deer. She'd even managed to coax a doe into the house with carrots pulled from cook's kitchen garden, only to have Mr. Reynolds, their horrid butler, shoo the animal away.

The boys would have been so impressed with her pet, as would her mother.

Sophia now watched the deer feed. A mature stag looked up and turned its head toward the carriage. Sophia felt as if the big male was looking straight at her, though she could not decide if he was welcoming her home or warning her away.

The carriage dipped slightly as the wheels jolted over a rut, and Sophia jerked with surprise.

"Are you all right?" Lettie inquired, reaching across the coach to steady her.

Sophia wished she could tell her companion yes. That she continued to feel convinced their trip was necessary.

To do so would be lying. "Lettie, I believe I will walk from here."

"We're still some distance from the house, my lady. And it looks as if we'll have rain soon enough. I don't know that setting out on foot to the manor house would be wise."

Sophia tapped the roof of the carriage and called to the driver to stop. The horses slowed to a walk then came to a full halt. "It would be entirely unwise if I did not. I need to stretch my legs and work the uneasiness from my bones."

Lettie dropped the book that she'd been reading onto her lap and fixed her gaze on the younger woman. "Apprehension is to be expected. Still, in light of the long journey, wouldn't a bath and a properly cooked meal do more good than a walk?"

"I cannot go inside the house—not yet," Sophia whispered, fearful that she would start to cry. "I need a bit more time."

After a moment, Lettie nodded with wordless understanding and gestured for the coachman to open the door. "I will be waiting for you at the house, my lady. Whenever you're ready. I'll be waiting," she repeated.

"Thank you, Lettie," Sophia managed to say to the dear woman before taking the coachman's hand and stepping down from the carriage. "Go on, John. Take Mrs. Kirk up to the house. I'll be along in a bit."

To his credit, the coachman only nodded, uttered "Yes, Lady Sophia" with unflappable calm, then resumed his post and urged the horses into motion.

Sophia watched the carriage roll forward and lumber down the sunlit drive until it swayed around a bend in the lane and disappeared from sight.

The lake was visible just to the east and Sophia set out for its banks, relieved to have her feet moving and her mind less engaged.

She concentrated on the beauty of the land around her and the quiet calm of the lake ahead. She'd forgotten how peaceful Sussex was. Even in the relatively quiet part of London where she resided, there were still city sounds to be heard at nearly every hour.

Petworth was vastly different from the hustle and bustle of the capital city.

A murder of crows broke the silence. Their raucous cawing was deafening as, without warning, they swooped low in formation then shot up suddenly and dispersed.

Sophia instinctively lifted her arms to shield herself from them, panic pricking her skin. Distracted, she stepped in a hole and pitched forward. Unable to keep herself from falling, she threw her hands out to break her impact, wincing at the sting of rocks against her palms.

The crows resumed their loud cawing and Sophia looked up. She saw them behind her, gathered in one of the chestnut trees, their sleek black bodies bobbing as the branches swayed.

She shuddered with renewed apprehension and a deep sense of foreboding. The birds' repetitive cawing pulsed in her ears and the grass and dirt beneath her felt as if it were bruising her bones.

A single crow flew low over her, nearly brushing the top of her head with its wings.

Sophia cried out, terrified, her gaze fastened on the bird as it flew high and picked up momentum. When it circled back, she staggered to her feet and bolted, tearing off across the field. She didn't bother to look up to assess the crow's progress, catching her skirt in both hands to run faster, harder, than she could remember ever doing before.

Her lungs burned and every muscle in her legs ached with fatigue, but she pressed on, dropping her hem and pumping her arms in an effort to put as much distance as possible between herself and the crow.

The shores of the lake, ringed in chestnut trees, drew nearer. Sophia ignored her dizzying tiredness and pushed on, not slowing until she reached the coolness of the lake's edge. Her breathing rasped as she struggled to draw oxygen into her starved lungs.

She looked up from the safety of the tree cover and searched the sky for the crow, knowing that it was a foolish act. Still, relief flooded her when she saw only gray clouds and not the darting black bird.

Her heart pounded and she drew in deep, gasping breaths in an effort to slow her pulse. She walked closer to the lake's edge and stared into the clear water, waiting for even a small measure of the comfort that the placid waters had always granted her when she was a child.

Now even the lake felt threatening in some way. Sophia dropped onto the soft, mossy grass and drew her knees up, wrapping her arms about her legs tightly, shivering in reaction.

"Sophia?"

She closed her eyes. Even her imagination was taunting her.

"Sophia, what the hell are you doing?"

Nicholas's familiar voice reached her ears a second time and she began to cry hot, angry tears. How she wished he were really there.

She rubbed her temples hard in an effort to banish the illusion, but when strong fingers closed over the curve of her shoulder, she looked behind her—and saw Nicholas.

He was crouched down, his head level with hers, a concerned, if irritated, look on his face. "Oh God, you're crying. I hate it when women cry."

His honest admission struck Sophia as terribly funny and she began to giggle.

"Have you gone mad?" he asked warily. "Because the only situation worse than a woman crying is a woman gone mad."

She could not help herself. She'd never been happier to see him—anyone, really. The giggles took on a life of their own and Sophia simply threw her head back and let the laughter rule until her sides ached.

Nicholas sat down on the grass beside her, his confusion over her current state clear as he watched her warily.

When Sophia felt the last of her laughter bubble up and escape, she let go of her knees and wiped at her tearstained cheeks.

"Are you finished?"

"I am," Sophia replied, taking a long, cleansing

breath and folding her legs daintily beneath her. "And I am sorry if I frightened you."

"Well, I don't know that 'frightened' is the precise word I would use," Nicholas replied, planting his hands on the grass behind him and leaning back on his braced arms. "Actually, come to think of it, yes, it is. What did you think you were doing hiking about the grounds when you've only just arrived? And clearly in an unstable condition, to boot."

Sophia felt the pressure of tears building behind her eyes as she suddenly realized Nicholas's presence *had* frightened her. "My letter requested that you not follow me to Petworth. Why did you come against my express wishes?"

"God Almighty," Nicholas muttered. "Do you think I wanted to come back here? I simply could not leave you to face returning all on your own."

His nearness only serving to upset her further, Sophia scrambled inelegantly away until an expanse of ground separated them. "I don't think it is wise for you to be here."

"I am trying to do the right thing, Sophia. Do not make it harder than it already is," Nicholas replied, his own rancor growing to match hers.

"Why must you *do* anything?" she countered with frustration, pulling at the grass until she felt the cool dirt beneath her fingertips. "Especially what is right. Isn't that best left to—"

Sophia regretted the careless, hurtful words the moment they left her lips. "Nicholas, I am so sorry."

"Don't be." He emitted a low, mirthless chuckle, then stood. "You are absolutely right. Such noble acts are best left to my brother. Langdon and I are nothing alike. He is the responsible one, the man who can be counted on to keep a level head and act in an honorable manner. I, on the other hand, know nothing of such things.

I've worked my entire life to be his polar opposite. Your words, and their weight, are precisely what I deserve. And it is Langdon who should be here with you, not me."

He looked down at her and gave a practiced smile, only his eyes betraying the pain she'd caused. "I'll go."

"Please," Sophia begged, her voice no more than a whisper.

Nicholas turned back toward the house and strode away, his strong shoulders slumped, his capable hands curled into fists at his sides.

"No, please don't," Sophia commanded, her voice growing with need. "Don't go."

She struggled to stand, her boots tangling within the drape of her skirts. Finally gaining purchase, she leapt up and rushed after him, running ahead before turning to block his path.

"Don't leave. I was wrong—I've been wrong all along."

She wrapped her arms around his neck, lacing her fingers together and pulling down until his head was level with hers. "Please, do not deny me."

Sophia closed her eyes as she leaned in and pressed her lips to his—afraid he might refuse her, but more afraid not to try.

⁂

At the time, Nicholas could not have explained precisely why he'd been exceedingly enraged at the thought of Sophia wandering about Petworth lands, other than he feared she might feel as he did about returning to Sussex.

Frightened. Confused. Even angry. And terribly alone. And he had been right.

He unclasped her hands from about his neck and

gently pushed her away. "You're upset, Sophia. Confused. You do not know what you're saying," Nicholas responded, stepping around her and walking on. "Only a moment ago you wished me gone."

"I was being stupid—and cowardly," she called out, running to obstruct his route once more. She planted herself firmly in front of him and reached up to cradle his face in her small palms. "You are as different from Langdon as two brothers could ever be, that much is true. Still, you've something in common with him."

He watched as her feathered brows veed with earnestness, and for a moment he let himself pretend she wanted him as much as he wanted her. He let himself grasp her lightly about the waist and pull until she fit snugly against his chest.

"Neither of you are a matter of black and white—none of us are. I see the good in you, Nicholas. You try so hard to cover it up. But it's there."

Goddammit, he was a scoundrel, he thought with self-loathing. A poor brother to Langdon. And a worthless friend to Sophia.

The realization was not new to Nicholas. It had never been more painful than now, though, with her in his arms.

He brushed his lips against the soft silk of her hair. "I wouldn't be so sure," he said bleakly.

Tension eased from her body and she settled more fully against him. "That is just it; I wasn't certain before. I didn't want to be, if you must know. But I am now. There is no going back."

Nicholas wanted nothing more than for the world to stop, right there and then, to hold Sophia close with her sweet words still lingering in his ears. And thank her for having some faith in him, no matter how minute.

Menacing clouds rolled in from the west, a thunderclap

parting the skies. Guinevere, tethered loosely to a chestnut tree nearby, nickered wildly.

"I would be a selfish coward were I to take you for my own," Nicholas said even while he tightened his hold about her waist.

"We would both be selfish cowards if we allowed Langdon to believe in something that was doomed from the beginning," Sophia countered, lifting her head from his chest and gazing into his eyes. "I do not claim to understand love, Nicholas. But now, with you here, I can recognize its presence. I want the same for Langdon, just not with me; my heart belongs to you."

The rain began to fall in earnest and Nicholas thought he heard Guinevere nicker a second time. Yet there was nothing more than Sophia in his arms. "Am I dreaming?"

"Kiss me."

He lowered his head to hers and kissed her left cheek and then the right, the tangle of words, "Don't wake me," ricocheting against reason in his mind as he turned to her mouth and captured her with a deep, soulful kiss.

# 16

Mrs. Kirk had taken one look at Sophia when she stepped over the threshold of Petworth Manor and taken charge, her efforts more fierce and accomplished than those of a seasoned general.

Sophia barely had time to greet the servants before Lettie bustled her up the grand staircase and down the hall of the south wing, stopping in front of the last door on the left. "We thought it best for you to sleep here," the older woman explained, failing to add the reason.

Sophia knew exactly why they'd chosen the room. It was the farthest from her parents' adjoined suites. Lettie opened the door and ushered Sophia inside, closing it behind them.

"Let's get you out of that dress," she urged, crossing the room to where Sophia's travel trunks sat. "And into a gown more . . ."

Sophia looked around her, trying to remember the rose-accented suite. "Dry? Less bedraggled?" she suggested absently as she frowned at the lovely tea-rose wall covering and attempted to harness her emotions.

"I did not want to comment, my lady," her companion began, unlocking the first trunk and lifting the lid back to rest on its hinges. "But you look as if you swam to Petworth."

Sophia would have laughed at the comment if not for

the very thing that had contributed to her current disar-
ray.

Nicholas.

She wasn't even sure where he was, having lost track
of him during the dizzying few minutes she'd spent in
the foyer.

Still, she felt him. His hands about her waist. His lips
upon her skin. The sensation had not lessened. In fact,
it had grown.

"I'm afraid the rain came on rather quickly. I'd forgotten the distance from the lake to the house. Silly of me,
really."

Lettie shook out a blue morning gown and folded it
over one arm. "Not at all, my lady. It's a wonder you
were able to remember anything, considering all that
you've before you."

"Quite right," Sophia agreed, thankful that Lettie believed her—and glad for the sympathetic ear.

"I did not know Mr. Bourne would be joining us,"
Lettie continued casually. "If I had, there would have
been a room prepared for his arrival."

"Nor did I," Sophia answered, wise to her friend's ulterior motive. "I swear, Lettie. You know I speak the
truth. Though I cannot help but think, if Nicholas had
not followed after us, there is every likelihood I would
still be standing by the lake, soaked to the bone and unable to muster the courage to move."

*And he would not know that I love him.*

If Nicholas had remained in London, would she, as
she'd planned, have taken her time at Petworth to exam-
ine her feelings for him? Weighed the outcome of hurting Langdon against her own need for Nicholas?

More than likely, no, though Sophia could not be
sure. His arrival had saved her from the elements and
her own overly practical mind.

"Besides," Sophia continued, sitting on an overstuffed

chair near the fireplace, "his mare was certainly useful in the end."

Lettie huffed with irritation as Sophia reached down to unlace her kidskin boots and hurried to her. "Well, that might be true, though the sight of you two galloping toward the house—astride, no less—is one I will not soon forget."

Sophia finished with the first boot and waved off the woman before setting to work on the other. "No more riding astride. Duly noted, Lettie."

The dear woman nodded in approval. "As long as you are open to suggestions, one more piece of advice, my lady; be careful around Mr. Bourne."

Sophia dropped the laces and sat upright. "Of course, Lettie. I wonder, though, do you have reason for your concern?"

Lettie laid the muslin dress carefully over the back of the chair opposite Sophia, then knelt down and finished unlacing the boot. "I've suspected for some time that the man harbors certain feelings for you—beyond those of friendship, that is. I worry the time you've spent in each other's company this past week might have encouraged him, you see."

Sophia slipped her foot from the boot and struggled to suppress a surge of fear. "Surely you're mistaken, Lettie."

The older woman collected the wet boots and rose from the floor. "My lady, you are a kind, thoughtful person. You've always been considerate and understanding of Nicholas Bourne, even when others were not," she said, turning to deposit the boots on the hearth and retrieve the dress. "And I can see it in his eyes when he looks at you—the man is in love."

*In love. The man is in love.*

And so was Sophia. Her heart soared, if guardedly. She was not ready to share Nicholas with the world.

Not just yet. She needed him to herself—craved the opportunity to learn everything there was to know before they faced the future.

She began to shake all over at the mere thought.

"My lady, you're shaking," Lettie said with worry, dropping the dress over the chair back once again. "I apologize. I've kept you talking when you should be resting. Let me help you out of that gown and into bed before I go and see about having your dress pressed."

"Yes, I believe a bit of a lie-down would be wise," Sophia agreed. She stood, legs trembling, to give her companion access to the buttons on the back of her dress. She steadied herself against the chair, gripping the rose-hued velvet until she scored the fabric with her nails.

Lettie finished freeing the buttons and tugged at the fabric with efficiency until it pooled at Sophia's feet. "If you'd like, I'll have cook send up a tray."

"Yes, thank you, Lettie. I believe a quiet night is just what I need."

※ ※

"What are you doing?"

Nicholas startled at the sound of Sophia's voice and slipped one stair tread down from where he'd been sitting. "I'm not precisely sure," he replied, watching as she came 'round to join him on the carpeted main stairwell of Petworth Manor.

The clock in the foyer below chimed midnight. "What are you doing skulking about at such a late hour?" he countered playfully, offering Sophia his arm as she settled against him.

"I was waiting for you—or waiting to go to you," she thought aloud, clearly not having decided. "And then I grew hungry. Waiting can do that to a person, you see."

Nicholas smiled and leaned in, intent on kissing her. "May I?"

"We're fools, aren't we?" Sophia asked, meeting him halfway and placing a sweet, hesitant kiss on his mouth. "Here we sit, waiting for the other. Thinking on our kiss by the lake, yet wondering if we've need to ask permission for another. Wanting to know everything about each other yet too shy to ask."

He moved his mouth to the shell of her ear and nibbled at the tender lobe. "I've waited nearly my entire life to touch you, Sophia. That many years of restraint does something to a person."

"For my part, I cannot claim years of yearning," Sophia answered with complete honesty. "But I want you—the whole of you. Your thoughts and feelings. Your heart. Your body. Everything. And I cannot let hesitation or embarrassment keep me from you."

Nicholas's mouth went dry. "I . . . You . . . Exactly."

Sophia sighed with amusement, an air of ease settling between them. "Well then, what do we do to regain some composure—some balance, if you will?"

Nicholas trailed a series of small, wet kisses down her neck, circling about the neckline of her blue dress and ending his travels with one last kiss on her mouth.

"Do you really want to know everything about me?" Nicholas asked boldly, though he felt stupid for doing so.

Sophia cupped his face in her hands. "I do. And more."

He felt ridiculously pleased. As a child might upon receiving the most wanted of gifts on their birthday.

"This is where you confirm your own desire to know everything about me, Nicholas," Sophia prompted, gently pinching his cheek before releasing him.

Nicholas eased back against the stairs, placing his elbows on the tread just above. "But I already do know everything. You always assumed I wasn't paying attention to you—when, in fact, I was."

"Is that so?" Sophia asked, arching one brow in disbelief. "My favorite color?"

"Green. Emerald, to be exact."

Sophia emitted a low "mmm." "What makes me the happiest?"

"Your work with the Halcyon Society," Nicholas answered succinctly.

"What makes me sad?"

Nicholas hesitated for a moment, not wanting to upset her. "The sight of a mother and daughter together."

Sophia turned to look down the long stairwell, a frown appearing on her lips. "Does that make me selfish? That I envy such girls?"

"It does not make you selfish," Nicholas assured her in a low, steady tone. "It makes you human."

He reached out and took her hand in his, rubbing the pad of his thumb methodically over her knuckles.

"Thank you," she whispered, turning her face toward him once more. "Now, I believe it is my turn."

"Ah yes," Nicholas confirmed, thinking back on her questions. "Rose, you, Langdon."

Sophia's eyes grew round with dismay. "You really are the most impatient man in all of England, aren't you?"

"Efficient, Sophia," he corrected her teasingly. "I am the most efficient man in all of England."

Sophia chuckled at his reply. "Well, that may be. Still, I'll require an explanation—especially the rose part."

"It's simple. The color rose reminds me of you—of your lips, to be precise."

"Oh, that is quite sweet, Nicholas," Sophia said, then leaned in and gently kissed his cheek.

"It is, isn't it?" Nicholas asked in all seriousness. "You appear to have a gift for bringing out the most detestable traits in me—sweetness, thoughtfulness, kindness. Really, everything admirable that ends in 'ness.'"

"Well, that is improvement. At least you didn't deny their existence."

"You're quite comical, you know," Nicholas teased, pulling Sophia onto his lap. "I nearly forgot where I was . . . Ah yes, what makes me happy. You. I believe my gut-wrenching speech delivered in front of the milliner's should suffice for explanation."

Sophia wrapped her arms about his neck and laid her head on his shoulder. "I suppose it will do. Now, for the sad bit."

"Must I?" Nicholas asked, only wanting to close his eyes and breathe in the scent of her. "I am not accustomed to laying my soul bare. In fact, I rather avoid it, if you must know."

Sophia tilted her chin until her mouth rested against his ear. "The sad bit, Nicholas."

He swore under his breath. "Langdon is my brother, Sophia. And despite all of the upheaval, the unnecessary drama and pain I've caused, he never so much as let me think he regretted it. He never once lost faith in me, unlike my parents—though, to be fair, I've absolutely no confidence that they ever possessed any to begin with. Langdon is my brother . . ."

Nicholas swore a second time, not bothering to hide it beneath a whisper. He swallowed hard and rested his cheek against Sophia's. "I want him to be happy. To be rewarded for the admirable life he's lived."

"As do I," Sophia murmured, tightening her hold on him. "And he wants the same for you, Nicholas."

Nicholas brought her as close to him as he could, memorizing the feel of her in his arms. "But at such a high cost? That is the question."

## *June 4*

"You hurt my feelings, young man, taking your dinner in your room. On a tray, no less."

Nicholas smiled warmly at Mrs. Welch, Petworth's cook. "Well, that is typically how one does it, though I would be most happy to entertain other ideas. Perhaps a horse's backside? Wide enough to accommodate all of the necessary dishes and such. Still, how would one ensure the nag did not wander off with one's meal?"

Mrs. Welch let out a cackle that could surely be heard on the Continent. "You well know what I'm unhappy about, you sly fox. But it is nice to know you haven't changed, Nicholas—oh blast! Mr. Bourne, that is. All these years and I can't think of you as anything else. Your own fault for not visiting us a time or two when you were grown."

Nicholas sat back, the heat from the kitchen fireplace pleasantly warm. "Then we have something in common, Mrs. Welch. For I cannot think of you as anything other than the young, beautiful cook who so cruelly denied my advances."

"You were a boy, Nich—Mr. Bourne," Mrs. Welch said, catching herself. "And the second son of an earl. Besides, it was only my tarts you were interested in," she finished, shooing away a kitchen girl with a wave.

Nicholas simply looked at the woman with a slight smile, arching his eyebrow as he took another drink of coffee. "Your *tarts*?"

"Ah! Go on with you, then," Mrs. Welch howled, her peal of laughter making the spurned kitchen girl titter with amusement.

"Dear me, I seem to have missed the joke."

Nicholas swung about in his chair. Sophia stood in the doorway that divided the kitchens from the servants' dining area. He'd woken that morning thankful that they'd decided against anything more than rest last night. Their conversation had taken a toll on both of them.

He stood and sketched a neat bow. "There will be another one shortly, never fear."

Mrs. Welch rose to her feet as well and curtsied, her excitement over Sophia's presence palpable. "Lady Sophia, I don't suppose you'll remember me. We are all so glad to have you here once again. Welcome home."

"Thank you, Mrs. Welch," Sophia answered, walking to the scarred kitchen table and taking a seat. "And of course I remember you—quite fondly, actually. You were my most stalwart supporter against Reynolds."

Mrs. Welch grimaced at the sound of the butler's name. "Well, I don't know if the news reached London. Mr. Reynolds had his comeuppance served to him on the horn of an angry bull. He was gored to death while chasing after a village boy who he believed had stolen from the manor's gardens."

"Good Lord," Sophia uttered, her eyes widening with horror.

"I beg your pardon, my lady," Mrs. Welch blurted out, looking pleadingly at Sophia. "I must learn to mind my tongue. It's just that we're not used to anyone else but the small staff, you see." She eyed Sophia carefully.

Sophia cocked her head, confusion flitting across her face, only to be quickly followed by a mischievous smile. "Oh, please do not misunderstand me, Mrs. Welch. I was merely thinking of the poor bull. That must have been quite frightening for him to find a man such as Mr. Reynolds affixed to his horn."

Mrs. Welch slapped the table with her large, worn hands and cackled. "Oh, Lady Sophia, you are still the sprite I remember from long ago. I'm mighty glad for that. We all worried, you see, when Lady Afton . . ."

Mrs. Welch peered down at the scarred table and

brought her fist to her lips, rubbing her knuckles gently back and forth. "I'll just shut my mouth, Lady Sophia, and have Daisy fetch your morning tea." She laid her hand on the tabletop and pushed herself to her feet, then snapped her fingers once in the kitchen girl's direction.

"Mr. Bourne," Mrs. Welch said with solemn formality. "If you would be so kind as to accompany my lady to the jade drawing room? Daisy will be there directly with a tray."

"Please, Mrs. Welch." Sophia reached across the table as if to grasp the cook's hand to keep her from leaving. "You've not upset me with talk of my mother. In fact, I was rather hoping you would be willing to share what you remember about her—and me. It was all so long ago, and I'm afraid most of my efforts have been aimed at forgetting Petworth."

"And why wouldn't that be the case?" Mrs. Welch asked, her sober countenance softening a touch. "Such a tragedy, it was. But let us speak of the happy times, yes?"

Nicholas watched Sophia smile appreciatively and return her hand to her lap. What a show the woman was putting on, he thought with admiration. She meant to question the cook right there, over tea and shortbread. All the while pretending to want nothing more than fond memories and touching stories.

"Wouldn't you be more comfortable upstairs?" Mrs. Welch asked hesitantly as she smoothed out her white apron.

Nicholas looked at Sophia, unsure of whether a change in venue would affect her plan.

"No, that won't be necessary," Sophia replied. "It's rather warm and inviting in the kitchen. And there's a pleasant hum of activity. So very different from the main floors."

Mrs. Welch snapped her fingers again and Daisy jumped, nearly spilling the hot water.

"Your mother made the very same observation, my lady," Mrs. Welch commented as she oversaw Daisy's efforts with the tray. "Oh, she loved life above stairs, do not misunderstand me. Still, there were many times she could be found down here, lingering after this or that errand."

The kitchen girl carried the laden tray to the table under the watchful eye of Mrs. Welch and set it down carefully. "Shall I pour, then, ma'am?"

"No, you shan't, you daft girl. Go on now and see if Jonah has returned with the supplies from town."

Mrs. Welch watched as Daisy turned a tidy curtsy then practically ran for the door that led to the outer yard.

"She's sweet on Jonah, so we should not be disturbed," she explained, a twinkle in her eye as she settled into her chair once again. "How do you take your tea, Lady Sophia?"

"A splash of milk is all," Sophia replied easily, and smiled graciously when the cook handed her the tea.

"And you, Mr. Bourne? How do you take your tea?"

Nicholas glowered dramatically at the woman. "I take my tea and pour it out in the nearest field, Mrs. Welch."

The cook tsked at his humorous reply and returned the pot to the tray. "As clever as ever. Do you remember, Lady Afton called you her crow? 'Smart as the day is long, crafty and cunning, and far more entertaining than any play could ever hope to be.'"

Nicholas noticed a brief shimmer of distress in Sophia's eyes, though it passed just as quickly as it came. "Is that right?" he asked Mrs. Welch.

"I remember," Sophia offered, looking kindly at the cook. "She had pet names for us all."

Was this really going to happen, then? Nicholas asked himself. A cup of tea, a biscuit or two, and a tragedy resurrected as though they were discussing the price of hay?

"That's right, Lady Sophia," Mrs. Welch chimed in, a fond expression lighting her features. "Young master Langdon was a buck, master Dashiell her red fox, and you, my lady—"

"Were her swan," Nicholas interrupted, the image of Lady Afton looking down at Sophia as she named her flashing in his mind's eye. "Beautiful and loyal, with a nasty bite when provoked."

Sophia smiled wistfully, as though picturing the exact image. "Yes, I do remember now," she said, lifting the dainty china teacup to her mouth and sipping. "Mrs. Welch, you mentioned that my mother spent a fair bit of time below stairs?"

"Yes indeed," the cook answered, looking about the kitchen. "She was very involved in the day-to-day workings of the manor, of course. And careful to keep up on the servants. She knew everyone's birthdays, all about our families—and more than once, all about our sufferings. A finer mistress I'll never find—nor a finer woman, I'd wager. And you can bet every last person in service to the Aftons would say the same."

Nicholas watched as Sophia tipped her head in thanks for the cook's appreciation. It was nothing they had not heard before—nor did not know to be true from their own time spent in Lady Afton's presence. But hearing it from Mrs. Welch, more than fifteen years after Lady Afton's death, was profoundly touching.

Nicholas rose abruptly, desperate to be away from the memories, if only for a few minutes. "I need to speak with the butler. Please, continue," he urged the two. "I'll only be a moment."

He walked to the door and stepped across the threshold, momentarily disoriented. He ground his teeth against the flood of melancholy emotions, his hands curling into fists.

He wrestled the grief with iron control and started down the hall, peering into what was clearly the house-keeper's office before continuing on. At last, he found the butler at the end of the hall, sitting behind a neat desk and consulting a series of sums in a ledger. "Good day," Nicholas said cheerily, walking into the man's office.

The butler snapped to attention and quickly rose from his chair, quill still in hand. "Mr. Bourne, I did not see you there. My name is Mr. Watson. What might I do for you?"

Nicholas had hoped Watson would be unavailable, preferably upstairs, so that he might have a moment's peace. Clearly, that was not meant to be. He glanced about the neat room, noting the nearly empty bottle of brandy sitting on a side table. "I was wondering if you might have some brandy sent up to my quarters," he asked.

"Of course, Mr. Bourne," the butler replied, walking around his desk and over to the side table. "In fact, I was just going to return this to the storeroom. I'll fetch you a new bottle and I'll send it up at once."

Mr. Watson picked up the brandy and turned to Nicholas, waiting for him to leave.

"I will take care of this one, Mr. Watson, if you don't mind." Nicholas held his hand out.

Mr. Watson did not even bat an eye. He simply handed over the bottle and bowed, then left the room.

So why did Nicholas feel . . . what? Embarrassed? He pulled the cork from the amber-colored bottle and lifted it to his lips.

Guilt, perhaps? He tipped the bottle up and drank, savoring the almost instant numbing quality of the smooth brandy as it slid down his throat.

God, this business was grueling. All he wanted was to lay hands on Lady Afton's murderer, not sort through everything he'd spent years trying to forget.

When the bottle was empty, he returned it to the side table.

That would be enough. At least for now.

# 17

Sophia had forgotten how much she liked Mrs. Welch. As she watched the animated woman share stories of Lady Afton with her, she could almost allow herself to enjoy being back in the house she'd once lovingly called home.

But the pain Petworth clearly caused Nicholas made Sophia heartsick.

She promised herself that it would not be in vain.

After Nicholas had abruptly left to find Mr. Watson, Sophia encouraged the cook to talk about Lady Afton's affinity for event planning. Their reminiscing had led naturally to a discussion of the house party during which her mother had been killed.

Of course, there had been nothing natural about the seemingly meandering conversation. Sophia worked hard to guide and manipulate Mrs. Welch's emotions and fondness for chatter for her own gain, even though it had felt dishonest.

She sipped her second cup of tea and listened intently to the woman's words. Witnesses so often left out important details when first interviewed; their nerves and the shock of seeing a crime affecting their ability to be thorough in remembering precisely what they saw.

In some ways, the time span between her mother's death and the present could work to her advantage. Mrs. Welch was not agitated nor upset over the death of her employer. She'd been given more than enough distance from the horrific event to recover from the shock—very unlike the witnesses Sophia had interviewed in past cases.

But with the benefits of time came drawbacks. Nothing about the day was fresh in Mrs. Welch's mind. And at what Sophia guessed to be fifty-plus years of age, the cook could not be relied upon to have the sharpest of memories.

Still, there did not seem to be any more reason to be pessimistic than there was to have hope.

"Do you recall what play the acting troupe was planning to put on for the house party?" Sophia asked, accepting a biscuit from Mrs. Welch.

The cook returned the plate of shortbread to the silver tray. "I'm afraid I don't, my lady. I can tell you that they recruited players from your parents' guests—which would have been quite fun to see, I suspect."

"Oh my, yes. That would have been terribly entertaining," Sophia replied, matching Mrs. Welch's smile. "And who were the unlucky souls?"

The cook squinted her eyes as she considered the question. "Oh dear, it's been such a long time, my lady," she replied, drumming her fingers upon the wood table.

"Of course, Mrs. Wel—"

"Wait! I remember—at least one gentleman." She slapped her hand on the table and cackled with satisfaction. "He was an unlikable sort—made me feel as though someone was walking across my grave every time I saw him."

"And his name?" Sophia pressed, careful to remain calm.

Mrs. Welch's eyes squinted again. "Oh, now that I can't tell you. I've never been good with names, I'm afraid. But his being picked for the play was talked about by the staff. Seemed an odd choice, considering how little anyone appeared to like him. Oh, if Mr. Reynolds were alive, he'd surely know."

Mr. Reynolds was *not* alive. And Sophia felt as if she were right back where she'd started in London, with hardly enough to go on. She folded her hands in her lap and swallowed the disappointment, intent on finishing the interview so that she might seek out another member of the staff.

"Yes, well, I wouldn't wish the man's resurrection on anyone," Sophia offered, earning a chortle from the cook.

"Nor would I," Mrs. Welch answered honestly. "You might remember the man. If you saw him, that is."

It seemed a rather obvious statement to Sophia, but she nodded her head to be polite.

"Have you forgotten about your sketches?"

Sophia pushed her empty cup and saucer away. "My sketches?"

"You have, haven't you?" the cook asked disbelievingly. "My lady, you couldn't be parted from your art supplies—not even for bath time, if I recall. Why, you even drew my likeness. I had it framed, it was that good. Would you care to see it?"

Sophia stared blankly into her empty cup and tried hard to remember, fragments of lines and shading, color and brushstrokes appearing, then regressing back into the darkness. "No, thank you, Mrs. Welch, it won't be necessary."

"Just as well, I suppose. Your favorite subject was your mother. Seeing those old sketches would only upset you more."

Sophia was confused by the cook's words. "I'm afraid I don't understand."

"I'm sorry, my lady," Mrs. Welch offered, smiling apologetically. "It's hard for me to keep my finger on

what you know and what I think you know simply because I remember it. If you understand my meaning?"

"Of course," Sophia agreed. "And I do not mean to
be impolite, but I'm quite curious about these other
sketches that you mentioned just now."

"There I go again, not explaining myself well at all,"
Mrs. Welch said with frustration, placing both hands
palms-down on the table. "All right, now. There are
sketches of yours here, in the manor house. Of master Nicholas and the other boys. Several of your father
and the servants. The majority are of your mother. Still,
there are a few you drew of parties and such. You'd
sneak out of bed at night and find a hidey-hole where
you could watch and not be seen. I knew what you were
up to—as did the rest of the servants, save Mr. Reynolds. We worked hard to keep the wool drawn over that
one's eyes so you might enjoy yourself."

Sophia belatedly realized that she'd brought her hand
to her mouth in astonishment.

"We did, and I don't regret going against house rules,"
the cook continued firmly, "no matter how out of line
we were. Besides, I'm almost certain you sketched at
least one night of that last house party. And if you did,
it'll be with the others."

"And where is that, Mrs. Welch?" Sophia asked, almost hovering above her seat.

"In the nursery, my lady," she answered, folding her
hands together and resting her chin on them. "I'll ask
Watson to have one of the footmen fetch them for you."

Sophia suddenly felt inexplicably cold. "No, Mrs.
Welch. I intended on visiting the room during my stay."

She *had* planned on going to the nursery. There was
no better place than the scene of a crime to understand
a criminal. Anyone who had ever read the research concerning such things would wholeheartedly agree. Though
Sophia would be willing to bet her great-grandmother's

pearls that none of the experts on the topic had intended for an individual to inspect their own mother's death scene.

Nor had they ever pondered the idea of a *woman* doing so, in all likelihood.

Which was their mistake, not Sophia's.

"I'll be fine," she assured Mrs. Welch again—and herself as well.

She hoped it was true.

※

Nicholas left Watson's office and stopped in the kitchen only long enough to learn Sophia had gone up to the nursery. He took the stairs two at a time. The irony of the situation was not lost on him. His last trip up to the Petworth nursery had been made with similar speed, though he had not been alone. Langdon, Dash, and himself had been trying hard not to lose a race— and to Sophia, no less. Failing to win would have been a brutal blow for the boys, especially Nicholas.

He reached the landing of the second floor and continued up the next staircase, lost in memories as his palm ghosted over the polished banister. On that fateful day, the boy he'd been had not yet known why losing to Sophia would not have been the end of the world. His love for her had been camouflaged by his boyish dislike for anything that flounced about in delicate shoes and hair ribbons. And he'd hated the idea of losing.

Langdon had persuaded the boys to stop running once they reached the final staircase, his common sense winning out in the heat of the day. They'd lost valuable time when Dash had managed to get himself stuck in the library window and it was impossible to think that the skillful Sophia had not sneaked past the ogre of a butler and run upstairs to the nursery.

Nicholas shook away the memories and quickened his pace now, not content to accept defeat this time, either. He reached the fourth floor, his breath coming hard and fast.

"Sophia," he called, striding to join her outside the nursery door.

She turned her head when he called her name and held up her hand in protest. "Nicholas, please. I know it was difficult for you to listen to Mrs. Welch's recollections. I cannot ask you to revisit the nursery."

"Then don't ask," he answered, blocking her from the door. "I've come of my own accord."

God, she'd nearly gone in there alone. The thought made him break out in a cold sweat.

"Why didn't you wait for me in the kitchens?" he demanded.

Sophia reached out and took his hand in hers. "I wanted to spare you the pain, Nicholas. I've seen what returning to Petworth has cost you."

"Far less than what you've paid," he answered softly. "You asked for my help and I'll be damned if I won't give it to you now."

Sophia squeezed his hand as she stared at the closed door in front of her.

"Ready?" Nicholas asked, reaching with his free hand for the brass knob, then turning it until the door cracked open.

"Yes," she whispered, her voice shaking.

Sophia placed the palm of her hand on the smooth oaken door and slowly pushed it open.

The door creaked as it swung wide, and she stepped across the threshold first—then, hand-in-hand, they walked to the edge of the rose-print rug.

"Why did they not throw this out?" Nicholas released Sophia's hand and paced to the bloodstain marring the otherwise cheery carpet. God, he'd never expected the household would have left something so upsetting as the very rug Lady Afton had bled to death on.

"It was packed away," Sophia answered distractedly, looking about the room. "I asked Watson to have it brought down and placed exactly where it had been when my mother died."

Nicholas stared at her in shock. "Why would you do such a thing?"

"Because I need everything as it was that day," she explained, moving closer to him. "Otherwise I risk missing something important."

It was difficult to focus on Sophia's words while standing in the same room where Lady Afton had been killed. "I won't pretend to understand you," he said, "but I will help. Tell me, what can I do?"

"Lie down on the floor approximately where my mother's body was found," she instructed.

Her neutral tone, clipped words, and brusque gestures mirrored that of a Bow Street Runner.

Nicholas was taken aback by the shift in her personality. Still, he pressed on. "Here?" he asked, stretching out on his back, his head just above the stain.

"Yes, that's it," Sophia answered, turning back toward the door. "Now I am going to step out, shut the door, and come back in."

Nicholas watched her leave the room, closing the door behind her, then appear again, having absolutely no idea how such behavior would lead to anything of use. "Why would this—"

"Please," Sophia interrupted him, stopping at the edge of the carpet as she'd done only moments before. "I need you to be absolutely quiet and still. Will you promise to do so?"

Nicholas nodded his head, and then turned on his side so that he could see her more easily as he remained still. Sophia closed her eyes and began to rock back and forth on her heels. "I am ten. It is the summer of 1798, and we are in the midst of our annual house party. I've just managed to elude Mr. Reynolds and reach the nursery in record time. I am tired and hot—and would very much like a glass of lemonade, which I will retrieve from the kitchen once I've entered the nursery and the boys catch up. Despite my discomfort, I am extremely pleased with myself. And I am very much looking forward to the play that will be put on for the guests' entertainment that evening. I open the door to the nursery and walk inside, closing it behind me."

Sophia opened her eyes and reached to shut the door. "Then I see my mother lying on the carpet. I pause, trying to make sense of her presence. She is not moving. Perhaps she's asleep."

She walked slowly toward Nicholas, her eyes looking at him, yet clearly not seeing him. "Why would she be in the nursery? Perhaps it does not need to make sense, I tell myself, and call out softly to her, walking forward. She still does not move, and I begin to feel afraid. I pull my crystal swan figurine from the pocket of my dress . . ."

Sophia stopped suddenly and closed her eyes again. "My crystal swan. The one my mother bought especially for me in London. She told me that it had been on display in a shop and she'd simply had to buy it as it so reminded her of me. From the very day she'd given it to me, I'd not let it out of my sight. I'd even begged Mrs. Kirk to sew a hidden pocket into each one of my dresses so I could keep it with me always."

Her eyes opened and she pretended to reach inside a pocket and pull something small from it. "I held the swan in my hand, clenching it tightly as I knelt down beside her. That is when I see her neck. It is ringed in blood and her head is turned at an awkward angle."

Sophia knelt down now next to Nicholas and moved his head to mimic the position of her mother. "It is not right. And I know it." She continued to stare at him, her finger tentatively touching his neck just underneath his chin.

She looked spellbound, her eyes glassy and her face devoid of any emotion. Nicholas wanted to reach out and wake her, stop his own growing fear and unrest from expanding, and return to London that very day. But he had promised Sophia his cooperation. And he would honor it.

"I startle at the feel of her warm, sticky blood on my finger and pull away, setting my crystal swan down in order to wipe my hand on the rug."

Sophia raised her right hand, her palm folded as if she held the swan in her fist, and placed it next to her feet. "I set the crystal swan down . . ."

She suddenly sat up, then stood, turning back toward the door. "Dash was the first one of you through the door, correct?" she asked Nicholas, her voice normal once more.

"May I move now?" he countered, doing so once she'd nodded in answer. "Yes, Carrington was the first, with Langdon second and me bringing up the rear. Why?"

Sophia tapped her finger on her chin as she stood approximately where the boys did that day. "And Lords Carrington and Carmichael, where were they?"

"Here," Nicholas answered, moving forward and to his right, "and here," he finished, pointing just ahead of himself.

"Then it is conceivable that the swan was not destroyed, but perhaps kicked out of the way?"

Nicholas thought for a moment, trying to picture the figurine in his mind. "I suppose. Tell me, why is the glass swan important?"

"I don't know," Sophia admitted, "at least not yet. Please, help me search the room, won't you?"

Insisting that she drop the idea of locating the silly

figurine would only prolong their stay. "Of course," he replied, attempting to hide his frustration. "I'll take the right side of the room, you the left. First, let me roll up the carpet, in case anything was covered, all right?"

"Thank you," she replied, then busily began to inspect a painted bookshelf running along the north side of the room.

Nicholas walked to the edge of the rug and bent down, grasping it with both hands and pulling upward. The physical exertion felt good and he put his back into it, his body and mind in desperate need of distraction. Slowly rolling the aged rug up into itself, he scanned the wooden floor for signs of broken glass.

Of course he didn't find anything—and damned if he didn't experience a small wave of disappointment. He reached the opposite end of the rug and stood, kicking it up against Sophia's side of the room.

"Anything?" he asked, looking at her. Her back was turned to him as she finished searching the bookshelf and started on a large toy box in the corner. "Not yet, no."

He could hear her disappointment and it gnawed at him. It was all well and good for him to lose hope, but not Sophia. For if she did, what then?

"Well, we've only just started," he said bracingly, walking to the window seat that straddled the imaginary line dividing the room in half. "There is plenty of time left—and room, obviously—to find any number of trinkets."

Sophia nodded her head slowly as she pulled a doll from the toy box, her hand smoothing its ratted hair. "I'm sure you're right."

"I am always right," Nicholas teased, hoping his pathetic joke would do something to lift her spirits.

He searched beneath the yellow-hued cushions padding the bench and the back of the window seat, finding only a tin soldier and a small child's top. He slipped the items into his vest pocket, not wanting to raise Sophia's hopes. Continuing on, he pulled back the heavy damask curtain, upsetting a vast amount of dust. "I believe the maids have been remiss in doing their job," he choked out, waving his hand in front of his face.

Sophia turned her head to look at him, her lips curving in a small, weak smile. "You always did know how to make me smile, didn't you?"

"Well, obviously," Nicholas replied, the dust finally settling.

Sophia returned her attention to the toy box, unearthing what looked to be a sheaf of papers. "Mrs. Welch said I would find these here," she explained, taking the yellowed sheets out carefully and setting them in her lap.

"What are they?" Nicholas asked, staring out the window at a vista he'd known by heart as a boy.

"Sketches—my sketches, to be precise," she answered, the crackle of stiff, aged paper being thumbed through accompanying her words.

"Oh yes, of course. You were always busying yourself with your portraits. I'd forgotten." Nicholas stared down at the gardens of Petworth House. Designed by Lancelot "Capability" Brown, they were, he'd been told as a boy, the finest in all of England. He hadn't cared one crown about the flowers. No, he'd sat on the window seat and watched Sophia with her mother, the two picking blossoms for summer bouquets and dancing about like faeries.

Or swans.

The sun emerged from behind a cloud and Nicholas held up one hand to protect his eyes from the suddenly bright light. Something off to his left caught a stray beam and reflected it brilliantly. He moved closer and squinted in order to see the source.

Nicholas reached out carefully, almost certain that if

he were to move too fast, it would disappear from the windowsill. "I'll be damned."

He lifted the tiny, delicate crystal swan and stared at it for a moment, the bevels in its wings creating glorious rainbows where the sun refracted off the fine-crafted form. "I believe I've something else for you to smile about."

He walked to Sophia, sitting with her legs tucked beneath her and the sketches spread out all about her on the floor.

"And what is that, Nicholas?" she asked dubiously, tracing the arch of her mother's brow on the sketch she held.

"This," Nicholas said simply, crouching down next to her and holding out the slim, fragile swan. "She was here all along."

# 18

Sophia was afraid to touch the fragile glass. She simply stared at the swan, perched on Nicholas's palm as if it belonged there. It had disappeared from her mind the moment she'd realized her mother was dead. And now it was as if she'd never been without the crystal bird, the sharp yet surprisingly soft contours of its delicate body as familiar to her as her own face.

"One of the servants must have found it on the floor and set it on the windowsill for safekeeping," Nicholas guessed.

"How could I have forgotten her?" she murmured aloud, reaching out to touch the swan's expertly carved beak. "She was a gift from my mother—to remind me how very special I was to her."

Nicholas looked at the figurine in his hand as if seeing it for the first time. "How have I never seen the swan? We four were together every minute of every day. Surely we boys would have attempted to steal her from you."

"And she would have met a horrible fate in your hands."

Understanding dawned on his face. "Ah, I see. Then you hid the swan from us in order to keep her safe?"

"Yes," Sophia confirmed, finally feeling brave enough to take the swan in her own hand. "And no."

She stroked the swan's head lightly with her forefinger, the sensation of cool, sleek glass beneath her fingertip achingly familiar. "I wanted something of Mother that was just for me. I suppose it was selfish, but when she gave me the swan it seemed the perfect secret between the two of us. Does that make any sense?"

Nicholas picked up the sketch of her mother that Sophia had been studying. "It makes perfect sense. And I must say I admire your ability to keep it hidden."

Sophia looked at the portrait in Nicholas's hands, then at the other drawings she'd examined and set aside.

"What is it?" Nicholas asked.

"I'm not sure," Sophia replied honestly, worrying the crystal figure between her fingers. "There is something missing—a piece that I've forgotten. I was certain everything would come together here at Petworth."

She looked about the room and frantically searched for something she must have missed—a clue her mother wanted her to find.

"Come," Nicholas said to her, his hands taking hold of her wrist and pulling her to stand.

Sophia attempted to turn away, intent on remaining in the room.

"Listen to reason, Sophia. Come away from here," Nicholas urged. "Continue questioning the staff downstairs—hell, dig up that bastard butler, for all I care. But please, leave this room now. For me?"

Sophia's mind stopped spinning for a moment as she considered his words. "You're right. I have lost my perspective."

Nicholas took up her hand and lightly skimmed his lips against her soft skin. "Then let me help you find it."

*   *

He was counting down the minutes. Nicholas looked at the clock on the fireplace mantel, then to the bottle of brandy sitting next to the candelabra on the small table near his bed.

"You're pathetic," he told himself with derision, returning his gaze to the window. It was a dark, moonless night. Petworth Manor and the grounds were cloaked in blackness.

He pressed his forehead to the cold glass, the sensation almost painful. Earlier in the day, Mrs. Welch and a senior footman who'd begun his service at Petworth as an errand boy had managed to remember the play that the traveling acting troupe had planned to perform—*Dido Queen of Carthage*. Actors never forgot their parts, and if any one of the troupe was still alive, they'd find them in Drury Lane.

He looked back at the clock. Two minutes until he could open the brandy bottle. Since Sophia's observation about his tremors, Nicholas had made a point of going longer than eight hours between each drink.

Sophia. He stared broodingly out the window once again. With each passing hour he felt more and more intimately linked with her, Petworth affording them the time and space to make up for all the years they'd lost.

Still, he hesitated to go to her now. Was he so weak that he needed her to seek him out instead of the other way around? To know once and for all that she desired him, body and soul, as much as he did her?

Nicholas turned away from the window and stalked toward the fireplace, ready to throw the clock across the room should it not show him the time he desired.

"You will live to see another day," he told the timepiece as it chimed the hour.

"Who are you speaking to?"

The soft, feminine tones startled him. Nicholas spun on his heel, relief and a profound thankfulness flooding his senses at the sight of Sophia in his chamber. She wore a blue silk wrapper, her bare toes peeping from beneath the hem, and her hair was loose. The dark wooden panels of the closed door outlined her slim curves.

"Sophia?"

"I waited for as long as I could, Nicholas."

She rushed toward him. The wrapper was unbuttoned below mid-thigh, and the white night rail she wore beneath was nearly transparent. Nicholas's mouth went dry at the clearly visible shape of thighs, knees, calves, and ankles as her swift movements pressed her legs against the thin linen. It wasn't until she reached him that he realized she held a large book clasped to her chest.

"What is that?" His voice was gravelly, even to his own ears.

"I was stalking about in the dark—as I am wont to do—and wandered into the library." Her eyes glowed with excitement, her face flushed. "I found this book of maps on the desk. When I was a little girl, my father let me press flowers and leaves in it. And, apparently, other things." She caught his hand and drew him to the small table near the bed.

She lay the book down and opened it. Tucked between the pages was a sheet of drawing paper.

Carefully, she lifted the sketch and showed it to Nicholas.

The picture, clear and concise, showed the Afton drawing room. A boy lay on a settee near the window; and outside, two children played in the snow. A girl stood next to the reclining boy, watching the others tossing snowballs just beyond the glass.

"I remember this day," Nicholas said, smiling at the fond memory. "Your mother wouldn't let me go outside. You volunteered to stay in and keep me company." The skirt of her wrapper brushed against his bare feet. He glanced at her. Her lashes were lowered as she studied the sketch in his hand.

She looked up and several dark strands of her loose mane of hair caught on the linen of his shirt. Her smile faded, awareness turning her eyes darker as she stared at him.

"If there is one sketch hidden away in Petworth, there may be more," she whispered. Her gaze flicked from his eyes to his mouth and her lips parted as she caught her breath. "Perhaps that is what I sensed in the nursery."

Neither of them moved.

"Is that the only reason you are here?" He barely breathed the words.

"No," she admitted, softly. "As I've already told you, I waited as long as I could."

His gaze on hers, Nicholas laid the sketch on the open book. Then he slowly lifted his hands to cup her face.

Her skin was soft and warm, so warm. He closed his eyes.

"We can't do this," he managed to get out. "We can't betray Langdon."

Sophia lifted her hands to cover his.

"Nicholas."

Her voice was a quiet command. He opened his eyes and looked into hers. He saw fierce, raw conviction in the green depths.

"I cannot marry Langdon. My feelings for you forbid it, in every way. Even if you make me leave this room, even if you never speak to me again, I will not marry him."

He believed her. The nearly violent joy that shook him was instantly followed by a wave of guilt.

"If I hadn't come home from India—if we hadn't begun the search for your mother's killer . . ."

"Stop." She laid her fingertips over his lips, effectively silencing him. "I do not love Langdon as a wife should. Whether or not you had returned, that wouldn't have changed. And I've come to realize that affection isn't enough for me. I want to spend my life with someone who feels much more for me. I want passion in my life." She smoothed her fingertips over the curve of his lips before her palm cradled his cheek. "I want what I feel with you, Nicholas. I want you—all of you."

"You deserve a far better man than me," he told her. "But I am yours. I've always been yours."

She was his. His heart constricted with the overwhelming knowledge. Every single point in his life, whether glorious or agonizing, had contributed to this moment.

He bent his head, his lips brushing against hers in brief, tasting kisses. Each kiss was longer, the press of his mouth against the soft, lush cushion of hers harder.

Her hands slid around his neck, her fingers threading into the hair above his nape as she held him closer. Beneath his lips, hers heated.

Nicholas cupped the back of her head in one palm, her hair a mass of silk beneath his fingers. He slipped his other arm around her waist to gather her closer. Her lush curves pressed against the harder angles of his and she shivered, her lips parting in a soft, breathy sigh of surprise.

He slipped the buttons free on her wrapper and pushed the edges aside to give him access to the smooth, bare skin of her shoulders. She hummed with pleasure, tilting her head back as he licked the curve of her throat. His lips traced the upper swell of her breasts and her fingers clenched in his hair.

Nicholas pulled her arms from around his neck and with swift efficiency shoved her wrapper off her shoulders, forcing the blue silk lower until it pooled at her feet. Sophia skimmed her hands over his shoulders and tugged at his shirt. Nicholas finished freeing the buttons on her night rail and yanked it up and off over her head, going still.

Her body was all lush curves and valleys, the full swell

of breasts narrowing to a nipped-in waist. The shallow indent of her navel drew his eye lower to silky dark hair, and thighs that gave way to firm calves and delicate ankles and feet.

"My God, look at you," he murmured reverently. He cupped one rose-tipped breast in his hand, smoothing his thumb over skin softer than the finest silk. The pad of his thumb found the ruched bud of her nipple and she swayed, catching at his arms to steady her boneless legs.

"Nicholas," she moaned.

"I've got you," he murmured.

He swung her up in his arms and carried her to the bed. She curled on her side, shifting one thigh over the other in a belated attempt at modesty.

"Don't," his voice rasped. Impatiently, he shrugged out of his shirt, his breeches quickly following. "Don't hide from me," he added, needing to reassure her.

Sophia only smiled, her eyes dark as she watched him undress, holding her arms wide and welcoming him into the sweet cradle of her body.

Nicholas was determined to make Sophia's first time memorable, to gently initiate her into lying with a man. She wrapped her legs around him, answering each stroke and kiss with tender, sensual replies of her own.

"If we finish this, I won't be able to give you up," he told her. "Are you sure it's what you want, Sophia?"

She stilled beneath him, her hands coming to rest on his shoulders. "I'm very certain, Nicholas," she solemnly assured him. "You're all I'll ever want."

He couldn't speak, every last word in his vocabulary simply unable to communicate what he felt at that very moment.

He settled between her parted thighs, nudging against her core before he caught himself. He needed to make her his—truly and in every way. With sheer force of will, he reined in his body and held himself still.

"A woman's first time can be painful," he told her, his voice husky with need. "I couldn't bear to think I'd harmed you in any way."

"I know you won't hurt me, Nicholas," she murmured, shifting beneath him, urging him on until they were fully joined.

"Are you all right?" he breathed in her ear.

"I am—please don't stop now."

Reassured, Nicholas bent his head, trailing kisses down the arch of her throat as he shifted his hips. Her inner muscles clasped him tighter, silently protesting as he nearly withdrew from her wet heat.

"Don't stop," Sophia pleaded, her hands clenching against his biceps to pull him nearer.

"No, my love, I won't," Nicholas managed to reply. His body protested the slow pace. But he wanted to savor Sophia, to tell her with his body all that she was to him.

He cupped the full curve of her breast in one hand and bent to take the rosy tip in his mouth, feasting on the soft, succulent skin. Sophia's breath caught in a gasp of surprise and her fingers threaded into his hair to press him closer. Beneath him, her body lifted, her hips moving to meet the thrust of his.

Sweat slicked their bodies, the scent of their lovemaking filling the air around them as Nicholas torturously tempted Sophia's desire into ruthless need. He withdrew from her and with openmouthed kisses traveled every delicious slope and curve of her body, tasting the soft skin of her throat, breasts, and the sweet indent of her navel. He moved his mouth to the apex of her thighs, his tongue flicking Sophia's swollen core until she moaned.

Her hands clutched his shoulders with desperation. "Nicholas, please. I need you." Her voice was throaty, drugged with seduction as she scored him with her fingernails.

He ceased his carnal assault on her luscious folds and slowly nipped his way up her, each and every last taste punctuated by Sophia's gasps of delight.

He loomed over her, watching as pleasure and raw yearning played across Sophia's face.

"Do not deny me," she begged, wrapping her arms around his neck.

"Sophia." Her name was a prayer on his lips. The answer to everything Nicholas had ever needed to make him whole.

He lowered himself and entered her again, the sensation piercing him to the soul. He was home. Well and truly home.

He stroked his hand down her body, over the sweet inner curve of her waist, to close over her thigh. He nudged her legs higher and she willingly, eagerly wrapped them around his waist, seating him even deeper. He palmed the curve of her bottom and she instinctively pressed her hips more tightly to his. She was made for him, her body meeting his thrusts with dizzying precision.

"I love you, Nicholas," she whispered, her lips seeking out his with a searing kiss.

The very passion she'd told him she craved caught them up and spun them about in a whirlwind of carnal desire.

Sophia threw her head back upon the feather pillow and cried out, her core pulsating with satisfaction as she gripped the bed linens in a vain attempt to gain purchase.

The sound of her ecstasy inspired a guttural growl from deep in Nicholas's throat. He hitched her knee higher on his hip and quickened his pace, his need now undeniable.

Sophia reached up and caressed his chest, her tender touch intensifying the moment. He drove deeper, closing his eyes as every muscle in his body flexed and tightened.

"Come to me."

Nicholas roared at the sound of Sophia's demand, the powerful release of his climax ripping through his entire being, his mind and soul shattering into oblivion.

"And I love you, Sophia. I always have, and I always will."

✥

The pieces floated as if in water, their jagged edges coming close to touching, but never quite forming a full picture.

Sophia swiped at the shards until they disappeared into the recesses of her mind. The fragments of memory frightened her, even while she dreamed of making love with Nicholas.

She'd never known such pleasure. Nor had any idea of the profound connection created between two people when they gave themselves fully to each other.

*He threatened to take my swan.*

He wore a mask, so she could not see his face, the red and black squares of the domino coming to life before her very eyes. He must have been one of the members of the troupe—or one of the houseguests chosen to participate. He discovered her hiding behind a large potted plant, drawing the performers as they practiced. He waited until everyone else had gone, then approached Sophia. He was angry with her for capturing his likeness. When he demanded the sketch she refused.

Sophia was back in the parlor, the man's grip on her arm hurting as he squeezed and bruised the skin. He took the swan and told her he would smash the figurine in front of Sophia if she did not turn over the drawing. The man frightened Sophia and so she did as he demanded. After he'd gone, she drew a second picture of the man and woman.

The feeling of resurfacing from deep water swept Sophia up, carrying her from the world of her dream to a fully awakened state.

She bolted upright in Nicholas's bed, taking the bed linens with her. "Nicholas, wake up. You must wake up. Now."

He rolled to face her, his arms raising above his head to flex and stretch. "Whatever for?"

"I know where the missing piece is."

✤ ✤

"Just up here, William." Sophia beckoned for the young stablehand to hurry.

Nicholas walked beside her, holding her elbow as they trekked over uneven ground, through the bracken and long, overgrown grass. "I haven't thought about the chalk cave for years."

"Nor have I," Sophia admitted, appreciating Nicholas's steady grip. "Obviously."

"Do not blame yourself," Nicholas warned in a lethal tone. "Beyond the fact that there was no real reason for you to remember the man, the incident coincided with the shock of your mother's death."

Sophia knew, on a very practical level, that Nicholas was right. But there was nothing simple about what was happening. Nothing at all.

"I cannot argue with you, Nicholas," she whispered, eager to focus on finding the cave—and with any luck, the sketch.

Sophia tripped over a thick tree root hidden in the grass and Nicholas tightened his hold on her arm. She welcomed his support, leaning into his strength. "Thank you." She moved closer to him.

"Just up there, my lady," William exclaimed, trotting past them. "Watch your step. Wouldn't do to have you falling down into the chalk cave. Mrs. Welch would skin me alive."

He halted where a bare patch stood out in the overgrown terrain. "Here it is, just as you said it would be."

Sophia rushed forward, forcing Nicholas to keep pace. "And so it is," she answered, staring down at the circular metal grate in the ground.

William knelt down, setting his satchel on the soft grass beside him, and examined the hole. "I've heard about these caves. Never seen one for myself."

"Unfortunately, I have—and more than once against my will," Nicholas commented dryly, staring at the grate. "It can get rather dark down there. You'll need your lamp."

The stablehand picked up the small lantern and smiled. "I thought I might."

"I remember a crude ladder of sorts cut into the side of the cave, William," Sophia said, dropping to her knees and pointing to the right side of the grate. "The holds are small, but they'll get you in and out."

She examined the manhole, brushing away bits of branches and other debris, most probably left by yesterday's storm. "Once you are in the cave and have oriented yourself, I'll tell you where to find the treasure. All right?"

"How did you manage to hide so much from the three of us?" Nicholas interjected, squatting down to join them.

Sophia gripped the grate. "You boys never bothered to bring a lamp with you. I'm fairly confident I could have hidden the contents of my father's library within the chalk walls and none of you would have been the wiser."

"It was more exciting that way," Nicholas muttered in response. "At least that's what Langdon always said."

Sophia pulled at the grate with all of her might, not

moving it in the slightest. "It must be stuck from lack of use," she assured the other two, trying again. "I had no difficulty opening it as a child."

"Why would you have come to the cave on your own?" Nicholas asked, gesturing for Sophia to move aside and let him try.

She released the grate and watched Nicholas take the iron bars in hand. "There were times I preferred to be by myself."

He tugged once, twice, and a third time, before the grate scraped from its hold and lifted. He grinned at her. "It simply needed a man's touch."

"Such as now," Sophia grumbled, turning her attention to William. "Are you ready?"

The stablehand smiled, a dimple flashing in his cheek. "I am, my lady, and looking forward to it. It's about time I saw what there is to see."

The lad's excitement over the experience lightened Sophia's heart a touch and she returned his smile with one of her own. "Well, remember that the goal is to bring you back *up,* so do be careful."

He nodded his head and stood, awaiting instructions.

"The footholds begin here," Nicholas explained, pointing into the lip of the cave just to the right. "Come along and step inside, then I'll hand you the lamp."

William walked around the hole until he stood directly in front of the spot Nicholas had indicated, then turned his back and lowered his right leg into the cave.

Sophia watched the young man's progress nervously, letting out a small scream when he faltered and nearly fell back.

"I'm all right, my lady," William assured her just as his head dipped below ground level.

Nicholas squeezed her arm for support. "He will be fine, Sophia. If four foolish children were able to climb in and out without incident, surely William can manage one trip—aided and supervised, no less."

"And what if we four were simply lucky?" Sophia asked, planting her palms near the cave entrance and carefully peering down.

Nicholas joined her, his body brushing against hers as he positioned himself over the hole. "We were never lucky, Sophia. That much I can assure you."

"I'm in!" William yelled enthusiastically, his voice echoing off the walls of the cave.

Sophia lingered against the heat of Nicholas, savoring the contact as it warmed her skin. "If we are to rely on your reasoning, then the sketch will not be found."

"Sophia," he turned to look at her with a mix of empathy and frustration, "we are leaning over a chalk cave, in the middle of Petworth's grounds, with nothing more than the hope of evidence in an old sketch standing between us and abject failure. If I do not have you to rely upon for optimism, who do I have?"

Sophia smiled. "All right, then. Since you've made such a valiant and convincing plea, I suppose I've no choice in the matter."

He grinned at her reply and gestured toward the hole. "I believe William is ready for further instructions."

"Oh yes," Sophia said, feeling foolish for having delayed. "William," she called, "are you near the footholds?"

"Yes, my lady. I'm standing right in front of them."

Sophia shifted her weight until she was looking into the cave once more. "Excellent. Now, bend down until you can see the very last hold."

The lamplight moved lower, indicating William's progress. "All right."

"Now walk your hand to the middle of the hold, then from that point, directly to the bottom of the wall. You should come upon a slightly raised section."

"Aye, there it is!" he yelled up to them. "It's a circle."

Sophia gripped the grass with tense fingers, wanting to join in William's excitement but afraid to do so quite yet. "Grasp the circle as best you can and turn it to the right. Then pull."

She held her breath, waiting for the young man to say something, fearing she'd only dreamed the second sketch out of sheer desperation.

"Breathe," Nicholas commanded, his voice thick with absolute conviction.

"I've got something," William reported, his enthusiasm audibly deflated. "Only a bit of paper, I'm afraid."

Sophia pushed up and launched herself at Nicholas with exuberance, her arms encircling his waist. "I was so afraid it would not be there," she said fervently.

"As was I," he admitted as he peered down at her, his full lips curved into an apologetic grin.

"Here it is," William announced as he emerged from the hole.

Sophia hastily released Nicholas and stepped back.

"No crown jewels, to be sure," William added, handing the roll of parchment to Sophia.

She tugged gingerly at the faded red ribbon around the paper, untying it with careful hands. "Oh, I don't know about that," she replied, unrolling the brittle parchment to reveal a complete, if sketchy, portrait of the masked man as he conversed behind a dressing screen with a woman wearing a ball gown.

## June 5

"I'm very angry with the three of you," Sophia said in a stern voice. "You know that, don't you?"

Nicholas continued to gaze up at the dark sky, amazed

by the seemingly million stars sewn into its swath of silken blackness. "Whatever for?"

The two lay side by side on the Petworth Manor lawn, basking in the hushed silence of the late hour.

"While I slept tucked up tight in the nursery, you boys crept from the house and had all sorts of adventures without me—that's what for," Sophia explained, slapping him on the arm.

Nicholas captured her hand in his and tugged until Sophia was settled against him, her head resting on his chest. "Oh that. Well, it wasn't my decision."

"Langdon's?" Sophia ventured, her arm wrapping about his waist.

Nicholas began to draw lazy circles along her spine with his finger. "Of course. Late night wanderings were far too dangerous for you. Even then you were his princess in a high tower."

Sophia squeezed him possessively.

"Even more so now," he lamented, the stars suddenly subdued.

"Nicholas?"

He'd dreaded this moment since they'd awoken in each other's arms that morning. Interviewing the remaining servants and making a final search of the attic for clues had occupied their day, while dinner and an impromptu dance in the kitchens had kept them busy throughout the night.

Nicholas breathed in Sophia's floral scent. Perhaps they might stay in each other's arms right there, suspended in time.

"Nicholas?" Sophia said again.

He sighed deeply. "We will have to tell Langdon— once we've captured the Bishop. We cannot put him in such a difficult position."

"How will we possibly keep our feelings hidden from

him?" she asked, rubbing her cheek against his linen shirt. "What if he grows suspect . . ."

Nicholas felt Sophia's breath hitch as she began to cry. "Shh," he murmured, tightening his hold. "I know this will sound cruel, but we cannot risk all that we've worked for by drawing attention to ourselves. Do you agree?"

"Yes," Sophia whispered. "You're right—I know it is for the best. I simply cannot bear to think what he will feel when he learns of us."

Nicholas looked up at the sky once more, his bloody emotions threatening to get the best of him. "He will feel betrayed, Sophia. Cuckolded. Taken advantage of."

It was precisely what would consume Nicholas if he were Langdon, the knowledge of his brother's impending pain piercing his chest like an arrow through his heart. "He will suffer whether we tell him now or wait until the Bishop is ours."

A tear ran from the corner of his eye and slipped down his face, reaching his unshaven jaw. "Goddammit."

Sophia released his waist and reached up, settling her hand on his cheek. "I am meant to be with you. Not Langdon. In time he will come to understand. He has to."

"And if he does not?" Nicholas asked, afraid of her answer.

"I will not give you up," Sophia replied with conviction, placing her palm on the ground and pushing up until she came eye to eye with him. "Not now. Not ever."

"Goddammit," Nicholas muttered a second time as more tears fell. "A happy ending. Is that what you're proposing?"

Sophia kissed him, the full intent of her pledge communicated in the soft, sacred gesture. "I would settle for nothing less—which means I have one more request. One that you might not like."

The sweet taste of her disappeared from Nicholas's mouth, replaced with bitter apprehension. "Is this to do with my drinking?"

"Yes. I told you I would not give you up, and I meant it. Not one moment of your life will be wasted in the company of brandy—not when you could be spending it with me."

"I'm afraid, Sophia," Nicholas admitted, the warm night breeze making him feel even more vulnerable than his words did. "I'm afraid I won't be able to stop."

Sophia lowered herself and rested her head once again upon his chest. "It's not a matter of stopping your drinking. It's a matter of starting to live the life you were meant to lead."

# 19

*June 9*
EN ROUTE TO BEECHAM HOUSE
MAYFAIR
LONDON

"How is your great-aunt?"

Sophia stared at Langdon seated across from her in the warm carriage and tried to decipher his words.

She'd returned from Sussex two days before and still could not regain the usual sensible rhythm of her days—to be expected, yes, but no less troubling.

"There has been improvement," Sophia replied vaguely, belatedly remembering she'd gone to Petworth under the pretense of visiting an ill aunt.

She discreetly wiped at perspiration beading above her lip while silently chastising herself. Why had she not prepared in advance for Langdon's polite inquiries? She'd frittered away the hours earlier in the day, occupied with a tray of letters and calling cards until there'd been barely enough time to dress for the Beechams' ball. Lettie had enlisted a housemaid's help in order to finish Sophia's hair and see to the jewelry.

"And yet, you seem disappointed," Langdon added thoughtfully.

"Oh no," Sophia assured him. "It is simply a pity to

see Great-aunt Harriett trapped inside. She lives for her garden, you see."

Langdon nodded in reply. "Well, I do hope I'll have the opportunity to meet her someday. Perhaps at our wedding?"

Sophia wanted to scream. Or cry. Or both.

"Oh, you have met her before, don't you remember?" she replied, fidgeting with her reticule.

"When I was a child, Sophia. And if I'm being completely honest," Langdon said, crossing his legs, "no, I do not remember her. Why has she never come to London for a visit?"

Sophia removed a painted fan from her reticule and attempted to cool herself. "Great-aunt Harriett was never one for travel. Nor for town. As she is so fond of saying, she 'prefers the fine fresh air in the country to the smoggy environs of the capital,' and at her age, I do not blame her. Better to stay comfortably settled in one's familiar surroundings, I say."

She held tight to the fact that she truly was in possession of a great-aunt named Harriett, who did indeed prefer not to travel. The woman was, as she always had been, healthy as the draft horses who worked her land, even at her advanced age of ninety and three. Still, one never knew when a cold or ailment of the stomach might strike.

Sophia closed her eyes and concentrated on the minuscule amount of relief the fan was providing from the evening's heat.

Langdon nodded. "Ah well, as I said, let us hope Great-aunt Harriett considers coming to London for the wedding. Speaking of our wedding, I'm planning a trip to Wales to visit your father."

Sophia's eyes flew open and she quickly turned to look at Mrs. Kirk—as if she might be of some use.

"Forgive me if I've embarrassed you by speaking of

our marriage in front of Mrs. Kirk." Langdon uncrossed his legs and leaned forward. "It's just that I think of her as family. Besides, I am sure she is as tired of waiting for such news as everyone else."

Lettie turned to take in Langdon, a polite smile curving on her lips. "My lord, it is happy news, indeed."

Sophia clasped her companion's hand under concealment of her skirts. She knew that Lettie could say no more on the topic; she had no right to comment beyond congratulations, and doing so would only look odd and improper.

"Are you speechless, Sophia?" Langdon asked good-naturedly, clearly unaware of the reaction his comment had elicited. "Surely you are as anxious as I to finally wed. Not that I see it as a burden, mind you. But setting the date for our union has eluded us for long enough, wouldn't you agree?"

The bodice of Sophia's cream silk gown seemed to slowly shrink, squeezing her chest uncomfortably. "Yes," she whispered, barely able to manage even that.

Langdon smiled brightly. "Was that a yes to being speechless, or yes to the idea of becoming my wife? I know which one I would prefer."

The Beechams' townhome came into view as the carriage turned up South Street. Sophia fixed her gaze on the stately home in a vain attempt to quell a rising tide of nausea.

"Are you quite all right, my lady?"

Sophia heard Mrs. Kirk's question. She could not answer, as the carriage began to slowly spin around her. She grasped the lacquered window frame in order to stay upright, barely aware of her fan falling to the floor of the coach.

Langdon reached across and steadied her. But his touch only deepened the growing sense of panic and dread in Sophia.

"Lettie, please," Sophia asked in a panicked plea as the suddenly intense heat and stuffiness of the carriage became unbearable. "Please, I cannot breathe."

"My lord, please look away," the woman instructed Langdon, reaching for the buttons on Sophia's dress. She made quick work of the row before moving on to the corset beneath.

Sophia panted, struggling for air. The sudden release of the ribbon ties allowed her to drag in several deep breaths and fill her lungs. She fell back onto the seat and squeezed her eyes shut.

The carriage slowed. Sophia heard Langdon yelling something to the driver, though she could not make out what, precisely, he had ordered the man to do.

And just as quickly, the carriage began to move again. Langdon's large, warm hand covered hers as he whispered indistinct words of comfort into her ear.

"Everything will be fine, my lady," Mrs. Kirk assured Sophia in her practical way. "We're returning home now. Soon enough you'll be in your bed with nothing, only the quiet to keep you company."

It occurred to Sophia that the only situation worse than what she found herself in presently was the one Lettie described.

### Beecham House

Nicholas stood near the orchestra in the Beechams' ballroom, nursing a cup of tepid lemonade. He watched Singh as the man entertained a group of people, including Lord Beecham, a particularly annoying sort who never tired of his own importance.

Nicholas smiled. Lord Beecham would be horrified to know that Singh was not the son of a Maharajah, as Nicholas had informed his hosts, but in fact a holy man of sorts who preferred a simple robe and bare feet to the colorful silk and linen Indian costume he currently wore.

Nicholas was not about to tell anyone the truth. And Singh was clearly enjoying himself. Rumors of his false identity as foreign royalty had spread throughout the ballroom and earned him a growing following. The man deserved a spot of fun. After all, he'd seen to the running of the house while Nicholas had been away—a house that now boasted a cook, a maid, and a footman.

If he was not careful, he thought with amusement, he would soon be seen as something approaching social respectability. "Blast you, Singh," he muttered wryly, then finished off the lemonade.

He could grouse all he wanted. Secretly, Nicholas was making plans. With Sophia at his side, anything was possible. Suddenly the world had opened up to him in ways he never could have imagined.

Laughter erupted from the group around Singh and Nicholas smiled at his friend. Perhaps he'd underestimated the man's wisdom, after all. Not that he would ever admit such a thing.

"Is that Singh?"

Nicholas turned to find Langdon behind him, his gaze fastened on the Indian man.

"Yes," Nicholas answered, turning back toward the crowd. "Though he is pretending to be royalty this evening, so do not spoil his fun."

Chuckling, Langdon stepped forward and clapped Nicholas on the back. "God, I have missed you."

"We reserve such thumps for Carrington, if you'll remember," Nicholas replied, handing his empty glass to a passing footman.

"Yes, well, Carrington is not here. So we must make do . . ."

"Nor are Sophia and Mrs. Kirk. Did you forget to fetch them this evening?" Nicholas asked.

Langdon's congenial manner disappeared at once, replaced by sober concern. "It was the oddest thing: Sophia became quite upset in the carriage. So much so that Mrs. Kirk and I decided it was best for her to return home."

"Upset?"

Langdon hesitated, his mouth opening and closing as if he did not know what to say. "I believe a physical ailment is at the root of the episode. It was most distressing for her; in fact, I do not think I've ever seen her more agitated. She claimed that she could not breathe and insisted Mrs. Kirk unlace her corset."

"Scandalous!" Nicholas said dryly, attempting to appear unmoved. "Did you fetch the doctor?"

"Oh yes, the doctor was sent for immediately. I stayed until after he'd examined her."

Nicholas tensed. "And what did he believe the cause to be?"

"Nerves."

"Nerves?" Nicholas repeated, thankful that Sophia was not physically ill, yet still filled with concern.

"Yes, nerves," Langdon confirmed. "The doctor inquired as to the subject of our discussion just before the episode and whether it might have been upsetting to Sophia."

Was Langdon toying with him? Had Sophia told him of their time in Sussex on the way to tonight's ball, then broke down from the stress of the admission? "And?"

Langdon looked at Nicholas with amusement. "Good God, little brother. You've not been this interested in Sophia since we were eight and you discovered she could whistle."

"She is to be a member of our family, is she not?"

Nicholas asked, an appropriate amount of sarcasm in his voice. "I am simply concerned, that's all."

Langdon shook his head. "I'm only teasing, Nicholas. The truth is, we were speaking about our wedding. And I won't deny that if her attack of nerves was a response to the thought of marrying me, it hardly puts my mind at ease."

"But you said you believed a physical malady brought on the episode," Nicholas pointed out.

Langdon nodded. "Yes, well, the doctor did hint at the cause being something feminine in nature. Still, I do not want to be a man that assumes every little irritation may be attributed to a woman's . . ."

For the first time that evening, Nicholas was thankful for Langdon's hesitancy. "Ah, I see," he replied. "While I commend your desire to be forward-thinking, perhaps the doctor is correct in his assumption."

"Yes, I suppose you're right," Langdon agreed, his expression easing. "And it is not as if our marriage should come as a surprise to Sophia."

"No, it should not," Nicholas confirmed, his heart aching for her. To engage in such a conversation so soon after returning from Petworth must have been torturous.

A footman approached, a tray laden with champagne flutes balanced carefully in his hands.

Langdon took a glass and waited for Nicholas to retrieve one as well.

Nicholas waved the footman on and smiled at his brother, eyeing the flute with envy.

"Are we not drinking this evening?" Langdon remarked casually, though he was obviously pleased.

Nicholas nodded. "We are not."

Langdon beckoned the footman to return. "I will not be needing this after all," he explained to the man, setting his glass on the tray. He turned back to Nicholas. "A woman?" he asked, clearly curious.

Nicholas was momentarily thrown by his brother's question. "Why would you assume a woman had anything to do with it?"

"Because they always do," Langdon replied, elbowing his brother in the ribs. "Now, anyone I know?"

Love was meant to simplify life, wasn't it? Nicholas had always assumed as much. Yet another bloody fallacy, he reflected, floated by poets and writers through the ages.

"A gentleman never tells," Nicholas answered, adding, "nor do I."

## 20

*Afton House*

Sophia sat up at the sound of her bedroom door being opened. "Lettie?"

The woman's tall form appeared in the doorway. The candlestick she carried illuminated a look of severe distress on her face. "My lady, I am sorry to wake you. Mr. Bourne insisted I do so."

She stepped inside the room, followed by Nicholas.

"Sophia, assure Mrs. Kirk my presence is acceptable," he whispered, glaring at her companion. "She threatened to send for Bow Street and insists she will go ahead with the hue and cry if you do not ease her mind."

"Lettie," Sophia began, beckoning the woman closer. "My wrapper, if you will."

Her companion handed the candle to Nicholas and retrieved the silk garment from the back of Sophia's desk chair. "My lady," she whispered, coming forward, "this is highly inappropriate."

"I am aware of that, Lettie," Sophia answered. She threw back the covers, swung her legs over the edge of the bed, and stood.

Lettie held up the wrapper while Sophia put it on. "The servants are bound to talk—"

"Then I will rely on you to curb their tongues," Sophia interjected, tying the sash about her waist. "Trust me, Lettie."

The older woman hesitated in front of her and reached out to straighten the two ends of the sash. "It's not you I do not trust."

"Enough," Nicholas ground out. "I'll not say nor do anything that Sophia may object to. You have my word, Mrs. Kirk."

Lettie released the sash and folded her hands together. "I'll go, then," she said, and turned toward the door.

Sophia reassured her with a loving pat on the back.

Nicholas offered the candlestick to Mrs. Kirk but she refused.

"Keep it, Mr. Bourne—and you would do well to light the others in the room," she informed him, pointing to each and every last candle in Sophia's bedchamber. "My lady does not like the dark, you see."

He nodded impatiently and opened the door. "Thank you, Mrs. Kirk."

Sophia watched as Lettie crossed the threshold and Nicholas swiftly closed the door behind her.

He turned the key in the lock. "If she did not hate me before tonight, she most assuredly does now."

"She does not hate *you*—at least, not entirely," Sophia answered, hurrying to meet him. "She hates the idea of a man in my room."

Nicholas set the candlestick on the fireplace mantel. "I don't blame her," he replied, his hands reaching out to lovingly cradle Sophia's face. "But when Langdon explained the reason for your absence from the ball, I had to see you."

The mere mention of Langdon's name set Sophia crying again.

"Please, Sophia," Nicholas murmured, pulling her close. "Come, sit with me."

Sophia buried her face in the warmth of his superfine

coat. She relaxed into his arms as he carefully picked her up and carried her to the end of the bed.

"His face beamed with happiness as he talked of the wedding—*our* wedding," Sophia began, settling onto Nicholas's lap. "I'd always assumed he'd viewed marriage much the same as I—inevitable, but agreeable enough. His face told me otherwise."

Nicholas felt her words like a blow and he froze for a moment, absorbing the impact. She belonged to his brother. It should be Langdon holding her, not him. But his heart refused to accept the thought and his arms tightened around her in instant rejection.

He kissed the crown of her head, breathing in the faint scent of lavender and soap. "I'm sorry, Sophia. If I were not so selfish, I would let you go."

She hugged him closer, her soft breasts pressing against his chest. "You're not selfish, Nicholas, not in the slightest." Her voice quivered with emotion. "But I'm a terrible person. I felt like the most despicable villain in that carriage—knowing I loved you, yet still allowing Langdon to continue as if I shared his enthusiasm for his plans."

She tipped her head back, her gaze searching his with mute appeal. "When I arrived home, after Lettie had helped me undress and prepare for bed, I recalled what I told you at Petworth: Langdon deserves to have someone love him with all the passion, respect, and tenderness I feel for you. I would never be able to offer him more than companionship and a friend's affection. It isn't fair to allow him to settle for less when he has every right to expect so much more from a wife."

A swell of fierce pride and admiration swept over Nicholas. Her willingness to face her emotions with unflinching honesty was a testimony to the depth of her character.

"I love you," he murmured. His voice was rough, his

throat clogged with too much feeling. "For everything you are—and all I am not."

Her beautiful eyes instantly welled with tears, dampening the thickness of her lashes. "And I love you," she whispered. "For everything *you* are, and I am not."

She lifted her head to press her lips against his in a soft, warm kiss that felt like a vow.

Nicholas loved the way her arms wrapped around his neck, claiming him, her fingers threading into his hair. The move brought her unbound breasts tighter against his chest, the rounded curve of her bottom shifting closer. A swift surge of lust hit him, swamping the pure affection, love, and commitment in their kiss that had shaken him to his soul.

*Wrong place, wrong time.* He couldn't strip her out of her night rail and take her, not after he'd promised to be a gentleman.

He lifted his mouth from hers and tucked her close as he struggled to maintain his composure.

Sophia turned her head and brushed openmouthed kisses against his throat.

Nicholas fought to tamp down his desire, the warm, damp movement of her lips over his skin torturous.

But then she stirred, planted her palms on his chest, and pushed back. He swallowed a groan as her bottom shifted seductively over his thighs. Her eyes were lambent with unhidden need as she reached for his cravat, her fingers busily unknotting the starched linen. He caught her hands in his, stopping her.

"Wait," his voice rasped, the tone deeper. "What are you doing?"

"I'm undressing you." She looked up at him, her green eyes dark with heat and need, before she gently tugged her hands from his and pulled the linen cravat free.

"I promised Mrs. Kirk that I would do nothing inappropriate." His words were strained and his hands restless where they gripped her waist. "I'm desperately trying to play the gentleman, Sophia."

"Please, Nicholas." Her soft voice trembled. "I need you." She slipped the buttons of his shirt free, pushed the edges back, and settled her hands against his skin.

The press and stroke of her fingers and palms against his bare skin was a brand. Fire and heat built beneath her touch.

"Tell me what you need from me, Sophia," he murmured, unbearably aroused by her touch.

She glanced up at him, her eyes gleaming through half-lowered lashes. Color flushed the high arch of her cheekbones and bloomed on her throat and the upper curve of her breasts, visible above the neckline of her night rail.

"I want you to touch me." Her gaze flickered to his chest, where her fingers stroked compulsively against his skin. When she looked back up at him, her eyes were smokier, clouded with need. "Like I'm touching you."

It took all his control to keep his hands on her waist.

"Where?" he murmured. "Show me."

The flush coloring her cheeks deepened. Nicholas felt her fingers tighten, pressing harder against his skin. But then she slowly lifted one hand, as if reluctant to break contact completely with him, and skimmed her fingertips over the swell of her breast, pausing over the silk-covered nipple.

"Here," she said softly, her voice husky with desire.

Nicholas shuddered, barely controlling the urge to rip the silk from her body and ravish her with no regard for finesse. But this was Sophia and she deserved more than a swift, hot ride. He refused to give in to the urgent demand.

"Whatever the lady wants," he murmured as he took her hand and placed it back on his chest, closing his eyes briefly at the sheer pleasure of her skin against his, "the lady shall have."

He nudged the tiny sleeves of her night rail off her shoulders and tugged the bodice lower until the ribbon-trimmed edge rested below her breasts. If he hadn't already been seated, the sight would have driven him to his knees.

"You're so beautiful." He heard the gravelly, barely audible words and knew she might not have understood him. He wasn't capable of pretty words at the moment. He would have to show her what the sight of her did to him.

He bent his head and brushed his lips over the satin-smooth curve of her breast, taking his time. The world narrowed to the woman in his lap, the feel of her in his arms, the taste of her skin beneath his mouth. Sophia murmured, her hands sliding around his neck to clasp the back of his head and press him closer.

"Please . . ." Her voice was desperate, fractured with need.

Nicholas closed his lips over her nipple drawn tight with desire, and Sophia gasped, holding him closer.

Long, heated moments passed, the silence in the room broken only by soft sighs of pleasure. When her slim body shifted restlessly in his arms and her breathless pleas demanded more, he caught the hem of her night rail and tugged it higher, up over her thighs until it pooled around her hips.

He lifted his head and took her mouth with his just as his hand closed over her mons, his fingers brushing the soft folds between her legs.

Sophia surged against him, her hands fisting in his hair before moving unerringly down his chest to stroke the rock-hard arousal beneath his breeches.

Her silent demand drove him over the edge, dissolving his careful restraint as if it had never existed.

Nicholas lifted his head, muttered an oath, and brushed her hand aside. Buttons gave easily beneath his impatient tugs and he shoved his breeches and smalls down, freeing himself.

Sophia brushed her tumbled hair out of her eyes and looked down. The thick head of his erection rose from the opening of his breeches, flushed with deep, rosy color. She closed her hand around the heavy length, rubbing her thumb over the moisture pearling on the top. Fascinated by the silky smooth skin over iron-hard muscle beneath, she stroked the length, feeling it stiffen even more as she caressed. Several more drops of the clear liquid gathered on the head and, curious, she brought her hand to her lips and licked a fingertip. The warm, faintly salty taste intrigued her.

Nicholas's harsh groan barely registered. Compelled to explore further, she closed her fingers around him once more but his muscles bunched and he brushed her hand aside again. With one easy, fluid movement, he caught her waist and lifted her, shifting her astride him. She caught her breath as the hot, heavy length of his erection slid between her legs.

Then the blunt head nudged her soft entry and she gasped, eagerly pushing back against his silent demand. He slid home, sealing them together, and Sophia shuddered with relief. Nicholas's mouth covered hers and he swallowed her cries as he lifted her and thrust upward, steeping her in pleasure again and again.

Sophia frantically obeyed the tight coil of demand building within her. She quickened the pace, sinking herself again and again onto the length of his hard penis. His buttocks came off the bed as he matched her speed and the coil broke, sending the heat of a thousand flames spiraling throughout Sophia's body. She cried out, small moans of both pleasure and peace shaking her.

Nicholas wrapped his arms about her and pulled Sophia down to his chest. "You're mine." He flipped her over to lie against the mattress, his penis still buried within her.

His mouth rested near her ear. Sophia heard his breath falter as he began to move his hips. She wrapped one leg around his waist and held on tight. Nicholas moaned deep in his throat, each ensuing thrust coming harder and faster than the last. Suddenly, every muscle in his body clenched and he stilled, his arms tightening about Sophia until they truly felt as one.

"No matter what happens, Sophia," he whispered, brushing his lips against her ear. "No matter what."

# 21

*June 10*
Drury Lane
Covent Garden
Westminster

Sophia's hackney slowed to a stop in front of Drury Lane's Gloriana Theatre. Nicholas stood with his back settled against the brick façade. He pushed off from the wall and sauntered toward the conveyance, opening the door and holding out his hand.

"I apologize for being late," Sophia blurted out, accepting his assistance and stepping from the coach. "The moment I received your note I made preparations to come."

Nicholas waited for the hackney to move into traffic before speaking. "Do not worry yourself. I only just received the information this morning. You've not delayed us more than an hour at the most."

"Nicholas Bourne," Sophia said skeptically, "no more than an hour? Really?"

"Are you calling me a liar?" Nicholas asked, settling his hat brim lower on his brow in an attempt to escape the light drizzle.

Sophia considered his question. "Well, yes, I suppose I am."

"I'm glad we've cleared that up," he replied with a wink. "Now, shall we continue?"

A fat drop of rain landed squarely on the end of Sophia's nose.

Nicholas reached out and tenderly wiped it away. "Come along," he urged, offering her his arm.

Sophia shivered. Even the slightest touch and she could feel him surrounding her, the memories more than mere images in her mind. It was as if her entire body had recorded their lovemaking—every touch, smell, taste, sensation.

Sophia slipped her hand through the crook of his arm and allowed him to gently guide her down the sidewalk. "As to these 'sources' you mentioned in your note . . . Are they truly reliable enough to warrant a visit to Drury Lane?"

"Really, Sophia," Nicholas grumbled, drawing her protectively nearer as a carriage rolled by and splashed the sidewalk with muddy water. "You are far too inquisitive today. Know that my sources are ones I trust. They tell me there are only three companies who've performed *Dido Queen of Carthage* within the last fifty years."

Sophia peeled a clinging, wet panel of her humble dress away from her leg and attempted to discreetly ring it out.

Nicholas cast a critical eye over Sophia's dress. "Now, are you prepared to play your part?"

Sophia shook out the soaked fabric and inspected her appearance as best she could. Lettie had done a fine job of finding a serviceable gown suited to the daughter of an actor. "Of course. I am Annabelle Farnsworth. My father, James Farnsworth, the wildly talented actor and equally errant sire, has inherited a tidy sum from his brother. It is my understanding that the last company he was known to work for was . . ."

"The Gloriana Acting Troupe," Nicholas prompted.

"The Gloriana Acting Troupe," Sophia repeated. "Therefore, I've started the search for my missing father in London, with you by my side. And you are . . . ?"

Nicholas adjusted the garish blue and red scarf tied about his neck. "Lucius McVeety, the toast of Edinburgh theatre and a dear friend of your father's."

"Your accent is spot-on," Sophia marveled, "I wonder, though, do you think it wise to adopt a persona so unlike your own?"

Nicholas arched one eyebrow in response. "And who says it is, lassie?"

Sophia attempted to smile at his antics, wanting to forget the real purpose for their masquerade.

"What is it, Sophia? What troubles you?" Nicholas asked, the tenderness in his voice catching Sophia off guard.

"I cannot decide whether I am excited or frightened by the prospect of finding the Bishop," she answered honestly, dodging the edge of a passing woman's parasol.

Nicholas pointed up ahead to the wooden sign marking the Gloriana Theatre. "Because once we find the Bishop, we'll be forced to tell Langdon? Yes, I feel precisely the same push and pull. But right now I need you to play your part, Sophia."

Her steps slowed as they neared the sign, watching as it swung lazily in the wind. "I always did enjoy a good play."

"Your answer, Sophia. Are you ready?"

She purposely slumped her shoulders slightly and scraped the side of her boot along the filthy walkway, smearing the cheap leather with mud. "There, now I am."

Nicholas patted her hand in silent approval and they walked the remaining distance to the theatre entrance. "And just in time," he replied, pulling the scarred door open and waiting for Sophia to enter.

"It's about bloody time, you two," a man barked, taking Sophia's arm and dragging her across the lobby. "Stratham said he'd have you here before ten. Last time I take the dishonest bloke's word. Go on with you. They're waiting in there," he said, nodding at the door he was about to push open. "You've cut into Beaton's morning pub call," he warned. "He'll be mad as a breeding bull by now. Best have your lines memorized."

Sophia looked over her shoulder at Nicholas for help, only to see him waving her on as he followed. "I'm sorry, sir. My lines?"

"From the balcony scene, love. Don't tell me you haven't got them memorized?" The man shook his head in disbelief, dramatically rolling his eyes at the very thought as he pushed the door wide. "There's scripts on the stage for you—'course you'll be lucky if Beaton allows you to finish. Interrupted ale and unprepared actors? I don't think his tiny little heart can take it. Still, you might as well have a go."

The man released Sophia's arm and swatted her backside, turning her toward the stage and giving her a shove when she dared to protest.

"And you too, Romeo," Sophia heard the man say to Nicholas as she narrowly avoided tripping up the narrow aisle.

"Here we are, Mr. Beaton," the man called out to a small group gathered in the front row. "Stratham recommended them both, so I thought it might be worth a wait."

Sophia turned to look at the group as she made her way to the stage. A man rose to tower above the rest, his mannerisms those of an overly proud peacock.

"I'll be the judge of that," Mr. Beaton answered imperiously, capturing Sophia with an icy glare. "If you want to be considered for Juliet, I suggest you take the stage. Now."

"As it so happens—"

"We apologize, Mr. Beaton," Nicholas interrupted, prodding Sophia forward with one finger against her spine. "Ach, if you'll just bear with us for a minute more, please."

"A Scottish Romeo?" Mr. Beaton demanded. "Well, now I have seen everything."

Sophia attempted to drag her feet and succeeded instead in almost tripping for the second time. "What are you doing?" she hissed in Nicholas's ear as he bent to help her up.

"You heard the man; he'll be off to the pub once we're through. Then we'll have the run of the place," Nicholas explained, righting Sophia and urging her forward. "He would have little time for Miss Farnsworth and her missing father in such a state."

"And I suppose you know Romeo's part?" Sophia pressed, lifting her skirts as she ascended the stage stairs.

"Why on earth would I?" Nicholas replied, bounding up the stairs and past her.

"We do not have time for the entire scene," Mr. Beaton bellowed. "We will start from the nurse's arrival. 'Yoo-hoo, Juliet,'" he cried out in falsetto, and then gestured for them to begin.

Sophia scanned the stage for the scripts that the burly man had mentioned out front. She knew Juliet's lines by heart, of course, the play being her favorite of all of Shakespeare's works. Still, Nicholas would need help.

> "O blessed, blessed night! I am afeard.
> Being in night, all this is but a dream . . ."

The voice, tinged with a Scottish brogue, was most definitely Nicholas's. Sophia turned to find he'd assumed a spot near the base of a newly constructed turret.

"Go on. Up the turret with you," Beaton hollered, his impatience growing.

*This is absolute madness.* Sophia caught up her skirts and trotted toward the turret, going around to the back, where she found a set of stairs. Relieved, she ran up the short flight and came out on a small landing, a view of Mr. Beaton and his men appearing through the hole cut for a window. Sophia looked down at Nicholas and glared.

*"Three words, dear Romeo, and good night indeed.*
*If that thy bent of love be honourable,*
*Thy purpose marriage, send me word tomorrow . . ."*

"Madam," Beaton's falsetto rang out, startling Sophia.

*"I come, anon.—But if thou mean'st not well,*
*I do beseech thee—"*

"Madam!"

*"By and by, I come:*
*To cease thy strife, and leave me to my grief:*
*To-morrow will I send."*

Nicholas tipped his chin up and closed his eyes reverently.

*"So thrive my soul—"*

"Skip to your last lines in the scene," Mr. Beaton demanded, his thirst—and perhaps, Sophia realized, their performance—getting the better of him.

She gazed upon Nicholas, much the same as Shakespeare must have envisioned his Juliet looking into the eyes of the fictional Romeo hundreds of years before. Despite Mr. Beaton's impatience, Sophia wanted to savor the moment and its pure emotion.

> *"Sweet, so would I:*
> *Yet I should kill thee with much cherishing.*
> *Good night, good night! parting is such*
>   *sweet sorrow,*
> *That I shall say good night till it be morrow."*

Nicholas opened his eyes just as she finished, tears welling up in them.

"Well, it was rather better than I was expecting," Mr. Beaton stated, as though he was disappointed. "Still, not quite what we're looking for. I always like to have a few attractive actors milling about, though—window dressing, if you will. Go see the costume mistress. If we have anything in your sizes, we'll find a small part for each of you."

"Thank you, sir," Nicholas replied, gesturing for Sophia to come down from the turret.

"And you'll do something about the bloody accent, yes?" Mr. Beaton added.

Sophia came around the turret and stood next to Nicholas. "Of course he will, sir. I'll see to it myself."

"Good girl," Mr. Beaton told her, then sauntered off without saying good-bye.

"You heard the man," Nicholas whispered. "Ach, it's to the costume mistress with us."

## 22

Nicholas took Sophia's hand and led her into the wings, only to find their way blocked by a massive papier-mâché sphinx. He turned about and stalked back across the stage and into the curtained wings on the other side, finding the stairwell to the pass-through quickly enough.

"Do you know where you're going?" Sophia asked as they descended the stairs and walked along the narrow passageway used by the actors and crew to travel from one side of the stage to the other.

"Yes—and no," he answered, mounting the stairs at the opposite end of the corridor. "Most theatres are situated in a similar fashion, with dressing rooms and the costume shop on the right, above the stage; props and director's office, etcetera, on the left."

They reached the stage level and Nicholas gestured toward a second set of stairs. "This way."

"I did not know you were an admirer of the theatre."

Nicholas was about to respond when he realized his explanation involved a particular actress. And nothing to do with her stage skills. "May I be honest?"

"I wish you would," Sophia replied, squeezing his hand.

Nicholas paused at the top of the stairs and pulled Sophia around to face him. "I am familiar with the general layout of a playhouse not because of my particular affection for the theatre, but because of my particular affection for an actress—an affection, let me be clear, that has since died a most dramatic and salacious death."

"I know."

Nicholas looked at the stairwell, then back at Sophia. "Did I not hear your question correctly?"

"No," Sophia murmured, a soft, dewy quality settling in her eyes. "You heard me correctly. I simply needed to be sure that you meant it when you swore absolute honesty."

He looked at the stairwell a second time and back at Sophia again, her gaze nearly doing him in. "Then that was a test."

"Of sorts, I suppose," she answered, furrowing her brow as she frowned. "Do you know, I hadn't thought of it as such, but that's precisely what it was. I'm sorry, Nicholas. It's just that with Langdon, every aspect of our relationship was assumed. There was nothing earned or sorted out. It simply was—like the Almighty," she explained, smiling shyly up at him. "I've never needed to prove myself, nor has he."

Nicholas swallowed hard. Yet another complication to their relationship he hadn't considered. "I know there is nothing simple about you and me—"

"Which is what makes me happy," Sophia interrupted, raising her hand to rest one slim finger on his lips. "Love is not meant to be assumed, Nicholas. It's meant to be discovered—even fought for."

"So you want to fight with me?" he asked, relief beginning where her soft, warm body touched his and spreading out to the end of each limb.

Sophia smiled, affectionate amusement returning to her eyes. "Amongst other things, yes," she said, taking her fingertip from his lips and holding up her reticule, which contained the sketches.

"Aye," Nicholas answered. He looked down the corridor before them. "This way."

He stepped forward and turned right, Sophia following closely behind. Scanning the closed doors, he found the one marked "Costume Mistress," just beyond the dressing rooms.

"Is there anyone about?" Nicholas called in a strong Scottish voice, rapping on the door with his knuckles.

A grumble of annoyance could be heard through the cheap wood panel, then a series of clicks as someone walked across the room and opened the door. "I thought the Scottish play had been postponed until next year."

A tiny woman stood before Nicholas, a pronounced frown on her lips as she stared at him. Her hair, a stark white that seemed to double as a light source, was piled on top of her head, the height extending her diminutive size. Her face was expertly painted, so much so that Nicholas suspected she was far older than she looked. A thick pair of spectacles threatened to slip off the end of her nose as she cocked her head to the right and captured him with her intelligent eyes. "Oh well, I'm afraid you've come to the wrong door. This is the seamstress's workshop."

"No, no, we're here for our fittings," Sophia answered from behind Nicholas.

"Is there someone with you?" the birdlike woman asked, peering around Nicholas and finding Sophia. "Ah, well, you I can work with." She gestured for Nicholas to move aside and grasped Sophia's hand, pulling her into the room.

"You've misunderstood. He is also here for a fitting," Sophia added, planting her feet firmly on the threshold and forcing the costume mistress to stop.

The elderly woman turned back and eyed Nicholas once again, her lips pursing into a makeshift beak. "Well, there is not a costume in all Britannia that will hide your brogue, but I'll see what I can manage. Come in, then, and close the door after you."

Nicholas stepped over the threshold after Sophia, pulling the door shut behind them.

"Now, then, I'm Camilla, though everyone calls me Mistress," the woman explained. "And you are?"

"Annabelle Farnsworth," Sophia lied smoothly.

"Lucius McVeety, at your service," Nicholas answered, sweeping a flamboyant bow.

Camilla let out a chirp of approval. "I adore the Scots. So passionate—so lively! Still, this is Romeo and Juliet, my boy. Can you manage an Italian accent? Or at the very least, an English one?"

"I believe so," Nicholas answered in his own voice, thankful for the chance.

"Perfect!" she replied, then turned to a rack of costumes. "Now, your parts?"

"Window dressing," Sophia said proudly, attempting to show some measure of enthusiasm for the inconsequential role.

"I see. Well, you must start at the beginning, I suppose," Camilla commiserated, pausing to inspect a dress.

"And Annabelle is doing just that," Nicholas replied. "She's gained some experience in York and Leeds, but nothing compared to the London stage."

Camilla whirled around and went straight for Sophia, holding a gown up to her and eyeing both dress and female critically. "This is hardly *the* London stage, Mr. McVeety. Still, I admire your positive attitude.

"Yes, this might do nicely. Go try it on," Camilla ordered Sophia, pointing to an oriental screen set up in the corner of the cramped room. "Now for you, Mr. McVeety. Something in green, I believe."

Sophia discreetly dropped the reticule at Nicholas's feet and walked to the corner, disappearing behind the screen.

"It might not be quite *the* London stage, Mistress," Nicholas began, watching her flit and fly from one stack of clothing to the next, her moves as precise and quick as a hummingbird, "but you'll be proud to know that, once upon a time, word of one of your productions spread all the way to Scotland."

Camilla grasped a folded linen shirt and a bolt of deep green fabric before returning to stand in front of him. "Is that so?" she asked, a gleam of curiosity in her eyes.

"Oh yes. I even have a sketch of the play with me," Nicholas said, bending low to retrieve Sophia's bag.

"You carry a reticule, Mr. McVeety?" she asked, arching one perfectly drawn eyebrow in amused disbelief.

Nicholas smiled at her and winked. "Annabelle was kind enough to shield the sketch from the rain."

He opened the small bag and lifted out the thick folded paper, then dropped the reticule on the floor. "It would have been a great pity to have damaged such a lovely sketch. Wouldn't you agree?" He held it up to Camilla's eye level and watched the woman's face fill with surprise and pleasure.

"Why, that is Maggie Pemble—and in my own creation, I might add," she exclaimed, reaching out to reverently touch the faded piece of paper. "Do you know, the troupe only performed *Dido Queen of Carthage* five times before the piece was retired? Such a shame. That dress was one of my favorites. In fact . . ."

Camilla abandoned the shirt and bolt of fabric on the floor and returned to the rack of costumes, thumbing through each one quickly. "Wait, that's right, I put it with . . ."

She swung around and came back toward Nicholas, shooing him out of the way and continuing on to a trunk shoved against the wall. She lifted the lid and set it back on its hinges, then bent over, nearly disappearing into the cavernous interior. "No . . . no . . . no . . . Aha!"

Sophia returned to stand next to Nicholas. The costume she'd donned looked odd. "I could not undo my own buttons," she explained, lifting up the hem to reveal her own gown below.

"Oh, my creation is as glorious as I remember," Camilla gushed, standing upright with a bundle of blue silk in her hands. She grasped the outer gown by the straps and let the fabric fall, miles of blue silk unraveling to reveal a bodice encrusted with beading that glittered in the light. "I hadn't been with the company for very long—and truth be told, I'd lied to get the job. This dress, though . . ." She paused as if remembering the very moment she'd stitched the soft fabric together. "This dress proved me right. Of course, it didn't hurt that I'd been blessed with Maggie. The woman could've worn a potato sack and looked beautiful."

"Maggie?" Sophia asked innocently, steering the conversation to what she instinctively felt was the important information.

"It's a sad tale—a tragedy, really. The troupe had traveled south for a scheduled appearance in Sussex. The day before the performance, the lady of the house was murdered. Murdered! Maggie was not back in London for a fortnight before she lost her mind over the ordeal. Most of us weren't even given the chance to say good-bye before they carted her off to Bedlam."

Camilla stared at Sophia as if seeing her for the very first time. "No, that color won't do at all."

Nicholas reached for the silk gown and held it between his fingers while he admired the beadwork. "Good God, that is tragic. And poor Maggie, is she yet alive?"

"Do you know, I've no idea," Camilla answered honestly, carefully tugging the fabric from his fingers and lovingly folding the gown. "I tried to visit her once—even brought a new night rail for her. They wouldn't let me see her. The guard said she was in confinement for attempting to injure herself. Only family and her doctor were allowed in."

"Family?" Sophia asked in a quiet, gentle voice.

Camilla finished folding the dress and returned it to the trunk. "Maggie had one sister living—Rosamund was her name. But she couldn't be bothered to come up to London for her sister. So that left her doctor. If she is still alive, would that mean that she'd only ever been allowed to see her doctor and no one else?"

Nicholas glanced at Sophia knowingly. "Aye, I suppose it does."

"That makes Maggie's story even more tragic," Camilla muttered, straightening the skirt of her own beautifully stitched gown. "Now, off with that dress, young woman. Thinking on Maggie has made me sad and I'm in no mood to dilly-dally."

*June 13*
## THE HALCYON SOCIETY

It had never occurred to Sophia that Bedlam would be difficult to visit.

Of course, it had never occurred to her to consider Bedlam at all.

Sophia watched as the women in the Halcyon afternoon sewing class perfected the buttonhole. She was glad that none in the Society's care had required the services of England's infamous mental institution.

During her time working with the Runners, there had been passing mentions made of criminals being sent to Bedlam rather than prison. She'd never been allowed to interview those men while they were in the court's custody and there was absolutely no chance anyone would reconsider once they were behind the walls of Bedlam.

The hall door squeaked, drawing Sophia's attention

away from her thoughts. Young Abigail appeared and hurried toward her.

"Beg pardon, my lady. Mrs. Mason asked that I fetch you. There's a man here to see you."

Sophia smiled at the girl. "Ah, Lord Stonecliffe," she explained, settling her hand on the girl's shoulder as they walked from the room.

"Oh no, this man is far more devilish than the earl, of that I am sure." Abigail's hand clamped over her mouth the moment the words slipped from her lips. "I'm sorry, my lady. I should not have said such a thing."

"It's all right, Abigail. And if it is the man I think it is, I rather agree. But we will keep this between the two of us, all right? Mr. Bourne has not had an easy life, you see."

"You can trust me to keep our secret, Lady Sophia," Abigail said solemnly, moving her hand to her heart. "I swear on my dead granny's grave."

Sophia dropped a kiss on the crown of the girl's head. "Thank you, Abigail. I knew that you would understand."

Sophia steered Abigail toward the stairs and waited while she took the first step down, then followed.

Nicholas waited in the foyer. Sophia and Abigail reached the landing and the young girl pressed onward at an industrious clip, reaching the foyer before Sophia.

"It is a pleasure to welcome you to Halcyon House, Mr. Bourne," Sophia commented as she joined the group. "May I introduce Abigail?"

"A true pleasure to make your acquaintance, Mr. Bourne," Abigail said cheerfully. She rolled her shoulders back and stood up straight. "Now, I'll see to the tea." She quickly curtsied and turned toward the stairs with military precision.

Nicholas chuckled. "She reminds me of a girl I used to know."

Sophia batted his arm playfully. "Come, have a seat in the parlor. We must talk of Bedlam. Have you made any progress in gaining entry?"

Nicholas caught Sophia's arm. "Yes, we will talk. First, though, now that we are . . ." He paused, then pulled her close.

"Yes?" Sophia asked, keenly interested to hear just what Nicholas would say.

"Friends. Lovers," he replied, his breath tickling her skin. "Soul mates. Have I forgotten anything?"

Sophia was vaguely aware that they should not be having this conversation in the foyer and attempted to gather her wits. "No, I believe you have thoroughly covered every point."

"Good," he growled, his lips nearly touching the sensitive lobe of her ear. "Because I do like to be thorough. But, as it so happens, I do not like tea."

"Tea?" Sophia asked, sure that she'd missed something important, but her mind was far too befuddled by Nicholas's nearness to ascertain what that might be.

He pulled back slightly and looked at her, mischief sparkling in his eyes. "Yes, tea. In the interest of absolute honesty, I feel it is time I told you that I do not like tea. In fact, I hate it."

"But you love me?"

"Well, yes," Nicholas replied automatically. "After all, you're not tea."

A solid rapping at the door startled Sophia and she squeaked with surprise.

Abigail came rushing down the stairs, slowing when she saw Nicholas and Sophia standing in the foyer. "Beg your pardon, my lady. There's someone at the door."

"Of course, Abigail," Sophia replied, stepping back to put distance between herself and Nicholas.

Abigail took the remaining stairs at a quick, efficient

clip, her boots making a small clacking noise as she hurried to the door.

Sophia noticed that Nicholas had not let go of her arm. "Mr. Bourne, my arm, if you please," she whispered, tugging gently.

Instead of obliging her request, Nicholas began to rub the pad of his thumb against the sensitive skin on the inside of her elbow.

Sophia sighed at the seductive caress, the circular pattern Nicholas traced and retraced lulling her into a carnal haze.

"Hello there, Abigail. I've come to see Lady Sophia. I trust she is here?"

Langdon's voice instantly pierced the bubble of sensation that Abigail's opening of the front door had not.

"Of course, your lordship. Do come inside."

## 23

There was no mistaking his brother's voice. Nicholas released Sophia's arm and took a step back just as the little maid opened the door far enough to reveal Langdon.

"Well, this is a surprise," Langdon proclaimed, smiling with pleasure at the two.

"Is it?" Sophia asked nervously.

Langdon removed his greatcoat and handed it to the waiting girl. "A happy surprise, I assure you. What brought you to the Halcyon Society, Nicholas? Am I correct in assuming you've not been here before?"

Abigail curtsied, then made haste for the stairs.

Nicholas watched as his brother took Sophia's hand and kissed it, his lips lingering against her soft skin. "Yes, you are—as always. I've heard so much of the Halcyon Society that I wanted to see the charity for myself."

"You are a kind man, Nicholas. For the life of me, I will never understand why you hide your good qualities," Langdon declared, pride beaming in his eyes.

Nicholas felt the weight of Langdon's thoughtful words as though they were bags of sand, tied to his wrists and ankles, intent on dragging him to the bottom of the cursed sea.

"Well, do not get ahead of yourself. After all, it is very poor form on my part to only now be visiting the Hal-

cyon Society, when I should have been supporting Sophia's charitable endeavors all along."

"Oh, I don't know about that," Langdon replied, finally releasing Sophia. "In fact, perhaps you'll do me a
favor and convince Sophia to devote herself to another,
more urbane charity."

Nicholas could not understand his brother's request.
"Whatever for? I cannot think of a more deserving organization. Can you?"

"Whether or not the Halcyon Society is deserving is
not the issue, Nicholas," Langdon explained patiently.
"The issue is Sophia's safety. Which I fear is compro-
mised by the Society's clientele."

"Well, you're mad if you think I will encourage Sophia to listen."

Sophia cleared her throat. "Gentlemen—"

"Then protecting Sophia is of no consequence to
you?" Langdon interrupted.

Nicholas gritted his teeth until his jaw hurt. "From
what, precisely? Life?"

"Langdon, I've just invited Nicholas to stay for tea,"
Sophia broke in, gesturing toward the parlor. "Won't
you join us? There will be biscuits as well. But no argu-
ments."

"Including the one we are currently engaged in?"
Langdon hazarded a guess.

"Especially that one."

Langdon breathed a frustrated sigh. "And we must
have tea?"

"I adore tea," Nicholas lied.

"You *adore* tea?" Langdon asked flatly.

"Boys," Sophia warned, then held out her hand to
Langdon and allowed him to escort her to the parlor.

*June 14*
BETHLEM ROYAL HOSPITAL
THE MOORFIELDS
JUST OUTSIDE LONDON PROPER

"Rather dodgy looking for a hospital that is meant to keep the insane on the inside, wouldn't you agree?"

Sophia looked up the long drive of Bethlem Hospital and found she could not argue with Nicholas's assessment. "It's my understanding the hospital was deemed unsafe in 1807. They are currently building a new location in Southwark, though work is not expected to be completed for another two years."

It was an unsettling thought, Sophia realized as she examined the cracked façade of the large building and broken balustrades on each side of the wide steps leading to the hospital. Six years had passed before the hospital's governing board had seen to the welfare of its patients. Which was not only dangerous, but downright inhumane.

"And why do their families not care for them?" Mr. Singh asked, his eyes focused on the statues of "Raving" and "Melancholy Madness" that crowned the gateposts of the hospital.

"Do you not have insane asylums in India, Mr. Singh?" Sophia asked, the crunch of their shoes on the gravel drive the only other sound to be heard.

Mr. Singh turned to look at Sophia. "We do, my lady. But it is not a place where people heal, despite what those in power would have you believe."

A guttural cry rang out from somewhere in the building, cutting through their conversation and echoing across the hospital grounds. "Then our two countries have even more in common then I'd originally thought, Mr. Singh."

"I suppose we do," he answered, then turned to look at the menacing statues yet again.

Nicholas slowed his pace as they neared the stairs. "Come, the time is at hand; we must focus our efforts if we're to reach Miss Pemble."

Sophia stared up at the building one more time, steeling her mind to block out her fear. "Shall we review?"

The two men nodded in agreement and waited for Sophia to continue.

"All right, then," she began, pausing as a second desperate scream sounded from the hospital. She shrugged off the discomfort the unearthly sound had brought with it. "I am Miss Pemble's long-lost niece. It was only recently that town records showed her to be living here. I came straightaway to London to inquire whether she is well enough to accompany me back to Hertfordshire, where my husband and I would gladly welcome her into our home."

"The husband," Nicholas added, raising his hand.

"And Mr. Pamuk, an expert in mental illness brought in to assess the aunt," Mr. Singh said, smoothing out the lapels of his new coat.

They reached the stairs and began to climb them slowly.

"Are we ready?" Nicholas asked, looking at Mr. Singh, then Sophia.

"I do not think we have any choice in the matter," Sophia answered, standing to the side as Nicholas pulled open the door.

"No need to be negative," he whispered. "It is only a mental institution. What could possibly go wrong?"

A multitude of things, Sophia thought as she crossed the hospital's threshold and waited for the men to join her.

"Follow me, please," Mr. Singh said with authority.

He stalked toward a woman sitting behind a desk just ahead.

Nicholas tucked Sophia's arm into the crook of his. "Well, let us look on the bright side, at least we're playing man and wife, which means I have every reason to comfort you should Singh be beaten senseless by Miss Pemble."

"Only you could come up with such a 'blessing,' " Sophia replied.

The two crossed the room to join Mr. Singh, where he stood talking with the woman.

"Come along, Mr. and Mrs. Felton," he instructed, his impatient tone perfectly suited to a man of his position. "Miss Dwyer requires the paperwork."

"Of course," Sophia said as they joined Mr. Singh in front of the desk. She loosened her reticule's drawstring and reached inside. "Here we are. Birth records, church affiliation, and the family tree from our Bible."

Sophia held her breath as Miss Dwyer examined the papers. Nicholas had procured the required proof. And while it had all looked very real to Sophia, she was hardly an expert.

"Wait here," Miss Dwyer told them in a flat voice as she pushed back her chair and stood. A ring of keys rattled as she walked to a door on the opposite side of the room. She untied the ribbon holding it, chose one, and fitted it into the lock. She pushed the door open and stepped through, slamming the heavy panel shut behind her.

The sound of the door being relocked on the other side reached Sophia's ears. "What does this mean?"

"I have no idea," Nicholas replied as he scanned the sparsely furnished lobby.

Hardly reassured by his response, Sophia began to mentally calculate how much time they would have to explain themselves should Miss Dwyer return, intent on discovering why one would attempt to break *into* a mental institution.

"I saw in Miss Dwyer a gentle spirit," Mr. Singh said. "I feel sure she is only following protocol and will return shortly with the answer we desire."

"Thank you, Mr. Singh," Sophia replied, "though I don't know that we can rely on the quality of Miss Dwyer's spirit should the papers prove inadequate. Therefore, do either of you have an explanation as to what we are doing here?"

A lock being thrown back rattled the door.

"Because if you do, I would suggest sharing it. Now."

Miss Dwyer appeared, the papers still clutched in her hand, with a tall, slim man following behind her.

"I apologize for the wait," she said, returning to the desk and sitting down. "I only started here last week and you're the first visitors I've met."

She handed Sophia the papers then opened a desk drawer. Pulling a form of some sort from a stack, she set it on the desk in front of her. "Now, let me sign here," she explained, dipping a quill into a tidy pot of ink and writing her name near the bottom of the form.

She offered the quill to Nicholas and turned the paper upside down so that he could read it. "Once you've reviewed and agreed to the following, please sign on the line just below mine."

Sophia purposely avoided looking at the document, reasoning the less she understood of their crime, the better.

"All right," Nicholas said, signing his false name and returning the quill to Miss Dwyer.

The nurse examined the paper one final time. "I believe everything is in order. Michael here will take you back to see Miss Pemble."

The orderly's long face twisted into a semblance of a

smile and Sophia returned the unsettling yet kind gesture with one of her own.

"Follow me," Michael said in an impossibly deep voice, turning and retracing his steps to the door.

Mr. Singh resumed his role and gestured for Nicholas and Sophia to keep up. "Do not lag behind, Mr. and Mrs. Felton. A mental institution is not a place where one would wish to be lost."

Michael unlocked the door and pushed it open. "It will be necessary for me to always take the lead. Impolite, but I'd rather you be safe than dead." He walked through the door, followed by Singh, then Sophia, with Nicholas in the rear.

Another orderly stood just inside, on the right. He pushed the door shut then threw a thick metal bar into place across it, securing it within a second band of metal before affixing it with a sturdy-looking lock.

"You mentioned death, Michael," Sophia said, following closely behind Singh as the orderly moved forward down a narrow corridor. "Do you refer to the violent nature of my aunt?"

They came to a second door and Michael paused to unlock it. "Miss Pemble? Violent?" he countered, waiting until they'd all made it through and he'd left the relocking of the door to yet another orderly. "No, ma'am. I've never seen Miss Pemble raise a hand to no one—and I've been here going on fifteen years. No, it's not Miss Pemble you'll need to look out for. It's the rest of the patients housed in the Incurable Ward. We're holding the building together with a bit of wire and paste. Who's to say when one of them will come busting right through. If we make it to the new building without an incident, it will be a miracle."

They started up a set of stairs; three more flights followed until they reached a landing that opened out into a much wider hall than those they'd traversed thus far.

Two signs were hung side by side on the wall they faced, one reading "Curable Ward" with an arrow pointing east; the other, "Incurable Ward," its arrow pointing west. A long line of people stretched the length of the entire hallway, three deep in some spots.

"You'll want to watch out for that lot," Michael said as he led them toward the Incurable Ward. "They've each paid a penny to see the mental cases—and the patients know it. My guess is, if anyone gets loose, it will be one of their numbers that's attacked first."

Sophia grimaced at the very thought. "And Miss Pemble is housed with the rest of the incurable?"

"Don't you worry, ma'am," Michael answered, approaching a set of double doors. "Miss Pemble's doctor says she's a special case. And special cases get cells away from the others. Still, there's—"

"Yet another set of doors that divides her from the rest?" Nicholas asked dryly.

Michael knocked this time, a panel at approximately eye level sliding open. A pair of eyes stared at them.

"Michael Morland, Orderly Number 26127. Brought visitors for Miss Pemble. Nurse Dwyer already cleared it with her supervisor."

The eyes looked at each and every one of them, then the panel slid shut just as quickly as it had opened. A jangle of keys sounded, then a lock gave way and one of the two doors slowly opened inward as if by its own accord. A cacophony of screams and grunting, rants and laughing met Sophia's ears. Nicholas reached for her hand and threaded his fingers through hers.

Michael entered first and the rest of the party followed, the routine becoming second nature.

"Jamie," Michael called above the din. A very small man appeared from behind the door, slamming it shut and seeing to the locks before acknowledging the orderly.

"Michael, will we see you at the tables tonight?"

Michael stopped to answer him, giving Sophia the opportunity to manage a good look at the second orderly. Jamie was standing on a tall stool, and for a very good reason: he was short. Perhaps half the size of Michael, though quite stout. He wore a clean gray uniform exactly the same as his friend's. A number of tattoos peeped out from beneath the pressed fabric. Sophia could not make out each one due to the poor lighting from the tallow candles. But there was a lion on one of his forearms and a poem engraved on the other, the words "love" and "regret" the only ones she could decipher.

"You could not keep me away, Jamie," Michael hollered, his twisted smile appearing again. "Must be off. They're here to see Miss Pemble. Don't want to keep them waiting."

Jamie smiled widely at the three of them, revealing several gold teeth. "Ah, Miss Pemble. Tell the dear that Jamie sends his love."

"I will," Sophia assured him just as something was flung from the first cell. It hit the wall and slowly oozed down it before settling into the crack between the mop-board and the wall.

"Come along, folks," Michael urged, putting himself between the three and where the liquid had been thrown. "Before Wild Willy decides it's time to toss another round."

"Keep your eyes straight ahead," Nicholas whispered to Sophia as they started walking down the hall. The wet splat of more material sounded again.

She was afraid, the guttural cries and screams compelling her to walk more quickly. She was also terribly curious.

Sophia turned her head and slanted a sideways glance toward the first cell. Wild Willy stood at the bars, completely nude and covered in what appeared to be his own excrement. His gaze was glassy and his hands reached out for her, the fingers on both hands mimicking a crawling spider as he attempted to touch her.

"You are the one I've been waiting for," the lunatic cried out. "Free yourself from those who would corrupt you and join me. Join me and we will find the answers you seek!"

"Eyes forward," Nicholas reminded her, pulling Sophia close.

She wanted to be unaffected by the man's words. She craved the ability to possess only a critical and scientific reaction. But her body began to tremble uncontrollably and her vision blurred in a visceral response.

Michael stopped in front of a second set of double doors and waited for the orderly on the other side to slide the eyehole open.

"The worst is over, then?" Nicholas asked him lightly, though he held on to Sophia as though Wild Willy's cell had crumbled from the weight of the man's own mental anguish and released the poor soul.

The door's peephole opened and Michael repeated everything he had told Jamie earlier, then turned back to Nicholas. "Let us hope so."

## 24

There appeared to be only a handful of patients in this wing. Nicholas scanned the hall as Michael bent over and looked through the eyehole into Maggie Pemble's room. Was it something good, or something bad that had earned these incurables rooms instead of cells? After walking the gauntlet past Wild Willy and the other mad-men under the short orderly's care, Nicholas wasn't sure that he wanted to know.

Michael reached for his keys and picked through the collection until he found the one he was looking for. Placing it in the lock, he turned it 'round until the lock clicked open. "Let me go in first and explain things to her. She's sure to be confused after so many years without visitors," he told the small group before pulling the key out and opening the door.

"Maggie Pemble, you are a sight for sore eyes," he exclaimed before going in and closing the door behind him.

"I believe those patients—back there," Singh pointed to where they'd just been, "I believe they would benefit from a more peaceful setting."

Nicholas looked at his friend. Singh's usual air of calm and serenity had vanished, a haunted quality now in his eyes. "I believe you would benefit from the same, my friend."

"It is true enough, sahib. I have heard stories of the

institutions in India. Still I could not have imagined anything such as Mr. Wild Willy and the others in their cells."

Nicholas agreed with Singh. He himself had spent time in arguably some of the most depraved and corrupt places in England and abroad, and nothing had shaken his nerves quite like Bedlam.

At least, not to date, anyway. Who knew what waited for them behind Maggie Pemble's door?

"I will pray for them," Singh said resolutely, which seemed to lessen the worry creasing his tanned forehead.

"As will we all," Sophia put in, looking kindly at Singh.

The door opened and Michael reappeared. "Sorry for the wait. Maggie needed a few minutes to freshen up."

He stepped back and beckoned them inside. Singh went first, with Sophia following closely behind, then Nicholas.

The light in the room was of a different quality than what they'd seen in the rest of the hospital. The flames of beeswax candles and natural brightness from the large barred windows cast a pleasant glow, soft and soothing, across the small but comfortably situated room.

"Don't be shy, you three," a shaky feminine voice called out.

Nicholas looked past the single bed and washstand to a small parlor of sorts. A large Sheridan chair upholstered in velvet stood with its back to them, a curled tuft of white hair visible just above the top.

"Go on and make yourselves comfortable," Michael said. "Maggie has requested tea. I'll see what can be done." Then he left the room, closing the door and locking it behind him.

Sophia moved to approach Miss Pemble first and Nicholas stopped her. He held up his hand and pointed silently at himself and Singh.

She glared, but relented, allowing Nicholas to walk forward. She waited for Singh to follow him before she herself moved.

Nicholas rounded the chair to stand in front of the woman—somewhat relieved to find she was just that, a woman. She was tall and slightly softer in areas where she most likely had not been in her youth. Fine, sharp cheekbones could still be seen beneath the wrinkled skin with its hasty application of powder and rouge.

She had been beautiful in her time, but the years of living in Bedlam had left their mark. Her faint blue eyes were dull and her smile faded to a shadow of what it surely once was.

"Miss Pemble, may I introduce myself. I am Christopher Felton, of Hertfordshire. This is Dr. Pamuk," Nicholas explained, purposely speaking in a slow, steady tone, "and that's my wife, Miriam Felton."

"And which one of you is my relation?" she asked, leaning slightly forward and squinting to see Nicholas better.

Sophia stepped forward and curtsied. "I am, Miss Pemble. Your sister Rosamund was my mother."

Miss Pemble gestured for Sophia to come closer. "Is that so?" She plucked a small pair of silver-rimmed spectacles from a table near her chair and held them up to her eyes. "You do look very much like Rosie. I was not aware that she'd had any children."

"Just me—and I was born some time after you'd left for London," Sophia explained.

Miss Pemble appeared to consider Sophia's words while she returned her glasses to the table and settled back into her chair once again. "We'd thought her barren. What is life without surprises, I suppose. Come, sit down."

Nicholas waited while Sophia chose a chair directly

opposite the woman, then took a seat near a cheery fire-place and watched Singh claim the final chair.

"Now, I'm afraid I have very little time before I must prepare for my seven o'clock performance," Miss Pemble said apologetically. "I would have requested that my understudy appear in my place if I knew you were coming, but there is no time to do so now."

Nicholas nodded in understanding, wondering why Michael had failed to tell them of the woman's delusion. "You continue to perform, then?"

"Oh yes, young man. I could never give up the stage," Miss Pemble replied dramatically. "It is who I am, after all."

A key connected with the lock and Michael pushed the door open, a tea tray in his right hand. He set it down on a low table situated in front of Miss Pemble, then left.

"May I pour, aunt?" Sophia asked.

The woman nodded happily and gazed at Sophia with fondness. "So like your mother . . ." she remarked, failing to give any particulars.

Nicholas watched Miss Pemble as her smile suddenly drooped into a sad frown and tears trembled on her lashes. "Rosamund was such a lovely girl."

The abrupt shift in emotions demonstrated the very fragile nature of Miss Pemble's state—and made Nicholas nervous.

"And the play you're in this evening? Would it be *Dido Queen of Carthage*?" Nicholas asked, anxious to secure the information they required before the woman forgot all about them.

Miss Pemble's eyes burned with anger and she let out a disgusted huff. "That is a play I've sworn never to act in again!"

Sophia handed a cup and saucer to the elderly woman

and returned to the tray. "Why ever not? I have heard such praise for the story."

"Well, that might be," the older woman countered, pausing to take a sip of her tea. "But did you know a woman was murdered because of that play? And—if you can even begin to believe—a dastardly fellow attempted to have me committed to a mental hospital when I told the truth of it. The nerve!"

Nicholas accepted a cup and saucer from Sophia, balancing them in both hands. "That sounds even more interesting than the plot of the play. Would you mind telling us the whole story?"

"Real life is often more exciting than fiction—at least for actors," Miss Pemble replied, taking a second drink of tea. "Now, let me think . . . The year was 1798. We'd been invited to perform in Sussex at a house party given by . . ."

She took a third sip and squinted. "By a peer of the realm. I'm afraid his name escapes me at the moment. When we arrived at the manor house, we were told the host had requested that some of the guests be allowed to participate in the play. Of course I thought such a request was completely outrageous. Still, one does not say no to a lord."

Miss Pemble looked at Sophia in particular. "I am sure that Rosamund taught you such, yes?"

"Of course, aunt," Sophia agreed, slowly stirring some sugar into her teacup. "You had no choice. And the play moved forward, with partygoers amongst the ranks of the actors?"

The woman's outrage burned anew. "Precisely. We had no more than three days to assemble our set, rehearse, and attempt to bring them into line. It was madness. Somehow we managed it—that is until the afternoon before the play."

"Is that when someone was murdered?" Sophia asked, her tone slightly tipped in urgency.

"Murdered?" Miss Pemble repeated, finishing her tea and holding it out for Sophia to refill. "Oh yes, that's right. The lady of the house was found in the nursery—I will spare you the gruesome details. But I saw the man who committed the crime . . . and the man who paid him to do it. I'd overheard them talking in the stables the day before the lady was killed. I was resting in the hayloft after a particularly strenuous assignation with one of the stable hands. The two men entered and began to review a plan of sorts; I was somewhat sleepy and am afraid I did not pay as much attention as I should have. Neither of them uttered the words 'murder' or 'kill.' Still, it was plain that they meant some measure of harm. I spoke with the troupe leader as well as the housekeeper, but without a name for either man, there was little that could be done."

Sophia set the woman's cup down quickly then reached for her reticule. "Was one this man?" she asked, pulling the sketch from her bag and showing it to Miss Pemble.

"The very one!" the woman exclaimed, clapping her hands together. "You are clever, just like your mother."

Nicholas set his untouched tea on the tray. "And you cannot remember his name?"

The imitation French Empire clock on the mantel struck three. "I am sorry but you really must go," Miss Pemble replied, struggling to stand.

"His name, aunt," Sophia urged, stuffing the sketch back inside her reticule and going to Miss Pemble's aid.

The older woman accepted Sophia's arm and allowed her to help her up. "Whose name?"

"The man in the sketch."

"Oh yes, that man," she answered, pulling Sophia toward the door. "He was just in the paper last week; or perhaps last month. I cannot remember his name now.

I will think on it and have it for you when you call tomorrow."

Nicholas rose and stalked after the women, with Singh close behind. "We cannot come back tomorrow, Miss Pemble. It is impossible."

"What do you mean?" she asked, turning on her heels with lightning speed. "You cannot deny me the company of my one and only relation. She is my niece," Miss Pemble wailed, her arms beginning to flail about as though she were drowning. "And I was going to order a special afternoon performance—just for you. Do you think my director would do that for just anyone?"

Her voice grew louder, the blood rushing to her face from the effort. Her eyes widened, gleaming with anger. "The answer is no! And now look what you've done. I should be resting my voice and reviewing my lines. Instead you've upset me greatly."

Nicholas shifted, inserting his broad bulk between Sophia and Miss Pemble. "I did not mean to upset you," he assured the distraught woman in a soothing voice. The sound of someone working the lock outside eased his frayed nerves. "We will come tomorrow. I promise."

Michael pushed the door open and entered the room, his twisted grin focused on Miss Pemble. "Come now, Maggie. Do calm yourself. You've a performance this evening and we can't have you losing your voice. Say good-bye to your visitors."

Miss Pemble stopped flailing her arms and quieted at the sound of Michael's voice. "Until tomorrow," she said to the three, her brain clearly addled from the outburst. And then she bowed an elegant, actorly curtsy that made her erratic behavior seem that much more surreal.

"Wait for me in the hall," Michael ordered them calmly.

Nicholas gently pushed Sophia through the open

door. He gestured for Singh to go next, then followed, stepping over the threshold.

"Do you know, Michael, she looks just as my dear sister Rosamund did at her age. Such a pretty girl, she was. But I had all the talent . . ."

Nicholas pushed the door closed and prayed for the strength to return again tomorrow.

꽃 ꙮ

"Thank you, Jamie. That will be all."

The orderly bowed and backed out of the room, closing the door behind him and locking it.

The Bishop held his candelabra aloft, illuminating the room. And, more specifically, the elderly woman asleep in the narrow iron bed.

He crossed to her, not relishing the task before him. But business was business. And Maggie Pemble threatened his livelihood simply by being alive and occasionally lucid.

Quietly setting the candelabra on a small side table, he sat next to Maggie on the mattress.

She had aged considerably since he'd last seen her. No more than fifteen or twenty years his senior, the faded actress looked more like thirty or forty years older than he. Her hair had gone completely white and her skin looked as though someone had taken a piece of parchment, crumpled it in their fist, then smoothed it out again, leaving a web of fine wrinkles.

The Bishop watched her sleep and felt a sick sense of nostalgia. Maggie Pemble had been bold enough to attempt blackmail, going so far as to offer him her body if he exposed the man who had killed Lady Afton. They would be partners, he and Maggie. She'd painted a pretty picture of what they could do with the money they'd receive once the man responsible for the murder was dangling on their hook.

She'd had no idea of the powerful people backing him, of course. But he'd suspected that even if she had, the fierce woman still would have attempted some scheme.

And he'd always admired her for it.

Maggie turned on her side toward him and slowly opened her eyes. "Is it morning?" she asked, as if she were expecting him.

"No, Maggie. It's the middle of the night. Don't trouble yourself," he replied, reaching out and giving her arm a reassuring pat.

She smiled in thanks. "Good. I am yet in need of rest," she said. Then a sudden smudge of concern tarnished her soft, pale features. "Tell me, who are you? And why are you here at such an hour?"

"You do not remember me?" the Bishop asked, surprised, and yet, not completely.

"Should I?" Maggie countered, squinting as she attempted to make out the features of his face for any familiarity.

He'd done this to her. The Afton murder was early in his career and he had not known the true nature of the men when he'd agreed to work for them. At least, not the full extent of what they'd done and to whom. Even so, it had been his decision to take up with the organization and it had made him a very rich man.

Maggie had simply been in the wrong place at the wrong time. The Bishop controlled his own actions. He could not control those of others—at least not without force.

And that afternoon, when the orderly had sent word that she had received visitors, he knew action was required. And he would be the one to take it.

"I suppose not, though we were friends once, very long ago," the Bishop answered honestly. After all, they had been fellow actors together, until that nasty piece of work Smeade had proved his ineptitude by approaching him in broad daylight, with no cover between them and the entire house party but an implausible excuse concerning his lines.

The stables had been their only option. And the Bishop had wanted to kill Smeade, not Maggie, when she'd come forward. Bedlam seemed a kinder choice for the woman.

At least, at the time it had appeared that way. The Bishop looked into the empty, dark eyes of Maggie Pemble and reluctantly realized he hadn't done right by her.

He was about to fix things, once and for all.

"Tell me, Maggie, did you have visitors today?"

She made to sit up, excitement flashing across her face. "Oh yes, indeed I did. My niece from Hertfordshire and her husband . . . And a doctor of some sort, though he was very quiet and altogether boring."

The Bishop moved his hand to Maggie's shoulder and gently pushed her back down until her head once again lay on the pillow. "And what did you talk about?"

"Oddly enough, they seemed surprised that I was still performing," she answered, her brows furrowing from the very idea. "And they wondered if I remembered anything of a certain play—a rather obscure one."

"What did you tell them?"

Maggie played with the end of her long white braid. "Everything. It's quite an interesting story, after all— murder, intrigue, and a narrow escape."

"Whose narrow escape?" he asked, confused.

Maggie captured him with a look of abject disbelief. "Why, mine, of course. He wanted to put me away in Bedlam. And all because I knew the truth. There was nothing wrong with my mind; the authorities could see that and let me go. Of course I had to watch out for him, which is why I am here. My servants keep me safe."

The Bishop nodded as if she spoke the absolute truth. "This man who tried to send you away. Do you know his name?"

"My niece asked me the very same question," Maggie answered, squinting until her eyes nearly shut. "I'd seen him in the papers; he's no longer an actor, I can tell you that much. No, no, now he's a man of importance."

The Bishop had heard enough. "You are a smart one, Maggie. Always were. I'm afraid you made a mistake this time around, though. And it's time to pay."

He didn't need to see her while she died. Killing was a necessary but gruesome business that he took no pleasure in. And so he reached for her neck with both hands and squeezed, closing his eyes until she stilled.

"Rest now, Maggie."

# 25

"It cannot be true."

Sophia stared at Mr. Bean, waiting for him to tell her she'd misunderstood him and that Maggie Pemble had not been murdered in her bed.

"I'm afraid it is, my lady. An orderly found her this morning at . . ." He paused, taking up the report. ". . . half past eight. She'd been strangled, from the looks of it."

"The question is, by whom?" Sophia asked, mentally reviewing the layout of the hospital. "It is impossible for just anyone to get in or out of the facility."

Mr. Bean read farther down the page. "A Mr. Quilby. Fellow incurable patient. He was sentenced to life in the hospital for killing his entire family."

"And how long has Mr. Quilby been a patient at Bedlam?" Sophia pressed.

"Thirty years."

A hard knock sounded at the door.

"I sent word to Mr. Bourne as well," Mr. Bean explained. "Come in."

The door opened and Nicholas and Mouse stepped inside.

"Mr. Bean, though I've sent my associate Mr. Singh

to Bedlam in order to verify your news," Nicholas said, abruptly gesturing for Mouse to take the seat next to Sophia, "I would very much like to hear it directly from you."

Mr. Bean returned the report to the desk and folded his beefy hands atop it, eyeing Mouse hesitantly. "Unfortunately, your friend will return from Bedlam with the information necessary to confirm my story is true."

"It is true." Sophia looked at Nicholas, carefully choosing her words in deference to Mouse's presence. "Miss Pemble will no longer be able to assist us with the matter. There is nothing that can be done about that now, though. So instead I suggest we investigate other options."

Nicholas raked both hands through his hair. "But that's just it; there are no other options. Tell me, Mr. Bean, have the orderlies been questioned? Did anyone see anything?"

"Of course my men spoke with those on duty. No one had a clue as to how Mr. Quilby was able to leave his room—never mind how the man gained entry into Miss Pemble's."

Nicholas turned to the window and braced his fists against the sill. "Of course no one knows. Because it did not happen," he said savagely over his shoulder.

"I understand your frustration—"

"Do not attempt to placate me, Mr. Bean," Nicholas ground out, turning back toward the group. "You will not like the results."

Mouse looked at Sophia, his eyes wide with concern. "Is there anything I can do, Miss Spoon?"

"No, Mouse," Sophia replied to the sweet boy's offer. "But thank you for asking." She smiled down at him and ruffled his soft, light locks with affection.

"All right," the boy replied, her lighthearted approach having put his mind at ease.

Nicholas stalked to the door and gestured for Mouse to join him. "I will return once Mr. Singh is back from Bedlam. I would ask that no decisions be made in my absence."

"Wouldn't dream of it," Mr. Bean said under his breath, picking up the report once more.

Mouse was halfway over the threshold when he suddenly threw himself backward, rolled until he was clear of the doorway, and slammed into Nicholas, effectively forcing the door shut.

"What in God's name has gotten into you?" Nicholas demanded, fingering a spot on his forehead where he'd connected with the wood.

Mouse scrambled on all fours and took shelter beneath Mr. Bean's desk. "It's him. It's the Bishop." His voice shook with fear.

Sophia ran for the door. "Get out of my way." She shoved Nicholas when he failed to move.

He responded by wrapping his arm around her waist to restrain her.

"He cannot do so," Mr. Bean said. "If it is indeed the Bishop, it's absolutely necessary for you to maintain complete anonymity."

Sophia was frantic. The seconds on the mantel clock ticked by with deafening sound. "We are wasting time. He could have gone by now."

"I will see who this man is. And then we will decide upon a course of action." Mr. Bean gestured Sophia away from the door. "Mr. Bourne, if you please."

Nicholas opened the oak door, careful to hide both Sophia and himself behind its varnished bulk.

Mr. Bean stepped over the threshold, pulling the door closed behind him.

"How could you let him keep me in the dark?" Sophia asked Nicholas, wringing her hands.

Nicholas's gaze met hers, his expression grim. "Because he was right. And you know it; otherwise, nothing would have kept you from clawing your way out that door."

Sophia was unable to deny it.

"Now, I suggest we keep ourselves occupied while we wait for Mr. Bean," Nicholas added, turning Sophia about.

She spied Mouse under the desk, his bird-thin legs tucked up against his chest in his attempt to disappear.

Sophia gasped, ashamed that she'd forgotten about him. "Mouse, my dear sweet boy. Everything is going to be all right. You must believe me."

Mouse shook his head at her words. "You don't know him, miss. If you did, you'd not make such claims."

*Billingsgate Wharf*
SOUTHEAST LONDON

It had taken Mr. Bean nearly five minutes of uninterrupted thought as he sat behind his desk before he told them the identity of the Bishop. He'd wanted to be careful, which was completely understandable when one was preparing to accuse a magistrate of crimes against the crown.

The very crown that said magistrate was employed to uphold and protect.

Mouse had agreed to come out from under the desk once Mr. Bean had assured him that the Bishop was gone.

"Is he the reason you were running when I found you?" Nicholas had asked the boy, who'd taken shelter on Sophia's lap and did not look as though he planned on leaving her anytime soon—if ever.

What had followed was the sad tale of one Mouse

McGibbons. And a sadder story Nicholas had not heard in quite some time.

From the day he'd been able to walk and talk, Mouse had been in service to the Bishop. In a drunken stupor, his mother had sold him to the organization, and there was no going back once such a deal had been struck. Mouse had seen her off and on, and clearly continued to love her despite all of her failings. The tavern owner—the same man Nicholas and Singh had met in the rookery—was more of a parent to Mouse than his own mother, and after she disappeared for good, he'd done his best to look out for the boy.

But Mouse had a gift for thievery. He was smart and quick, small and slim, making it easy for him to sneak about, fit into tight spaces, and lift anything he wanted from unsuspecting individuals. The Bishop appreciated a talented employee, and Mouse was one of his best.

There'd been talk amongst the gang that the Bishop was taking more than his fair share of the profits. Mouse wasn't even sure that he cared about such things, a dry bed and food in his stomach were all that mattered to him. Besides, the Bishop had shown him a kindness or two, telling Mouse more than once that he hoped to groom the boy for a more important role one day.

He'd not intended to follow the Bishop's men that night, Mouse had told Nicholas, Sophia, and Mr. Bean. Then the other lads he was with called him a coward. And he couldn't put up with such an insult. So they'd trailed along through the rookeries, past London Bridge and beyond to Thames Street, until coming to the wharf.

Mouse had known they should turn back when he caught sight of the ships in the harbor. He'd never been able to look at one of the hulking carriers without feeling as if someone had walked across his grave. He had kept his thoughts to himself, afraid the other boys would only tease him further.

"Here we are, sir," Mouse announced now, slowing to a brisk walk as he intruded upon Nicholas's thoughts. "I've no idea when the Bishop's men come and go, so we best keep to the alley."

Mouse picked up speed and trotted down St. Mary Hill, turning right into the alley that ran along the west side of the building. "Here," he whispered, motioning to Nicholas. They halted in front of a wall with a large window in it, some distance from the ground.

"How do you propose we access the window?" Nicholas asked, staring up at the dirty glass.

Mouse lifted his foot and gestured for Nicholas to give him a leg up. "The same way we did that night, only we weren't planning on breaking into the warehouse. Just wanted to see what was inside."

Nicholas boosted the boy onto his back. Mouse scrabbled up to sit on his shoulders, and then slowly stood. "The door is just a touch down the alley. Give me five minutes and I'll have it open."

Mouse pulled a rag from his pocket and covered his fist with it, testing the panes here and there before picking a thin spot and bashing his fist through. His arm disappeared inside the jagged hole for a moment, then he pushed the hinged panel open. "I'll see you in a jig."

The boy's negligible weight eased from Nicholas's shoulders. He looked up in time to see Mouse's fingers gripping the sill before they disappeared, too. A muffled thump sounded as he landed on the floor inside the warehouse.

Nicholas went down the alley and located the door just beyond a timbered loading dock. The building at his back blocked most of the moon's light—both a blessing and a curse. If the Bishop's men were anywhere within the warehouse, it would presumably be more difficult for the henchmen to locate Nicholas and Mouse. Of course, it also meant it would be slower going for the two once they were both inside. Their single lamp was little match for the large building.

The door abruptly popped open and Mouse's small frame appeared in the opening. "Come in, quick."

Nicholas shooed the boy back inside and followed, reaching behind to quietly push the door closed. "Any sign of company?" he asked in a low tone.

"Not that I can see, but it's a big building. Best to keep on our guard," Mouse replied in a whisper, gesturing for the lamp. "Here, I'll lead the way."

Nicholas handed the light over. "Now will you tell me why we're here?"

Mouse nodded. "Remember I told ya some of the boys thought the Bishop was up to something?" He walked quickly down a large aisle that ran down the middle of the room.

"Hardly surprising for someone like the Bishop," Nicholas commented, looking at the shelves on each side of him. They reached nearly to the ceiling of the warehouse and were filled with boxes and wrapped packages of all shapes and sizes.

Mouse continued on down the aisle. "True enough. Stealing is the man's business—only we didn't know he was taking the same thing twice."

They reached the end of the aisle, coming to a bank of high windows that mirrored those on the opposite end.

"What do you mean?" Nicholas asked.

Mouse turned around and held the lamp up. "Do you see all of this?"

Nicholas looked back and scanned what he could see of the shelves. The items near the front were not boxed, that much he could decipher, but little else.

"Give me the lamp," Nicholas said. He walked toward the shelving on the right side of the room, peering at the items that sat waist-high. There was a set of diamond and emerald jewelry. A Fabergé egg. Several antique snuffboxes inlaid with ivory. He angled the lamplight so it illuminated more of the shelving, too many similar items to count glittering in the dim glow.

"So this is where the stolen goods are kept until the Bishop arranges for them to be resold?" he asked, running his fingers across the diamond and emerald necklace.

Mouse suddenly appeared at his side, proving he deserved his nickname. "That's just it. This ain't the place where we deliver the goods. We're told where to go, sometimes what to take, then we steal the valuables and return to the warehouse in Marylebone. This warehouse doesn't figure in what we do. Not at all."

"So the Bishop keeps the most expensive items for himself?" Nicholas pondered aloud, shining the lamp on the emerald necklace. "Why wouldn't he sell them and keep the money?"

Mouse reached out and touched the beautiful necklace, pulling his hand back quickly as if he'd been burned. "It didn't make any sense to me, either. But now that I know he's a magistrate, it does."

"What difference does that make?" Nicholas asked, turning toward the aisle and walking back the way they'd come.

"People we rob pay good money to the magistrates to track down their belongings. More than you'd get reselling," Mouse replied, hurrying to keep pace. "Much more."

The two reached the end of the aisle and moved quietly toward the door. "So your boys were right. The Bishop is up to something. Keeping back the choicest pieces for the reward money—"

"And maybe even for himself," Mouse interrupted, looking back at what amounted to thousands of pounds in items. "There's too much here. He'd be far behind in returning things, and that's not like the Bishop. My guess is he fancies some of these bits and bobs and plans on keeping them for his own."

Nicholas opened the door and stepped out into the cool night air. "Lock up behind me, then come out through the window. I'll be waiting to catch you."

Mouse quickly closed the door and threw the lock, the sound of his small feet running to the window all that Nicholas could hear.

They had the Bishop's name, his hidden warehouse, and the boy who could destroy everything the bastard had worked so hard to attain.

It was only a matter of time.

## 26

*June 17*

THE FARNSWORTH RESIDENCE
MAYFAIR

Sophia looked out at the crowd gathered for the Bow Street benefit, a mixture of impatience, frustration, and sheer nerves washing over her. She should have been pleased with the turnout. Many of the ton's most prestigious families were in attendance, the Farnsworths' ballroom comfortably full. She forced herself to take another sip of lemonade, letting the cool, tangy drink slide down her throat.

"Impressive attendance."

Sophia jumped at the sound of Mr. Bean's voice.

"I apologize, Lady Sophia," he added, looking slightly chagrined. "I did not mean to frighten you."

"Please, there is no need to apologize, Mr. Bean," Sophia answered. "My mind was elsewhere."

He clasped his hands behind his back, a thoughtful look on his face. "Ah, am I to understand that you have not had the opportunity to speak with Mr. Bourne yet?"

"You are," Sophia confirmed, frowning at the mere mention of his name. "I received a letter this morning informing me that both he and Mouse were perfectly safe and that he would see me at this evening's benefit."

Mr. Bean nodded his head in understanding. "I too received a letter, containing the address of the warehouse they visited," he paused as Lord Winthrop said hello to Sophia. "And the property is registered in the magistrate's name."

"Then you will arrest him this evening," Sophia quickly replied, turning to look at the man. "You've proof to tie him to the Kingsmen's thievery. And I will have a confession from him, I promise you. Give me an hour in the Bow Street office with the Bishop and he will admit to my mother's killing."

Mr. Bean released a heavy sigh. "I would like nothing else, my lady. But for reasons I am not at liberty to disclose, we must wait."

"Wait?" Sophia asked, sure she'd misheard the man, then realized how loud she'd spoken. Lowering her voice to nearly a hiss, she said, "You have enough proof to arrest him. There is no reason to delay."

Mr. Bean scowled. "Have a little faith in the Runners, won't you, my lady?"

"I do have faith in you, Mr. Bean—otherwise I never would have come to you for help," Sophia countered angrily, forcing herself to take small sips of cooling lemonade. "I believe it is time to refill my glass."

"Let me, my lady."

"No, thank you," she replied. "Mrs. Kirk has been too long in returning from the retiring room. She was not feeling well earlier today and I should check to see if it is necessary for her to return home."

Mr. Bean bowed before Sophia and waited until she'd curtsied to reply, "Very well. Do let me know when Mr. Bourne arrives, won't you?"

"I will," she answered, then strode toward the refreshments. A few ladies of her acquaintance attempted to ensnare Sophia in conversation, but she simply smiled politely and continued to walk, needing distance between herself and Mr. Bean.

She reached the lemonade table manned by a liveried footman and waited while he refilled her cup. The orchestra began to play "The Sussex Waltz" by Mozart, Sophia's favorite.

She turned to watch the musicians and discovered Nicholas standing near the entrance. He was speaking with a man Sophia did not recognize.

She abandoned her cup and hastened toward the two men, stopping next to Nicholas.

"Mr. Bourne, there you are," she said, hopeful that her cheery tone hid her frayed nerves.

Nicholas wasn't happy to see her, that much was clear. He gritted his teeth, the muscles in his jaw taut beneath his tanned skin. "Lady Afton, I did not know that you were looking for me. Is there something you require?"

Of course he knew she'd been waiting for him. He himself had stated in his early morning letter that he would see her at the benefit ball. Why was he playing such games?

Sophia looked at the man to whom Nicholas had been speaking and smiled politely. He was attempting to look as if he was not listening to their conversation, turning his gaze to the merry gathering of elderly ladies two groups over from theirs. She discreetly examined his profile, his nose capturing her attention.

"Why, yes, I do require something—an introduction."

Nicholas grinned at her, but his eyes had gone black. "Of course. Where are my manners? Lady Sophia Afton, may I introduce to you Mr. Philip Ambrose."

The nose—his nose. She recognized it from her sketch. His hair had thinned and his jowls had grown more pronounced, but there he was, come to life.

Sophia was standing before the Bishop.

Her mouth went dry and she felt her knees begin to buckle as the man bowed before her. Nicholas caught her hand in his.

"A pleasure, Lady Sophia."

She curtsied, demurely lowering her lashes so that she might collect herself. "Thank you, Mr. Ambrose. And what brings you here this evening?"

Sophia concentrated on breathing in and out, the man before her seemingly stealing each intake of air from her very lungs.

"As I was telling Mr. Bourne, I am a magistrate— St. Giles district," he replied, his voice surprisingly soft. "The Bow Street Runners are very important to the work that I do, so I wanted to show my support for the men. And you, Lady Sophia? What is your connection to the Runners?"

"No connection, really," she blurted out, willing her heartbeat to slow.

*Do not fumble in front of this man, Sophia. Do not give anything away.*

She began again. "That is, I support a number of charities and worthwhile endeavors. The Runners are amongst those."

"I must say, myself and my fellow magistrates are thankful for your generous nature. The rewards offered by the members of the ton allow us to provide support to a larger area of London," the Bishop replied appreciatively, though not overly so. "And as you must be aware, the city is in desperate need of such services."

Was he toying with her? Sophia's head began to spin. If she'd been prepared to meet the man face-to-face, then perhaps she could have managed to converse with some semblance of intelligence, allowing her to observe his behavior.

She forced a polite smile in response to the man's false flattery. "You are too kind, Mr. Ambrose, which makes what I must do even more inexcusable. Mr. Bourne, I'm afraid Mrs. Kirk is not feeling well. Might you help me arrange for our carriage to be brought around?"

"Of course, Lady Sophia," Nicholas answered, concern clouding his face. "Let us be off, then. I do not like the idea of Mrs. Kirk being kept from her bed because of me."

"Mr. Ambrose," Sophia said, curtsying again.

"A brief but particular pleasure, my lady," he replied, bowing politely. "And you as well, Mr. Bourne."

The Bishop held his hand out to Nicholas.

Sophia noticed Nicholas hesitate for a split second before he briefly shook the man's hand.

"Lady Sophia," Nicholas murmured, steering Sophia by the elbow. "Do not say anything until we have reached the next room."

Sophia did not bother to argue with him. All she wanted right then was the comfort that his nearness afforded.

"Where the bloody hell is an empty room?" Nicholas growled in a low tone as they left the ballroom and moved down the hall.

Sophia tripped on her hem and stumbled, a quiet cry of anguish escaping her lips.

"I have you," Nicholas reassured her, his arm an iron bar of support at her waist. "Here, Lady Farnsworth's drawing room."

They crossed the threshold and he shoved the door closed. "Lie down. You've had a shock."

"I don't want—" Sophia objected as Nicholas gently placed her on a sofa. Bracing her hands against the cushions, she struggled to sit up. "I don't want to lie down," she protested, falling back as her hands slipped on the cool, smooth silk.

Nicholas knelt down next to her and enclosed her cold fingers in the reassuring warmth of his. "Only moments ago you spoke to the man who decided when and where your mother would die. Be patient with yourself."

"How can I be patient, Nicholas?" Sophia asked angrily, rolling toward him until her cheek rested on his forearm. "And why were you talking to him?"

"We arrived here at precisely the same time. Lord Farnsworth thought it clever to introduce the lowly magistrate to a peer," Nicholas explained. "I had no choice. Either I talked to the bastard or abandoned him for no good reason whatsoever—which seemed a rather risky proposition. We do not want to make him suspicious."

Sophia moved back so she could look into his eyes. "Precisely. Still, I've mucked it up, haven't I? Apparently I can keep my wits about me only when dealing with killers who have attacked other people's families."

"Nothing was amiss," Nicholas assured her. "You were polite and charming, if a bit rushed. He knows nothing more than that you are a lady with a sickly companion. And that is all he ever will know."

Sophia wanted to believe him. She needed to believe him, or she might never convince herself to get up from the sofa. And she would not give the Bishop such power over her. "You must speak with Mr. Bean," she urged. "He is waiting for you."

"Not until you and Mrs. Kirk are safely home. Then I will return and speak with the Runner." He placed a soft kiss on her lips. "We are so close, Sophia. Do not lose hope."

"I could never give up hope," she murmured, more cavalierly than she felt. "It is all I have ever had."

## 27

### The Albany

Mouse waited in the small gazebo, precisely where the note he'd received earlier had told him to be.

A small greenbelt ran behind the Albany building and provided a buffer from the noise of Piccadilly Street. The manicured garden with its flower beds, trees, and walkways was also well suited for concealment. The Bishop's men had slipped into their assigned hiding places the moment he'd sent young Daniel into Mr. Bourne's apartment with a note telling Mouse his mother would meet him in the garden.

The boy's whereabouts had been an educated guess on his part. The Bishop took one last inhale of his cigar before dropping it to the ground and flattening it with his foot. Mr. Bourne, on his own, had set off no alarm bells in the Bishop's mind. Bourne had been distant, hesitant to continue their conversation, and mildly distracted. But that was all perfectly normal. The titled liked to believe that their hearts were full of acceptance, when in reality they wanted nothing more than to wash their hands of the lower classes and be done with them.

The Bishop stared at the back of Mouse from his vantage point behind the gazebo. The boy glanced furtively about. Still, he didn't leave the steps.

The Bishop smiled and decided to draw out the tension a bit longer.

No, he thought in retrospect, Mr. Bourne had not made the Bishop wonder. But Lady Sophia had. She'd done an admirable job hiding her surprise, but she'd clearly not expected to meet him. It must have been quite a shock for her. And he felt sorry for the woman, as strange as that seemed.

He felt sorry for himself as well. He'd been an actor and playwright before the Kingsmen—and a damn happy one at that. But one debt he could not afford to repay had led him down a path from which there was no return.

The Bishop raised his hand and donned his hat, adjusting it at a slightly tipped angle as was his custom. There was no point in torturing the boy further—at least, not yet. He stepped out from behind the gazebo and quietly walked toward him, the soft grass masking each footfall.

"I'm sorry to say I'm not your mother, Mouse," he called out, watching as the boy whirled to face him. "But I am sort of a father to you. And that's something, wouldn't you agree?"

Mouse scanned the park, looking ready to run.

"Don't bother trying to hightail it out of here, Mouse," the Bishop told him matter-of-factly. "I've men in every nook and cranny, so you won't get far."

He stopped in front of the boy and sized him up. "You've grown, Mouse. Might be time to give you a new name."

"Daniel said my mother had come back," the boy spat out, a tremor in his voice. "I was to meet her here, in the park. What have you done with her?"

The Bishop closed his hand over the boy's shoulder. "Don't be angry with Daniel. He broke into Mr. Bourne's apartments and told you of your mother's return because I insisted that he do so. And you know how persuasive I can be."

Mouse ducked away from under his hand and put more space between them. "How did you know 'bout Mr. Bourne?"

"Mouse," the Bishop chided, "you had to know that it was only a matter of time until I found you. You are far too important to me, to the organization, to allow you to leave."

"So now you're gonna kill me? Is that it?" the boy asked, crossing his skinny arms across his small chest in an attempted show of strength.

The Bishop looked at Mouse, mindful of all the boy's promise and intelligence. And remorseful that he'd more than likely never see any of it come to fruition. "Not just now, no, Mouse."

Mouse's eyes grew round with fear but he did not attempt to run. "I see."

"First we will have a conversation about what you've told Mr. Bourne," the Bishop explained. "It is very important that I understand exactly what he knows and what he doesn't."

"A conversation?" Mouse asked irreverently, indicating he'd come to terms with his fate. "Is that what you call it when Topper tortures someone until they tell him what he wants?"

The Bishop smiled. "There's my Mouse. Now come along before you catch your death from the cold."

"You're to leave Mr. Bourne out of this," the boy demanded as if he had any power to bargain. "I'll come along and tell you what you want, but in return I want your word that Mr. Bourne and Miss Spoon will be safe."

God, the boy was admirable. Such pluck for one as young as he was. "I feel it is important for you to know that he was interested in you beyond kindness. Your loyalty should be decided based on all of the facts."

"You won't turn me against Mr. Bourne. He's been good to me, too," Mouse answered, unfolding his arms and planting his hands on his hips.

The Bishop chuckled at the boy's bravado. "I promise you, Mouse, I've no desire to turn you against anyone. In my own way, I respect you. Therefore you must know the truth of the matter; Mr. Bourne has reason to want me captured. That is why Mr. Bourne was in the rookery when he found you. He was looking for me—not that his decision to rescue you should be in any way diminished by this knowledge, but the entire time you've lived under Mr. Bourne's roof, he has been furiously working to apprehend me. Or perhaps even kill me."

"Did you steal from him?" Mouse asked, his brow furrowing as he took in the unexpected information.

The Bishop contemplated the boy's words. "In a manner of speaking, yes, I did. And something much more important than jewels or art, something I should most likely pay for with my life. And while I am a fair man, if it is to come down to my life or his, make no mistake, Mouse, I will always choose mine."

If he'd had the time, the Bishop would have allowed the boy to remain in the park to puzzle out just what he thought and felt about Mr. Bourne now that he knew the truth.

But he could not wait any longer. "We must go, Mouse."

"You'll leave him alone, then, if he stays far away?" the boy demanded.

"That all depends on how he chooses to respond to your absence. And that even I cannot predict."

Nicholas wanted a drink.

He stared out the window of the hired hackney and counted townhomes in an effort to ignore the incessant need. It ebbed when he was with Sophia, as if she made him stronger, even better.

"As if?" he asked himself out loud, losing track of how many homes he'd counted and beginning again.

Ignoring his need for a drink when he was alone, his mind and body idle, had always been more difficult. Now thinking about life after the Bishop's capture, when Sophia would be his forever, made it easier to deny the urge.

A conversation he'd had with Carrington began to replay in his mind:

"I've broken nearly every law within the Corinthian code—and a few outside of it as well. Carmichael could not overlook such things. But I've come to terms with the possible consequences."

"And those are?" Nicholas had pressed as a fine misting of rain began to fall.

"My expulsion from the Corinthians," Dash had answered simply. "Still, we'll have captured Smeade. And that's what matters."

The bay's hooves had slipped on the wet street, but he'd recovered and held his stride. Nicholas had called reassuringly to the horse and kept his hands firmly on the reins. "Are you sure?"

"What on earth do you mean?" Carrington had countered.

It had sounded to Nicholas as though his friend genuinely wondered at the question, though he'd found such a thing hard to believe. "Your whole life has been dedicated to the Young Corinthians. How could you surrender it so easily?"

Carrington considered the question while he'd swiped at the rain gathering on his greatcoat. "Elena."

"Come, now. Everything for a woman?" Nicholas had pressed, unconvinced.

"Yes, Bourne. We're capturing Lady Afton's killer not only for justice, but a second chance at life. Elena is my second chance."

It had been inconceivable to Nicholas that any man would think it a sound idea to put his entire future in the hands of a woman.

"I see," Nicholas had replied dryly, then slowed the bay with a tug on the reins. "Well, as for me, I'm looking forward to a second, third, and perhaps even fourth chance at *life* with Lady Whitcomb. Widows are rather generous, I find."

Carrington had arched an eyebrow sardonically. "You'll never change, will you, Bourne?"

Nicholas had by then brought his horse to a stop and jumped down. "Did you honestly think I would?"

The memory faded now as Nicholas considered Dash's words in a different light—one that involved Sophia.

"Goddammit all to hell," he muttered with vague disbelief. Dash had been right—about everything.

Somehow Sophia had expanded his horizons beyond drink and eventual death. She'd given him a future, just as Elena had for Dash.

Nicholas lost track of the number of townhomes yet again, but this time around he did not mind so much. It felt good to admit he'd been wrong. Not that he had any plans to inform Dash. Still, the revelation was satisfying all the same—unexpected, slightly intimidating, and more than he had ever allowed himself to believe could be true.

The hackney rolled to a stop in front of the Albany. Nicholas opened the door and stepped out, paying the driver his wage and a tip. Just as he turned toward the steps, Singh burst through the building's front door.

"Sahib, you must come at once," Singh cried out,

clearly very upset. "It is young Mouse. We cannot find him."

Nicholas took the stairs two at a time and met Singh at the door. "What do you mean?"

"Just that, sahib. I went to check on him at midnight as I normally do and he was not in his room."

"He has a tendency to hole up in the most unusual spots," Nicholas answered, stalking down the hall toward his apartment. "Did you look in my dressing room? He often sleeps on the servant's cot there."

Singh trotted beside him. "Yes, sahib, I looked in all of the usual places that young Mouse prefers."

Nicholas reached his front door and shoved it open with enough force to send the oak panels bouncing back off the wall. "It is possible that he is simply playing a game with you," Nicholas suggested, scanning the front room before continuing down the main hall. "He is a boy, after all."

"Mr. Singh, is that you? Have you found him, then?" The cook's voice carried clearly up the servants' stairs, followed shortly by the woman herself. "Oh, beg your pardon, Mr. Bourne. I thought perhaps Mr. Singh had some news of Mouse."

Nicholas did not want to believe that the boy was actually missing. A game of hide-and-seek was far less threatening, and did not twist at his gut the way—

God, if the Bishop had him . . . That would mean Nicholas had tipped his hand at the benefit. It would be his fault if anything happened to Mouse. And if the Bishop knew that the boy was connected to him, then he surely had figured out Sophia's involvement as well.

It was time to call in assistance.

"Mrs. Clark, gather Molly and Edwin, please, and meet me in the front drawing room in five minutes." His words were grim, clipped with command.

Mrs. Clark nodded her head quickly and disappeared back down the stairs.

"And what would you have me do, sahib?" Singh asked.

Nicholas rummaged in his vest pocket and pulled out a number of bills, handing them to his friend. "I want you to go and collect Lady Sophia and her companion. Tell them they must return with you to the Albany at once—and do not take no for an answer, Singh. Tell the driver to take you to Number Five Balfour Place, in Mayfair."

Singh embraced Nicholas, hugging him tightly. "I will not disappoint you, sahib."

Before Nicholas could respond, Singh turned on his heels and ran down the hall, the thud of the door opening loud in the still apartment.

Nicholas stared at the wall, wondering if they'd failed Mouse. He felt sure there was nothing they could have done differently, short of imprisoning the boy, which would have made no sense.

*There was nothing they could have done differently.*

*They*. Nicholas had included himself in the pardon.

"Goddammit, Singh," he said out loud, fighting a surprising and unwelcome swell of emotion. "You've managed to teach me to be kind—and to myself, of all people."

Nicholas leaned against the wall, his legs suddenly weak. He was scared for Mouse. Thankful for Singh's presence. And humbled by Sophia's love. All of his life, he'd run from emotional entanglements, certain such things would lead to his undoing. And at that very moment, he proved himself right. He was undone. Anxious and angry, in love and loved.

And he was still alive. Nicholas beat his fist against the wall and bowed his head. He was more than still alive. He'd been reborn.

Footfalls on the stairs signaled the servants coming up for the meeting.

Nicholas pushed off from the wall and ran both hands through his hair, the tingling of his scalp clearing his mind.

"We'll find the dear boy," Mrs. Clark said to Nicholas as she passed him on the way to the drawing room. "Don't you worry one bit."

"You are absolutely right, Mrs. Clark," Nicholas replied, following behind her. "We will find Mouse and bring him home."

"Oh yes, we will," a voice chimed in behind Nicholas. "And the bloke responsible for this will pay harshly!"

Nicholas had formed a family of sorts. "Goddammit, Singh," he said out loud, "you bloody, blessed man."

## 28

*June 18*

Sophia stood on the threshold of the front parlor in Nicholas's apartment. Singh gestured for her to enter. She hesitated, the gathering of men and the push and pull of their serious conversation foreboding.

"Mr. Singh," Sophia began, stepping tentatively into the room, "are you at liberty to explain yourself now?"

Nicholas rose from the sofa, where he had been deep in conversation with a young man whom Sophia vaguely recognized. "Sophia, Mrs. Kirk, thank you for coming. I apologize for the early hour."

"Please, will you tell me what this is all about?" Sophia asked as she hurried toward Nicholas. "Mr. Singh gave us very little information."

Nicholas took her arm. "Come with me."

"Of course," she replied, her nerves hardly soothed by his serious demeanor.

Lettie moved to follow her. "No, I will speak with Mr. Bourne—alone," Sophia told her.

Lettie nodded soberly and looked about the roomful of men. "I'll make tea, then."

"None for me, thank you," Sophia replied, smiling assuredly at her dear friend. "I will come and find you in the kitchen when Mr. Bourne and I have finished."

She allowed Nicholas to steer her through the gathering. "I am growing impatient."

"I understand, Sophia," Nicholas said, heading for the back of the house.

Yet another man, his identity unknown to Sophia, blocked the closed study door.

"I really must demand an explanation now," Sophia whispered, her fingers tightening on Nicholas's arm as they stopped in front of the stranger.

"Lady Sophia," Nicholas told him.

The other man remained silent; the only discernible sign he'd heard Nicholas was a slight nod.

Nicholas released Sophia's arm as the man reached behind him, opened the study door, and stepped aside.

"Sophia." Langdon looked up from his seat behind Nicholas's desk, his voice as stern as the look in his eyes. "Please come in. You too, Nicholas."

Langdon gestured for her to take one of two leather chairs situated in front of the desk.

"Langdon?" Surprised and confused, Sophia braced herself momentarily against the supple leather before sitting. "What is going on?"

Nicholas dropped into the chair next to her, his face as grim as his brother's. "Mouse has disappeared and we believe he's been taken by the Bishop. I thought it best for you to be brought here—for your own safety."

Sophia's heart missed a beat. She was terrified for Mouse and startled by Nicholas's decision to tell his brother about the case—so much so that when she opened her mouth to reply, nothing came out.

"Langdon knows, Sophia," Nicholas added. "I've told him all that we know about the Bishop. When we discovered Mouse was gone, I knew that even with all of my connections, I could not fight the Bishop on my own. I needed the Young Corinthians—we needed them."

"You told the Corinthians, without consulting me?" Sophia whispered, angered and hurt.

Langdon thumped his fist upon the desktop. "And you went after your mother's killer without consulting me, Sophia. It seems you are both at fault."

Sophia started at Langdon's unexpected show of emotion. "I am sorry. I truly am. But if I had told you what Dash and Nicholas had discovered when they caught Mr. Smeade, would you have allowed me to be involved in the search?"

"Of course not!" Langdon shouted, slamming his fist against the desk a second time. "And do you know why? Because of where we are now. One boy missing, your life in danger, my brother's life in danger . . ."

Sophia watched Langdon pause and take a deep breath. She had never heard him raise his voice. "I never meant for it to turn out this way, Langdon. You must believe me."

"Whether I do or do not is hardly the concern now. You've embroiled yourself in a deadly game. And the Bishop is an expert chess player, Sophia. Some might even say the best."

Sophia looked at him for an explanation.

"The Corinthians have known of the Bishop and his involvement in the Kingsmen gang for years." Langdon picked up a document from one of the piles spread out before him. "It was only recently that his identity as a magistrate was brought to light. Corruption is widespread within the magistrates, and we've not managed to find one who would give up the rest. We'd hoped to convince the Bishop to cooperate by threatening his gang.

"There are many channels of business that a gang such as the Kingsmen must rely on to keep turning a profit, including syndicates on the Continent. If the Bishop did not agree to help us, we were going to reduce the channels available to him until he saw the error of his ways."

"You were going to blackmail him?" Sophia asked, beginning to understand the ramifications.

Langdon nodded. "That was the plan. Your Mr. Bean was told to stand down. We had an agent in place, prepared to approach the Bishop. And then I heard from Nicholas."

"Do not be angry. We were only doing what you would have done in the same situation," Nicholas told his brother.

Langdon stared hard at Nicholas, his thinly veiled frustration obvious. "You've endangered Sophia, brother. I believe that gives me the right to be angry."

"Her safekeeping was always my top priority," Nicholas replied. "Surely you must know this."

"Frankly, I believe I don't know anything about you."

"Enough," Sophia said. "There will be time to discuss such matters after Mouse is found. Langdon, has our investigation ruined all hope of you apprehending the Bishop? Or is there something that can be done?"

Langdon looked at the papers he still held in his hand. "As for Mouse, yes, I believe there is something yet that we can do for the boy."

"And capturing the Bishop?"

"You will not be involved in his apprehension," Langdon said, his voice hard. "Do you understand? I will have your word."

Sophia looked at Nicholas. "Don't let him do this. Tell him he is wrong," she begged.

"He's not wrong, Sophia," Nicholas answered. "We are not spies, you and I. Hell, he'll most likely regret allowing *me* to accompany the Corinthians."

She wanted to argue; wanted to tell both men that they could not do such a thing.

But it was a lie. The two loved her. And Sophia could not argue with love.

"Can she at least see him when he's brought in?" Nicholas asked on her behalf.

Langdon looked at Sophia, reluctant understanding in his eyes. "Once he is safely behind bars, you will have the opportunity to voice everything you've ever wanted to tell the Bishop. Is that enough?"

"It will have to be," Sophia replied.

*Covent Garden*

Nicholas's mount spooked at a drunken reveler, dancing nervously sideways. He tightened Guinevere's reins and murmured gently to the mare, settling her. "Despite Mouse's connection to the Bishop, he had no clue where his headquarters were. We searched his secret warehouse for a clue to the location, to no avail. How did you find it?"

He and Langdon had ridden through the backstreets of London to Drury Lane. A host of Young Corinthian agents did the same, coming in twos and fours from wherever it was that spies came from.

Langdon pointed down Blackmore Street and turned his horse. "It was not easy. Members of the Kingsmen gang are not eager to give up information concerning the Bishop. And he prefers to stay unpredictable. The man spends no more than a night holed up in one of his establishments before moving to another. Luckily, we finally found a member of the Kingsmen who valued his life more than his boss's."

"You threatened injury?" Nicholas asked. He'd learned enough details of his brother's secret life that evening to make him wonder what more could be lurking behind Langdon's calm façade. He hoped there was much more; it made him less perfect—and far more like Nicholas.

"No, Nicholas. We are not in the business of killing," Langdon answered, clearly disappointed that the thought had entered his brother's mind.

Nicholas shrugged his shoulders. "Rather less exciting than I'd hoped."

Langdon smiled for the first time that night. "Well, most of it is, and this informant was no exception. He had quite a history with the Runners, including burglary, assault, even murder—though there was not enough proof to charge him on that count. Still, when the Corinthians were brought in to interrogate him, he cracked. Gave us the location of the Bishop's headquarters as long as we kept him off a ship bound for New South Wales."

"So you let him go?" Nicholas pressed, trying to see the honor in such an act.

Langdon's horse tossed his head. "It's a balancing act, Nicholas," his brother told him, patting the horse on the neck. "As you should well know, nothing in life is ever all right or all wrong. There are the gray spaces in between, where one has to figure out for themself the best course of action that will lead to the most positive outcome."

"Sounds tricky," Nicholas replied, mindful of the parallels between the situation Langdon referred to and his relationship with Sophia.

Langdon nodded. "You have no idea just how tricky. The Corinthians test me as a man on every level. It makes me a better person—and, eventually, will make me a better husband to Sophia."

Nicholas had never known his brother to be anything but honest and forthright. So was he imagining the subtle comments and references? Or was Langdon implying that he suspected something between his fiancée and his brother?

If the evening had revealed anything to Nicholas, it was that he did not know Langdon nearly as well as he'd always believed.

He looked at his brother and waited for him to do the same before speaking. "Is that right?"

"Of course," Langdon answered, no detectable emotion on his face. "I imagine that in every marriage there are times when the other does something you thought could never be forgiven. My work with the Corinthians has taught me to think before acting, to consider all of the information, including the effects the issue will have on others."

"Are you trying to tell me something?" Nicholas asked, hardly able to stand his and Sophia's secret any longer. "Because if you are, I wish that you would simply spit it out rather than wrapping it in—"

Langdon raised a finger to his lips. Two men on horseback appeared in the roadway. They came slowly toward the brothers, prompting Nicholas to reach for the knife tucked into his boot.

"My lord, the men are in place," the man on the dappled gray reported to Langdon.

Nicholas loosened his grip on the knife. "Are we close?"

They'd been riding the back alleys of Drury Lane for nearly the entire length of the theatre district, leaving Nicholas to wonder where they were going.

"The Bishop owns the Gloriana Theatre. According to our man, he will be there. It is the last building on the Lane," Langdon answered. He clucked his horse into a walk and gestured for the men to follow.

"Bloody hell," Nicholas murmured, unsure of whether he should be thankful that he and Sophia had not encountered the Bishop when they'd visited the theatre, or angry that they had come so close and still not discovered him there.

"What was that?" Langdon asked.

Nicholas brought his horse even with his brother's. "Nothing. Now, what is the plan?" he asked, genuinely curious . . . and thankful for the distraction.

One of the Corinthians cleared his throat. "Sir, do you think it's a wise decision to allow Mr. Bourne inside the theatre? The Bishop is never without at least two of his men, and there is the cast and crew to take into consideration as well."

"Cast and crew?" Nicholas repeated, confused.

"There is a dress rehearsal for the troupe's upcoming play tonight," Langdon explained. "Hopefully, the hour is late enough—or early enough, as is the case—that they have finished and are gone by now. If not, then yes, there will be the cast and crew to contend with—though I highly doubt any of them will stand with the Bishop. We have no proof that anyone connected to the theatre knows anything more of the man than that he is a magistrate."

Nicholas pictured the interior of the theatre as well as the back of the stage. There were many places to hide a young boy, especially given the added benefit of a busy rehearsal.

"As to your question, Damon," Langdon continued, turning his head to look at the young man. "My brother, with very little help, managed to track down two of the most vile men to walk the earth. And while it was necessary for him to ask for our help, that only proves to me that he is smart, as well as capable. So yes, I do think it's a wise decision—and one that I will stand by should any other choose to foolishly ask."

Damon cleared his throat, but wisely followed up with silence rather than words.

"Here we are," Langdon announced, pointing to a

hitching post outside a darkened butcher shop. "Leave the horses. We will walk the rest of the way."

The men halted their mounts in a line, each dismounting with silent ease.

"How will we get inside?" Nicholas asked, looping his leather reins about the post.

Langdon finished tethering his horse and pulled a pocket watch from his vest. "Do you recall Topper, the man who gave us the Bishop's whereabouts?"

Nicholas nodded as he completed the knot.

"He should be waiting for us at the back door of the theatre," Langdon offered, returning the watch to his pocket. "The Bishop knows nothing of your ties to the Corinthians. So, with any luck, he believes that only you will be coming for Mouse—he won't expect an entire unit of trained spies."

"I'm afraid luck is not often on my side, brother," Nicholas answered dryly, the weight of Mouse's welfare heavy on his shoulders.

The two Corinthians stepped back from their horses and Langdon gestured for them to fall into line. "Not to worry. It is always on mine."

## 29

### The Gloriana Theatre
#### DRURY LANE

He did not enjoy *Romeo and Juliet,* the Bishop reflected as he examined a playbill for the upcoming production. Never had, and most likely never would. He wondered if Shakespeare's plays were often performed in America—a question he planned on soon being able to answer for himself.

He looked at Mouse, who sat across from him in the tidy theatre office on Drury Lane. The boy's feet dangled from the high seat of the battered wood chair as he fidgeted with his hands.

"Do you know, Mouse, in America there is plenty of opportunity for all—even a young boy such as yourself."

Mouse looked at the Bishop as if he'd spoken in Latin. "What do I care about America? There's Indians there who cut off your scalp and wear it like a prize. And that's only if you make it across the ocean—which most do not."

The Bishop smiled at the boy. "I have a sound ship, Mouse. One fit to transport everything you saw in the warehouse—and more. And I have a mind to bring you with me."

"So you're not going to kill me?" Mouse asked disbelievingly.

"No, I don't think so," the Bishop answered, nearly as surprised as Mouse. "You have grown on me. Besides, I will need help setting up my business in America. And I believe you might make a good partner."

The boy slid forward in the chair until his feet rested on the floor. "What do you want with America, anyway? Just take your money and get out of London. Mr. Bourne won't follow you. I'll make sure of it."

"Oh, Mouse, if it were only that easy," the Bishop replied, a loud crash reverberating in the back of the house downstairs.

Both startled at the noise, the Bishop's gaze sliding toward the closed door.

"Who practices plays in the dead of night?" Mouse asked, looking down at the floorboards as if he could see the actors below.

The Bishop stood up from his chair and leaned over his desk, pulling the window curtains open and staring out at the dark street. No one was there.

"America, sir?"

The Bishop returned to his seat. "Yes, America. You see, one way or another, word is going to get out that I've kept the choicest pieces of the organization's plunder for myself. And that will not please my boss. Not at all. But an ocean between us should keep me safe."

Another crash ripped through the theatre, this time followed by yelling and several grunts of pain.

"I believe your Mr. Bourne has come for you," the Bishop told Mouse, standing again.

Mouse jumped up from his chair and moved toward the office door. "He's no match for the boys. You've got to call them off before somebody gets hurt."

"It's as I told you in the park, Mouse," the Bishop answered, opening the top desk drawer and removing a thick-handled, wickedly sharp knife, "even I cannot predict what others will do. If Mr. Bourne chooses to come for you, he must go through Paddy and the boys first. It is only fair."

Heavy footfalls sounded in the hall, then Paddy's deep, Irish brogue yelled out, only to be cut off mid-sentence.

The Bishop pointed the knife at Mouse, gesturing for him to move back. "Stay behind me, Mouse, and no harm will come to you."

Someone threw themselves against the door, their weight rattling the hinges. Another battering followed, and another, until the upper right panel of the door gave way.

"Stay behind me. Do you hear?" the Bishop yelled at Mouse as he backed up toward the wall.

A second panel was crushed to pieces, then one more charge from whomever stood on the opposite side and the door fell into the office, nearly hitting the Bishop before it landed at his feet.

"Stay back," the Bishop ordered, but Mr. Bourne charged over the threshold and came straight for him, then continued on past. The Bishop swung around in time to see the man lunge across the desk and grab for what looked to be the bottom of a small boot at the open window.

He didn't see *Mouse*!

Suddenly the room filled with men and the Bishop was shoved against the wall, one man holding his wrists together as another tied them with a length of rope to restrain him.

Bourne roared and slammed his fist on the desktop.

"We have him, Nicholas," another man assured him, physically turning Mr. Bourne until he was looking straight at the Bishop.

"Is the boy dead?" the Bishop asked, the rope beginning to cut at his wrists. "Tell me."

Bourne spared only a moment to capture him with a look of pure fury before running from the room, the sound of his footfalls on the stairs quickly muffled by the screams and confusion from the actors below.

*June 19*
YOUNG CORINTHIANS HEADQUARTERS
LONDON

Sophia stared at the man sitting across from her, a wooden table all that separated them. She had been blindfolded, loaded into a carriage, and driven the good Lord only knew where, only to be unloaded from the carriage and led into a building. From there, someone had taken her hand and pulled her along, down a set of stairs and then another, through a room that smelled of alcohol and medicinal supplies, until she was finally allowed to remove her blindfold.

Sophia would do it all again, ten more times, for the opportunity to interrogate the Bishop. After all, she had been through hell and back to get to this point; what was a bit of discomfort in comparison to such a journey?

She knew hers were not the first set of questions the man had faced. Langdon and Nicholas had returned to the apartments at the Albany at half-past three in the morning, leaving the Bishop in the capable hands of Lord Carmichael and a few of the more senior Corinthian agents. It was now nearly nine a.m. The Bishop looked tired. He'd revealed very little in his first interview, admitting only to the crimes he'd committed as a magistrate.

But Sophia had knowledge that neither the Bishop nor the Corinthians did. And she would use it to her full advantage, no matter what.

She did not expect the Young Corinthians to value her work; after all, how could they when they knew nothing of it? Sophia stared at the Bishop, watching him study her, and decided that if she was successful in convincing him to talk, she would make sure the Corinthians came to appreciate the value of scientific forensic work.

She had to break the man first.

"Do you have news of the boy?"

Sophia tilted her head and looked at the Bishop. "Have they not told you?"

She watched as his bound hands, placed on the table-top, trembled slightly. "I see," she said mournfully, casting her eyes down in a mournful pose. "Mouse worked for you, correct?"

The Bishop blinked hard. "Yes. He ran errands, that sort of thing."

"Oh, do we have to play this game?" Sophia asked sadly. "It is hardly respectful to lie when speaking of the dead—particularly when you played a part in their demise."

"I told him to stay behind me." His voice was controlled, even, but a tic was developing in his right eyelid.

Sophia pursed her lips with disdain. "Did you really expect him to listen? After all, you stole him away from his family when he was only a very small child."

"His mother sold Mouse to me," the Bishop offered, resettling in his seat. "And he was far better off with me than with his prostitute mother."

"Are you sure? You had the boy picking pockets by the age of five; stealing from homes and businesses by seven because he was inordinately skilled and small for his—"

"The boy was nine," the Bishop spat out, "get your facts straight."

Sophia looked down at the papers she'd brought with her, flipping through each as though searching for something. "Really? I feel certain he was seven."

He pounded his fist on the table, shaking the stack of

documents. "He was nine. I think I would know better than you."

"I absolutely agree," Sophia answered, looking up from the stack and offering him an apologetic look. "I'm sorry. Of course you would remember. He spent most of his life in your employ—as a member of the Kingsmen. To Mouse, you were family. Tell me, was he as dear as he seemed? I spent very little time with him, but he made an impression."

The Bishop flexed both hands then folded them together. "Why are you doing this?"

"I'm afraid I don't know what you mean," Sophia replied in a low, even tone.

The Bishop gazed at her, a haunted quality in his eyes. "The others asked after businesses, bank accounts, who I run, who runs me. Not you; you seem intent on making me suffer."

Sophia listened to the timbre of his voice. It was growing wearier with each syllable, as if he was running out of will.

"You assume I'm a monster, but I am not," he continued. "I never wanted any part in this. Do you believe me? You should. All I ever wanted to do was act; oh, maybe own my own theatre one day. Acting made me happy. Until I made a mistake. It was a small something. Still, it changed my life forever—and turned me into what you see now. I am cold and calculating—one cannot exist in my world and be anything else. And now I only want the things I do not have."

Sophia measured her breathing and sank slightly in her chair, effectively almost disappearing from the room, but still present enough so that the Bishop would continue his confession.

"It was the death of your mother that destroyed any hope I had of escape."

Her heart stopped for a split second and Sophia willed herself to remain calm. "In what way?"

The Bishop's voice was failing him. Even so, he looked determined to continue. "I didn't understand at first how the Kingsmen worked. I thought that one could work off their debt, then be released. Your mother's murder was to be my last job. I hadn't killed anyone up to that point—nor did I have any desire to do so. I took advantage of Smeade's recent recruitment and convinced my superior to allow him to do the deed with my supervision. But they twisted my involvement around, you see. Once I'd played a part in a murder, they had me for life. Stealing and cracking a few skulls was nothing the Runners had time for. The death of a lady, though? Now, that was something to build a career on."

"They blackmailed you," Sophia replied, her eyes locked with his. "And you exacted your revenge by stealing from those who'd stolen from you."

The Bishop closed his eyes for a moment and sighed deeply. "That's far more poetic than I deserve. But yes, I continued to act. I rose in the Kingsmen's ranks, played the loyal lieutenant, and quietly robbed the organization blind. And I nearly got away with it, too."

Sophia bit the inside of her cheek to keep from crying. "Then you are not the man responsible for my mother's death?"

"I am to blame, at least in part," he answered, opening his eyes again. "Understand me, though. She would have died even if I'd refused. And I am sorry for that. As I said before, I'm not a monster."

"Prove it to me."

The Bishop furrowed his brows in confusion. "How can I, my lady? What's done is done."

"Tell me who you work for," Sophia urged him.

"If I do that, I'm a dead man."

"Not necessarily," Sophia replied simply. "You tell me

the name, and I will see what can be done about your American dream."

The Bishop unfolded his hands, placing both palms on the table, understanding lighting his eyes. "You lied to me. Mouse isn't dead. That is the only way you could know of my plan."

"I never told you he was," Sophia countered, "merely that it was rude to speak so of the dead."

He looked down at his hands, a small smile appearing on his haggard face. "You're better at this than all of those men out there combined."

"I too had my life taken away," Sophia answered the man, then rose from her chair. "Which left me with an abundance of time to plot my revenge. That is where our similarities end. For I have every intention of reclaiming mine."

## 30

*June 20*
STONECLIFFE HOUSE
MAYFAIR

Climbing from the hired hackney, Nicholas realized he had been home in England for nearly two months, but this was only his second visit to the family townhome. He stood on the sidewalk and looked up at the impressive pile. He had very good reasons for staying away, Smeade and the Bishop the most obvious two. Still, he had to admit, even without the search for Lady Afton's killer, Nicholas was fairly sure that he would have avoided the townhome one way or another.

The sky above him opened up and large, fat drops of rain began to fall in earnest. Still, Nicholas remained standing in front of Number 3 Grosvenor Street. He was waiting for the sense of dread that always appeared whenever he set foot on his father's property. The dread was habitually accompanied by the humbling realization that he was nothing compared to Langdon, and the inescapable truth that he never would be.

Nicholas brushed his wet hair from his eyes and continued to wait. His greatcoat grew heavier and wetter by the second, soaking up the rain as if it were made to do so, and yet he waited.

"Nicholas!" Sophia stepped from her carriage and

joined him on the sidewalk, followed closely by Mrs. Kirk. "What on earth are you doing out here? You are soaked from head to toe."

He ventured one last look at the exterior of the house, daring the old, tired feelings to return. But they were gone. "Saying farewell to the past, as it happens."

"Isn't it possible to do so in front of a warm fire?" Sophia asked, adjusting her parasol to cover Mrs. Kirk.

"I suppose so," Nicholas answered, smiling widely at the woman he loved. "I do like a bit of drama, though. Besides, I've always let the past define me. And now that I am embracing my future, I want to leave it behind. Out here, in the pouring rain, where it belongs."

"A future?" Sophia asked, either hesitation or excitement in her voice, Nicholas could not quite tell which.

"Yes," he answered, "a future. Or, to be more precise, our future. I don't know why Langdon summoned us here, but I am not going to waste the opportunity. We owe it to my brother to tell him the truth. And we owe it to ourselves. I do not want to spend one more day without you—nor you, Mrs. Kirk," he added dryly.

"Then I suggest we go inside before we're all swept away," Mrs. Kirk said, picking up her skirts in an attempt to keep the hem somewhat dry.

Nicholas gestured for the women to go first, then followed them to Langdon's front door. The footman, who had been patiently waiting to assist them, bowed and opened the door wide.

"Good God, have you all drowned?" Langdon exclaimed, rushing to Sophia's side and relieving her of the dripping silk parasol.

Nicholas allowed a footman to remove his greatcoat, then shook his head. "Almost," he said meaningfully, discreetly locking glances with Sophia.

"Yes, well, from the looks of it we're readying for a biblical flood in the entryway," Langdon replied, handing the parasol to the footman who had assisted Sophia in removing her pelisse. "So if you wouldn't mind, Mrs. Kirk, James here will show you to the parlor, where tea and a seat by the fire await you."

Mrs. Kirk curtsied before the duke and dutifully followed James down the hall, looking over her shoulder and giving Sophia a supportive smile.

"As for you two, come with me," Langdon continued, calling a maid over and asking that she bring drying towels to his study before walking on.

"You have news of the Bishop, I hope," Nicholas said as he followed his brother past the green drawing room, Sophia by his side.

Langdon sighed at his impatience. "All will be revealed, Nicholas."

They reached the study at the back of the townhome, the maid Langdon had asked to bring the towels hurrying toward them from the servants' stairs.

"My lord," she said in greeting, handing one length of linen to Sophia and one to Nicholas. "Will there be anything else?"

Langdon gave her a brief smile. "Yes, please. Have tea sent up in thirty minutes. That will be all."

"Of course, my lord," the maid dutifully replied, bobbing a curtsy before turning back down the hall.

"Shall we?" Langdon asked, waiting as Sophia entered the study, and then Nicholas.

Sophia took her seat in front of Langdon's large mahogany desk, patting dampness from her cheeks and chin.

Nicholas took the opportunity to swipe his towel across his face and neck. "Don't remain standing on my account," he told Langdon, who appeared to be waiting to take his seat.

Langdon nodded in understanding and sat down, settling into his chair. "As to the Bishop . . ."

"Starting right in, then," Nicholas commented, tossing the linen onto a nearby chair and dropping into his seat.

"He was found dead in his cell this morning," Langdon continued, his face somber, disappointed. "An apparent suicide."

"I'd told him I would see to his plan for America," Sophia blurted out, sitting forward on the edge of her seat and reaching out to grasp the edge of the desk with one hand. "He was going to tell me the name of his superior! He was not suicidal, I am sure of it."

Langdon looked at Sophia. "I do not know what happened between you and the Bishop yesterday—yet something else about you, Sophia, that seems to have slipped my notice." He frowned down at the crystal paperweight sitting on his desk. "Still, I have to agree with you. I find suicide unlikely. A full investigation is under way. But he is dead either way, and with him, the search for your mother's killer, I'm afraid."

Sophia slumped back in her chair and covered her face with her hands.

"Surely there is more the Corinthians will uncover?" Nicholas asked, watching Sophia absorb the painful truth and knowing he could not do a damn thing about it.

"I cannot say, Nicholas," Langdon answered, his tone turning cold. "I can tell you that even if there are new leads uncovered in the future, neither you nor Sophia will be allowed to continue the investigation."

Nicholas turned to take in his brother, anger flaring. "You yourself admitted that our work led to the Bishop's capture. How can you presume to make such a decision on our behalf?"

"Do you love her, Nicholas?" Langdon asked simply.

Nicholas froze, Langdon's question catching him off guard. He swallowed hard, his mind racing for a response. In the end, he decided upon the simple truth. "Yes. I always have. And I always will."

Langdon picked up the paperweight and appeared to be testing the weight of it in his right hand. "And you, Sophia? Do you love my brother?"

"Langdon, how did you know?" Sophia asked, her voice tortured.

Langdon turned and looked out the French window. "I'm smart enough to see when two people are in love. In fact, I suspect I've known for some time—since we took tea at Halcyon House together. My suspicions were not confirmed until the night Mouse was abducted."

"We never meant for this to happen. You must believe me," Sophia begged.

"You know, I do believe you. And that's what makes it worse. If you'd purposely set out to deceive me, then I would have every reason to be angry. But I know the two of you too well. You'd never do such a thing—not even you, Nicholas. I'm sure you both struggled to come to terms with your love."

Nicholas reached out and took Sophia's hand, grasping it tightly. "What can we do, Langdon? How can we make amends?"

He watched his brother, wanting so badly to do *something* to make things right.

"You will marry, of course," Langdon replied, turning back to face them. "With my blessing, so I don't appear a complete ass. And you will abandon the murder case, forever. I'll have your word. That is what you can do—the both of you."

Sophia squeezed Nicholas's hand, beginning to cry. "Are you sure, Langdon?"

"I've never been more sure of anything in my life," he replied.

*July 10*
PETWORTH MANOR

"Here, now, that is still my job, isn't it?"

Sophia looked up from the pearl bracelet she'd unsuccessfully attempted to fasten four times. "As long as you'll have me, Lettie."

Sophia's dear friend smiled at her as she crossed the room and joined her. "Oh, you won't be rid of me so easily," she said, reaching for the two ends of the antique piece. "Mr. Bourne does not scare me. Never has, and never will."

Sophia chuckled at the woman's wit. "And what of the ton? News of our marriage will set society tongues wagging the moment it reaches London. You'll be in service to the *infamous* Bournes."

Lettie picked up one of Sophia's pearl drop earrings from the dressing table. "Is that why you two decided to have the ceremony here, at Petworth Manor? To hide from the scandal?"

"It is a scandal, isn't it?" Sophia asked dubiously, pulling her hair back away from her ear.

"Honestly? Yes," Lettie answered simply. "As far as the ton categorizes such things. But I've never been overly concerned with their opinion—not when it comes to your happiness, anyway. And you shouldn't be, either."

Sophia stood still while Lettie affixed the platinum-set earring onto her lobe before letting her hair fall back into place. "Is that so? Then I'll tell you something: returning to Petworth was a defining moment for me— and Nicholas as well. This house and the grounds . . ."

She paused, searching Lettie's face for understanding. "It may sound mad, but Petworth held the key to my memories—every last one that I'd kept at bay for the past fifteen years. Many were agonizing, as you already know. Still, when we returned to London, snippets of my life here at the manor began to surface—happy times with my family and friends, some of the happiest of my life. And I realized that facing the worst of my past had unlocked the very best. I can no longer live life looking behind me."

"Then you'll let the search for your mother's killer go?" Lettie asked, locating the second earring.

"I told Langdon that I would—"

"That does not answer my question," Lettie interrupted, gesturing for Sophia to hold back her hair. "You are prepared to give up everything you have worked for nearly your entire life? And finally allow yourself to be happy?"

It sounded much more monumental when Lettie put it in such a way. And a small part of Sophia paused, wondering if she had thoroughly thought things through.

"Would you think less of me if my answer was yes?"

Lettie stood back from Sophia, the beautiful pearl earring dangling from her fingers and tears in her eyes. "Oh, Sophia, I would think less of you if your answer was no. It takes far more courage to change course than continue along the same path, hoping for the best but fully expecting the worst. Mr. Bourne loves you with all of his heart—and from what I can tell, you feel the same."

Sophia felt the telling sensation in the back of her throat that always preceded tears. She nodded in agreement. "You are going to make me cry and I haven't even left my room."

Lettie started fastening the second earring. "Well, it would not be a proper wedding without tears, my lady. Not proper at all."

❦

"Might I loosen it? It's choking the life from me, sir."

Nicholas looked down at Mouse, who was grimacing as he attempted to destroy his cravat with one hand. "Welcome to manhood, young Mouse," he replied, adjusting the sling that held the boy's broken arm. It would heal in time. Still, Nicholas would never forget how lucky they were that he'd not been killed. Even the doctor could not quite believe how few injuries the boy had sustained as a result of his jump from the second-story window.

Sophia had called it a miracle. And Nicholas had to agree—just not when anyone else was around.

But on a day such as this, with the sun shining down on Petworth Manor, and the lake a ridiculously beautiful shade of blue, Nicholas was forced to consider whether God's wedding gift to him was not just one miracle, but a series of them.

Singh rushed up the aisle toward Nicholas, his traditional long silk banyan robe rustling in the gentle breeze. "Sahib, I have been told that Lady Sophia and Lord Carrington have left the main house," he announced, excitement twinkling in his eyes.

"Why don't he have to wear a noose?" Mouse asked, looking at Singh with envy. "I think I'm owed *something* for being lied to about Lady Sophia, after all."

"You are a proper English boy now, young Mouse, to be brought up the son of sahib and Lady Sophia," Singh replied, placing his hand on the boy's shoulder. "It is 'Why *does* he not have to wear a noose?' And it is not polite to accuse another of lying."

Mouse eyed him suspiciously, though his fondness for the man shone in his eyes. "You didn't answer my question, Mr. Singh."

"Perceptive, young Mouse. And an answer is unnecessary at this juncture. Come, we must find our seats," Singh urged, gently pushing the boy forward to where the household staff and Mrs. Kirk sat on chairs from the manor brought down to the banks of the lake.

The pounding of horse's hooves, accompanied by the rattle of wheels, sounded just beyond the trees separating the lake from the surrounding land. Nicholas looked with relief at Singh. The vicar had finally arrived.

Some moments later, the thick tree branches parted and Langdon appeared, followed by Lord Carmichael and the vicar.

"I am sorry for my lateness," the short, wide man apologized, walking quickly to where Nicholas stood. "The wheel on my cart broke some distance from Petworth Manor and I was forced to walk. Thankfully, Lords Stonecliffe and Carmichael came upon me, or we might not have had a wedding to celebrate."

"This way, Vicar Hawkins," the housekeeper trilled, standing from her seat across the grassy expanse and beckoning the man toward her. "Just a few details to discuss, you see."

Lord Carmichael cleared his throat. "I believe I will take my seat. First, though," he said, offering his hand to Nicholas, "congratulations, Bourne. I do hope you plan to devote yourself entirely to Sophia's happiness."

He referred—in part, at least—to Lady Afton's case, the subtle warning delivered in classic Carmichael style.

Nicholas offered him an astute stare. "I would be angry, Carmichael," he began, taking the man's hand in his, "if not for the fact that I plan on doing just that."

"Good to hear, Bourne." He tipped his hat in recognition and left in search of a seat.

Nicholas watched Carmichael walk away, then turned to look at his brother. "Will you stay?"

"I said I would, didn't I?" Langdon answered brusquely. "It would not do to have the servants gossiping about my absence."

Nicholas shook his head. "That is not why you're here. You are here because you are a decent, noble man."

"As are you, brother," he replied, his gaze sweeping the lake and beyond. "Sophia would not have fallen in love with you if you'd proven yourself to be anything else."

"Thank you," Nicholas murmured.

"I love you, Nicholas. I always have and this will not change things," Langdon said as he looked out over the land he'd nearly owned. "Still, I will require time."

"Take all the time you need, brother. I owe you that, at the very least."

# 31

"Do take care with her dress, my love," Elena instructed Dash from her place next to Sophia.

Dash stood outside the Afton carriage in the Petworth Manor drive. His valiant attempt to arrange Sophia's wedding dress had not proven particularly fruitful. "Would it truly be a tragedy of monumental proportions if the gown somehow managed to be caught in the carriage door?"

"Yes!" Elena cried.

Dash grinned with impudent pride. "You, my dear, are far too gullible."

He held the skirts in one hand and pulled the door with the other, slamming it shut only a moment after removing his arm. "You see? We men can be useful."

"'Can' being the operative word," Elena whispered to Sophia.

Dash climbed up to the box and joined the driver. "To the lake, Joseph Wends, and with care if you please."

"Aye, Lord Carrington," the elderly man replied with a laugh. "'Tis no other way I know."

Sophia smiled at the old driver's lilting voice, glad that he could be part of her day.

"Sophia?"

"Yes," she replied, still thinking fondly on Mr. Wends's presence as she turned to look at Elena.

"Is there anything . . ." Elena paused and demurely

cleared her throat. "That is to say, do you have questions regarding . . ."

The woman's fair skin began to glow with embarrassment.

"Oh!" Sophia cried as understanding dawned. "Regarding marital relations?"

Elena sighed with appreciation. "Precisely. To be frank, I had no idea whether Mrs. Kirk—"

Sophia could not help herself this time. She took Elena's hand in hers and giggled. "There are books for such things, and from what I understand, a certain inborn understanding will present itself at the necessary time. But I thank you for the kindness."

"Books, you say?" Elena asked sheepishly.

Sophia arched a brow. "Oh yes."

Both women fell victim to a fit of laughter then, the sound of their shared amusement reaching the men.

"Better a laughing bride than a crying one," Mr. Wends opined loudly.

Sophia covered her mouth with the palm of her hand and waited for the tickle of mirth to cease.

Elena sighed with contentment, one last bubble of laughter escaping her lips before she settled back upon the seat cushion.

Sophia peered out the window at the giant chestnut trees that lined the drive. "I do have a question for you, come to think of it."

"Of course," Elena replied. "After I fumbled the last topic so badly, I owe you at least one good answer."

"Tell me," Sophia began, "has Dash succeeded in building a new life with you—one free from those things that had consumed him entirely before you met?"

"It is a bit of a daft question, isn't it?"

Sophia blinked and abruptly turned her head, unsure if she'd heard the woman correctly. "Did you just question my intelligence?"

"No, not in general," Elena answered. "And it is an assumption that Dash made as well, so you are in good company. Honestly, though, the very idea that one could simply throw over essentially what they've lived for as if tossing out an old dress and embracing an entirely new life without any bumps along the way? I am sadly mixing my metaphors, but you do understand what I mean, don't you?"

"Eventually, the bumps and the old dresses smooth out?" Sophia pressed.

Elena sighed good-naturedly. "You are quite like Dash, aren't you?"

Elena's words were both disappointing and elating at the same time. For as long as she could remember, Sophia had assumed her life would flourish and thrive once she'd found the person responsible for her mother's death. It was quite a lot to ask of her future and, she realized now, impossible to fulfill. "Then there will always be difficulty, no matter what I choose?"

"Precisely!" Elena exclaimed, clapping her hands together. "No matter how dedicated we are to building the perfect life, there will always be bumps and old dresses. After our first fight, Dash was terrified that he'd somehow failed to do everything that he should, despite the fact that he'd all but left the Corinthians and moved to Verwood with me."

"So I should lower my expectations?" Sophia said, her lips tilting up into a smile.

The woman considered Sophia's words and nodded. "In a manner of speaking, yes. Life was always going to be difficult at times, even if your mother had not been taken from you. Because it is the bumps and old dresses that force us to grow and come into our own. It is how you found Nicholas, and I discovered Dash."

"How did you become so wise?" Sophia asked, returning her gaze to the window.

"My share of bumps and old dresses, Sophia."

A second carriage sounded just beyond the trees. "That will be Carrington and Sophia," Nicholas said to his brother, straightening his cravat.

"Carrington?" Langdon asked. "Where is her father?"

"Lord Afton sent word that he was too ill to attend," Nicholas explained, not bothering to hide his disappointment.

"Do not think too harshly of him. Not every man is as strong as you and I, Nicholas," Langdon told him, with a smile. Then, turning a little, he pointed to the aisle and said, "Now it is time for me to find a seat and for you to join the vicar, I believe."

Langdon left first, walking to take the empty seat next to Carmichael.

Nicholas followed after his brother.

The vicar looked past Nicholas and his eyes grew wide with pleasure. "Come along, Mr. Bourne. Your bride has arrived."

Nicholas turned around and walked the last few steps backward, the sight of Sophia on Dash's arm making the world melt away.

"Here, Mr. Bourne," the vicar urged, his plump hand pulling Nicholas into position.

The music of a single violin filled the air, though Nicholas could not be sure if it was real or his imagination. All that was real to him was Sophia.

Sophia. The one he had loved for so long. The one who had belonged to another. The one he had never dared to dream would be his.

She was the woman walking down the aisle toward him. Her dress, a frothy concoction of silk and antique lace, shimmered in the sunlight as she took each step forward. Her hair was pinned up, partially exposing the dainty pearl earrings that had once belonged to her mother. And her face . . . Her lips were curved upward in a small smile that Nicholas knew was only for him. And her eyes possessed the very love and devotion that he felt pulsing within his heart and soul.

She was no more than two steps from Nicholas. Still, he could bear the wait no longer. He moved forward and reached out to take her hand.

Dash grinned at Nicholas, shaking his head as he released Sophia and stepped back to take a seat next to Elena.

Nicholas lifted their linked hands and kissed Sophia's palm before looping her arm through his and turning back to the vicar.

"We are ready," Nicholas told the stout man, looking at Sophia. "Are we not?"

Sophia stifled a small laugh at his nerves, resting her head momentarily on his upper arm. "For the future?"

"Not precisely," Nicholas drawled, his heart disgustingly full. "For *our* future."

"Together?"

"Forever," Nicholas insisted, tightening his hold.

Sophia raised her head and captured him with a fierce look of possession. "I would not have it any other way."